The tragic mystery at the heart of their family has finally surfaced . . .

When Presbyterian minister Ellen Wakefield O'Connor is confronted by a young man armed with a birth certificate that mistakenly names her as his mother, she quickly sorts out the truth: his birth mother listed Ellen on the certificate to cover up her own identity, but also because Ellen was, in a way, related to the child.

The birth father is Ellen's troubled husband, Tom.

Twenty-four years earlier, only months before Ellen gave birth to her and Tom's daughter Sarah, his son, Brian, was born to Tom and the mystery woman, whose identity Tom now refuses to reveal. She may have come from Ellen's own hometown.

Shattered, Ellen heads home to Wakefield, West Virginia—named after her prosperous and respected family. She enlists her mother and sisters to help her comb through the memories of a turbulent past there, searching for clues about Tom's affair and for reasons to save their marriage.

What she finds is a web of sorrows that entangles everyone she loves.

Dedicated with love to my parents, who
taught all their eight children
to be voracious readers:
Dr. Robert M. Todd and
Dr. Jeanne M. Todd, 1932-2010

In lumine tuo videbimus lumen.

the year she fell

ALICIA RASLEY

Bell Bridge Books
PO BOX 300921
Memphis, TN 38130
ISBN: 978-1-61194-000-8

Bell Bridge Books is an Imprint of BelleBooks, Inc.

We at BelleBooks enjoy hearing from readers.
Visit our websites — www.BelleBooks.com and www.BellBridgeBooks.com.

10 9 8 7 6 5 4 3 2

Cover design: Debra Dixon
Interior design: Hank Smith
Photo credits:
Sky © Javarman | Dreamstime.com
Woman (manipulated) © Branislav Ostojic | Dreamstime.com

:Lwe:01:

CHAPTER ONE

Ellen

June

I couldn't help but think of him as "the love child."

It was an old-fashioned term, more genteel than "bastard," more evocative than "biological son", with an origin not in genetics but in passion.

He walked into my life when he walked into the Second-Rushmore Presbyterian Church—my church, or at least the Virginia church where I was currently serving as minister. Janitor, too, that June afternoon the boy came in.

I was just tidying up the pews after the Genesis Choir rehearsal, wandering down the aisle, grabbing up a paperback some child had left behind, a discarded baseball card. I'd gotten about halfway down before I saw the man half-hidden in the shadow near the big arched oak door. I slipped the book into my jacket pocket and called out, "Hello?"

He stepped out into the light filtering through the rose window. I felt a flicker of recognition, but with no name or context attached. Probably I'd seen him around town. A student from the university, maybe—he had the requisite camouflage jacket and ripped jeans and scraggly goatee, and that hard scared look young people have these days. At least he'd noticed he was in a church and pulled off the baseball cap. There was a quarter-inch of dark bristle left on his head.

He came forward, his sneakers making a sucking noise on the marble floor. His hands were jammed into his baggy cargo pockets, and for a moment I was frightened. There'd been a rash of church robberies and arsons during the winter, but the elders had agreed that a church just couldn't lock its doors until late in the evening. You will find Him among the murderers and thieves, I reminded myself, and walked down the aisle to meet him.

He stopped back at the last pew. "Mrs. O'Connor?"

A serial murderer wouldn't know my name. I walked closer. "Yes—I'm the minister here."

"I know."

His voice was deep but it wavered, echoing in the stone sanctuary. He stood there irresolute, his shoulders bunched, his hands knotted into fists in his pockets.

I knew that stance from years of counseling church members and students. He was in trouble of some kind, and embarrassed about it. "Is there something you want to talk about?"

He yanked his hand out of his pocket. He was holding nothing lethal, just a folded piece of paper. He thrust it across the yard or so divide between us. The paper felt rough and official as I smoothed away the wrinkles. A notary's raised seal rubbed under my fingers.

It was a birth certificate, with the state seal in the middle of a field of marble green. The first line read *Adam Paul Wakefield*.

On the line labeled "mother" was my own maiden name. *Ellen Elizabeth Wakefield*.

Unknown was named as the father.

There were other words and numbers, but the paper was rattling in my hand and I couldn't read any more. "I don't understand."

"I'm Adam. Or I was. When I was adopted, my parents—my adoptive parents—named me Brian Warrick."

I kept staring at the birth certificate, but still it made no sense. "I don't know why my name is on this."

Suddenly he was curt, almost disrespectful. "Isn't it obvious? You're my birthmother."

As that echoed off the high ceiling of the sanctuary and through my disordered thoughts, I realized dimly that this wasn't a good place for such a conversation. At any moment the session moderator could come by to warn me about the great pew controversy at the meeting tonight. My position here as the church's first woman minister was precarious enough already without allegations of—of whatever this boy, this love child, signified.

"Come into my office. I don't know what this is, but—but let's talk there."

Silently he followed me out the side door and up the narrow steps to the third-floor warren of offices. Taking the upholstered seat across from my desk, he watched as I scanned the birth certificate, looking for the clue that would make this all make sense. The birth was registered in a county in southern Pennsylvania, about a hundred-fifty miles northeast. I didn't recognize the name of the hospital or the attending doctor. I did, however, recognize the entry on the "mother's birthplace" line.

He was studying me closely enough that he knew what I was reading. "You were born in Wakefield, West Virginia. Just like it says."

I could hardly deny it. It was true, and besides, the town was named for our family. "How did you find that out?"

"I did a search on the Web." Bitterness crept into his voice. "I sent a letter to you there. There in Wakefield. And you didn't answer."

I felt defensive. "I never got any letters. I haven't lived there in twenty years." I set the birth certificate down on the open Bible on my desk and stared again at my name, my hometown. It made no sense.

Then I noticed the date.

I fumbled in my purse and came up with my leather wallet, solid and heavy with coins and credit cards. In a pocket I located the little plastic folder of photographs and took out one of Sarah. With relief I saw the date stamped on the back by the developer.

"Look." I shoved the picture towards him. My hand was trembling. So was his as he took the photo from the desk blotter.

We were both frightened of this.

He studied the picture some hospital photographer had taken when Sarah was six hours old. She had her eyes open and didn't look happy about it. Little Winston Churchill, Tom and I always called that pugnacious image of our only child.

"That's my daughter Sarah."

"So?" He said it rudely, but from the way he was staring at it I suddenly realized there must be no creased and cherished photo of his earliest hours.

"Turn it over."

He did as he was told. He read it slowly, already recognizing its meaning: "August 2, 1986."

"Your birth certificate says April 15, 1986. I couldn't have given birth to you and then Sarah four months later."

He looked up. There was something wild and sad in his eyes, and I knew he wanted me to be his mother. It was heartbreaking. At that moment, I wanted it to be true too, and damn the deacons and elders. To be wanted like that—

But it wasn't true. "I'm sorry."

"You could be lying—that could be . . . your niece."

"She's my daughter." I said that gently, but I also wanted to sound firm. I wanted to make it clear. I wasn't his mother, though I must admit it gave me a start to see my name there on the Mother line, just as on Sarah's birth certificate.

"Why—why would someone else put your name down?" He pushed the photo folder back at me and took out the birth certificate again. "It has your name right there."

"I don't understand it either. But when you were born in Pennsylvania, I was living in Washington and already pregnant."

He wouldn't let it go, this quest of his. And I guess I couldn't blame him. He would be searching for himself, not just his mother. He said stubbornly, "But it must have been someone you knew. To use your name like that. You must know her somehow."

"Well, I don't know who it could be." I looked up at him, saw the longing, and said, "I know this is important to you. But you have a family already."

"Adopted. Not really mine."

"My sister Theresa is adopted. And she's just as much my sister." This didn't convince him, and I tried to infuse more certainty into my voice. "Really. The family you're raised with counts too."

He nodded his head, but his eyes were still on the plastic sleeve that held Sarah's baby photo. "Yes. I understand. But I still want to know my origins. And you must know something about my mother, if she used your name."

He was right. But he was wrong. "I really can't think who would do that." I started to put the little folder away, but as I flipped open my wallet; I saw another photo and stopped. The young man saw it too. I didn't breathe for a moment or so, staring down at the old picture, taken at that first Pulitzer ceremony. Then I looked back at Brian—at Adam.

This young man was harsh and shorn and stubbled, deliberately ugly, all slack belligerence in form and face. But in the afternoon light streaming in from the tall window, there was a pure line to his cheekbones, and a straight blade of nose, and under the scraggle of beard his jaw was square. He could be beautiful, I knew.

I knew.

Slowly I slid my wallet back into my purse and rose. He rose too, with the involuntary good manners his mother—his adoptive mother—must have taught him.

"I don't know who your mother could be." The words cramped in the tightness of my throat. "But I think I can introduce you to your father."

I gathered up my things, found my keys, led the way out.

"Where are we going?"

"Home," I said.

Home.

Home was an old Federal-style farmhouse on the edge of town, on a hill surrounded by new developments. The farm was long gone, and the house was in a constant state of restoration. As I opened the front door, it slammed into a box of slate tiles that would eventually be laid down in the hallway. Grimly I moved the box a few inches away from the door, and headed through the front parlor to my husband's study. It was empty.

Tom was supposed to be home. He was teaching now, after all those years as a foreign correspondent, but summer semester didn't start for a couple weeks. He'd told me at breakfast he was planning to spend the day working on his book.

Just as Brian pulled into the gravel driveway, I left the front door open for him, and tracked my husband upstairs by following the sound of running water. His running clothes and shoes were dumped on the floor outside the shower. As always, the shower door was open a foot or so, and I could see his lean form through the steam on the glass.

I wanted to punch through the door and shower his naked body with glass. But of course I didn't do that. I just opened it all the way, said, "Get out. We have to talk," and closed it firmly.

My demand was unprecedentedly assertive, I guess, because a couple minutes later he was out in the bedroom, wearing jeans and a startled expression and a t-shirt getting wet on his chest. "What's troubling you, sweetheart?"

It was the warm, concerned tone that ordinarily melted me. But not today. "You have to come downstairs."

"Why?" he asked as he pulled on his shoes.

The sensible, non-confrontational thing to do would be to warn him about the boy and let him explain. But I wasn't feeling sensible. There was something about seeing my name on that birth certificate as "mother" that incensed me. Of course, whoever that Pennsylvania woman was couldn't have known that later I would end up with only one child—an ectopic pregnancy treated in a substandard hospital in Amman left me infertile when Sarah was three. But still, her putting my name there seemed like a taunt of some kind, a challenge.

I didn't know what Tom had to do with that taunt, besides fathering the child in question. But grimly I decided that surprise was my best weapon in ferreting out the truth from the man who had somehow hidden it for almost two decades, all the while letting me believe that we were that rare married couple who knew each other totally.

All I said was, "There's someone waiting to meet you."

He followed me down, silent now. He was prepared for something . . . but not, I thought, for what waited in the front parlor.

The boy was standing by the window, looking at the view—a spectacular one of the valley, green and pink and purple under the afternoon sun, and worth the hassles of owning this old house. But he turned quickly as I entered, Tom right behind me.

"This is my husband Tom O'Connor," I said.

Tom stopped just inside the room. He nodded at the boy, but warily. "What's going on, Ellen?"

The boy was watching us carefully, and I saw his eyes widen when he heard Tom's voice. Tom had spent most of his childhood in Ireland, and traces of the accent still livened his speech. I switched my attention to my husband. Did he recognize himself in the boy? Did he have that moment of realization that I'd just had? Did he even know Brian existed?

"This is—" I couldn't say Adam O'Connor. "Brian Warrick. He has something to ask you."

Tom was regarding both of us with that wary neutral regard he always assumed when he didn't know what was going on. He didn't see himself in this young man. Maybe I was the only one who could see the resemblance. But it was there—the square jaw, the perfect straight nose, the gray-green eyes. The boy wasn't as tall as Tom yet, but he had that same wary leanness. But Tom didn't see it. And neither, I realized, did the boy.

5

"Go ahead," I said gently.

Brian—Adam—hesitated. He jammed his hands into his jacket pockets and I heard the crinkle of paper, but he didn't pull out the birth certificate and fling it in my husband's face. I realized I was the only one who really understood what was going on here.

I held out my hand. "Give me the birth certificate."

He responded to my teacher's voice, the authority one, and slowly withdrew his hand from his pocket. I grabbed the certificate, unfolded it, and handed it to my husband.

I could see the moment when comprehension dawned on his face. But still he said nothing, only studying the paper as if there were secrets encrypted in its watermark.

Impatiently I said, "Do you see the date? And do you see the name in the mother field?"

"Yes."

"And you know what that means. I'm not the mother. You know that and I know that, and this young man knows it too."

"I know that this is wrong," he said. He glanced up at Brian, standing tense by the door, and then back at the birth certificate, and finally back at me. "You couldn't be the mother."

His face gave nothing away. That was his prisoner face. I'd seen it before, on the rare occasions I confronted him—remote and controlled and ungiving. Had he known about this child? You'd think I could tell from his face, but I saw only wariness. He was closing himself off again.

I couldn't let him do this, pretend this way. "Brian. This is your father. Tom O'Connor. I'm sure he can tell you more."

I don't know what I expected. But I knew what Brian expected, and he didn't get it. Tom just studied him, as he might study someone who looked slightly familiar. No greeting, no comment, no explanation.

The boy just stood there with a stricken look on his face. He couldn't even speak. I realized he never expected to find a father, only a mother, and he had prepared nothing for this eventuality. I felt an unwilling sympathy for him. I'd never expected this either.

So, grimly, as if I were counseling a dysfunctional family, I said, "I'm sure there are some things you want to ask, Brian."

He looked at me, surprised—grateful, I thought. "Yes. I want to know—if—if you are not my mother, who is? And where is she?"

I directed the question where it belonged. "Yes, Tom, who is she?"

Tom moved then, just an uncoiling, as if he'd been drawn in by tension. He looked down at the birth certificate again. "I don't know," he said finally. "We didn't get as far as names."

I gasped. It sounded so cynical. And the way he said it revealed something terrible about our marriage. I was bleak suddenly, as if an abyss had opened up a few inches in front of me. He knew what this was about;

maybe not her name, but at least when she must have slipped into his life. And never, in eighteen years, had he told me anything about that, or about the son he had given away.

Brian's face suggested the same vertigo had overtaken him. "You don't know her name? Then how—how can I find her?"

Tom regarded the birth certificate more closely. Now his voice was helpful, mildly concerned. "There must have been an adoption agency involved. I'd suggest you start there."

"But—but that's how I got the birth certificate."

Tom nodded, judicious now. "Maybe they have more information." He held out the birth certificate, and Brian automatically stepped forward and took it.

I couldn't stand this strange spectacle. "Tom!" I said sharply. "Tell us what happened. How this came to happen."

He'd started towards the archway back to the front hall, but stopped and turned as I spoke. "The usual way, I suppose." He'd gone back to callous again. He sounded bored.

"The usual way." I almost choked on that. It was too vague and too graphic, all at the same time. "When? And where?"

He shook his head. "Washington, I guess. It's hard to remember. When I started at the *Post*."

"Where did you meet her?"

"I don't remember. A bar. Look—sorry, kid," he said, flicking a glance at Brian. "It wasn't a relationship. You understand? It was just a one-night stand."

"How do you know it was a one-night stand?" I demanded.

"Because that's all I had that summer."

That hurt—stabbed deep. That summer . . . that summer I'd been so devastated after our pre-graduation breakup. I'd been so foolish. I'd turned down even a date with my high school boyfriend, because I couldn't imagine being with anyone but Tom. And he was having one-night stands all over Washington.

"But—" Brian said hesitantly, "but if that's all it was, then how—how did she know about your wife?"

"Ellen wasn't my wife then," Tom said quickly. "We weren't even together."

This apparently he wanted on the record, as though that technicality was all that mattered. It was aimed at me, I knew—an excuse, not an explanation.

"But she said you two were married. When I was born. How would anyone know to put her name on the birth certificate, if she didn't know you and didn't know you'd gotten married?"

This stopped Tom. It stopped me too. I didn't know what it meant.

Tom recovered first. "I said I didn't know her. She might have known me. She must have known me. I had bylined articles in the *Post* even then.

And marriages—that's public record. Maybe she looked me up in some database and found the marriage record."

Database. It sounded so impersonal. Not to mention implausible. In 1991, you couldn't just do an Internet scan for someone's name.

Besides, no woman whose name he didn't know would go to this much trouble to implicate him. "Tell us the truth." My voice, embarrassingly, quavered with intensity.

But Tom didn't even seem to notice. He shook his head, impatient, I gathered, with us both. "I've told you all I know."

Brian's eyes narrowed. I was reminded of that first, frightening impression I had of him, when he emerged from the shadows of the church sanctuary. Carefully he said, "Do you know even which one she was?"

"Which one?"

"Which one of your one-night stands?"

"No." Now, finally, there was some emotion in his voice. Regret. "No, I don't. I was drinking a lot then. I don't remember much at all."

I saw Brian's eyes, wide with something like shock, and I wanted to tell him it was a lie, that my husband was lying, that this woman meant something to him, so much that even now, when it couldn't matter except to us, he protected her identity. But I couldn't say it. I didn't know if that was because of some stupid residual marital loyalty, or because the boy would be better off thinking Tom truly didn't know—but I couldn't accuse him outright of lying.

Brian made an abrupt gesture with his hand and started towards the door. But he stopped under the staircase and looked up. "Where is Sarah? My . . . sister?"

Oh, God. The realization hit Tom as it hit me. He wouldn't just walk out the door, this boy, and disappear. He wouldn't. He was bound to this family of ours—and he wasn't going to let us forget it.

And he was right, I told myself. He owed the boy something—an explanation, at least. And he owed me that explanation too.

I just didn't want Sarah involved—not till we had sorted this out to my satisfaction. Before Tom could respond, I said quickly, soothingly, "Oh, she's a camp counselor this summer. We won't see her for weeks." And then pleasantly, to defuse any threat, "Are you staying in town?"

"I don't know. I haven't decided."

"You could stay here. We have room." It was an insane idea, I knew even before the words were out. But I suspected he had no money and would end up sleeping in that beat-up Escort.

He stopped at the door, turning to look at me. His eyes were wary but bright now. Then he glanced over beside me at Tom, and Tom stared back, giving nothing.

"No. Thank you." Brian opened the door. "I'll contact you if I want to." And then he was gone.

Tom walked off in the other direction, towards the kitchen and the back door.

"Wait! Goddamnit, Tom, you're not going to walk out now."

He stopped in the doorway to the kitchen but didn't turn around. "I'm sorry if this hurts you. I'm sure it does. But it doesn't have anything to do with you or our marriage. It happened before we married. Just a stupid mistake."

In a couple quick steps I was next to him, and I grabbed his arm. "Don't you say that to that boy. He's not a mistake, and he won't want to hear his own father say that."

"I'm not his father," Tom said, gazing through the kitchen, out the big window to the meadow. "He has a father—whoever adopted him. I've got no claim on him, and he has no claim on me."

"It doesn't work that way! Not anymore!"

"When someone's adopted, the original obligation is severed." The cool legalism gave way to his more usual gentle tone. "Your own sister is adopted. And if you've given two thoughts in twenty years to where she came from, I'd be surprised. Families live together. How they got into the family isn't important." He wrenched away from my hand. "Look, whatever this is, it's between me and the boy. Not you. I'll handle it."

"You'll handle it?" It sounded like some logistical problem, how to sneak a video camera past Libyan customs officials, or get a fake passport for a valuable source. "But it's not just your problem. Our marriage—do you understand? I've never known about this, and if I had—" I stopped short. I couldn't finish the thought.

"What? You wouldn't have married me? For something that happened before?"

"For not telling me. It's something I deserved to know."

"You're assuming I knew."

"I know you knew."

This he hadn't expected. But he must have known I wasn't bluffing. "You can believe what you want. I've told you everything relevant. I told you back then, when we got back together. Not this specifically, but in general."

"What? What did you tell me?"

"That things got out of control that summer. That I didn't do it well—freedom. You remember. When I called you that day in August."

I didn't remember anything about that phone call except a sudden proposal, a bright light in an escape route from a life I didn't want. It didn't matter. "The specific—that some woman was even then carrying your child—didn't matter? You didn't think I might have changed my mind if I knew?"

"I didn't know. You can believe me or not. But I didn't know."

"Then."

He didn't answer.

9

"So you found out later? When?"

He shook his head. "This is going nowhere. I'm sorry this happened. I'll take care of it. You don't need to worry about it." He walked through the hall to the kitchen. "I'm going for a run."

"But you just got back from a run—"

My protest followed him out the back door. I saw him bend to tie his shoe, and then he was off, running again, away, as he always did since Tehran, running.

on Main Street was red and gold with zinnias the size of goblets.

If I were a stranger, I'd have thought this was the healthiest town in a blighted state. Maybe I would even stay to lunch at one of the tea rooms on the courthouse square, and wander through the campus of the college that allowed us to claim to be an oasis of knowledge in the desert of ignorance.

But I grew up here, and coming back evoked guilt—guilt that I left, guilt that I wasn't building the community, guilt that I felt so trapped in the town that was supposed to be my legacy.

Growing up a Wakefield in Wakefield, my parents always reminded me, conferred some obligations. Our great-great grandfather had founded the town, or at least founded the bank that funded the town, and ever since, for most of the town's infrastructure—the city council, the library board and the schools foundation and the Rotary and the Philomathean society and the garden club and the philharmonic— you'd always find a Wakefield in charge . . . until my generation. Mother was still on half the boards in town, and a cousin ran the family bank. But my sisters and I scattered as soon as we got old enough to catch the early bus out.

I wondered, as I drove down the street winding along the river, if Mother blamed herself for that.

Not likely. I was the sort of mother who blamed myself. Margaret MacDonald Wakefield, however, was made of sterner stuff. She would tell me, if I asked, that I had to take responsibility for my own actions, and if I regretted leaving Wakefield, perhaps that was a sign that I'd made a mistake.

I didn't want to hear that.

From the time I was thirteen or so, all I wanted was to get away—away from the narrow-minded little town, away from my mother's velvet domination, away from the desperation that huddled back there in the hills, held back from overwhelming the town only by the combined authority of my family and other genteel types.

I always wanted to be a teacher, but I didn't want to struggle against the poverty and the illness and the suspicion in Loudon County. Many children in the hills didn't even get immunizations because their parents suspected the government doctors, and they didn't trust the public schools either. When I did a student-teaching internship in the local grade school, one child came to me, sullen, anxious, with a social-studies textbook he'd brought back from home. His father had ripped out every page that dealt with the rise of manufacturing in the 19th Century. Why? The boy couldn't explain. Perhaps machines were against Pa's religion. There were some very odd religions back in the hills—snake handlers and dowsers and Sethians. Maybe there was an anti-technology one too.

I found it much harder to teach those kids than the ones I later taught in the inner city of Washington. At least the parents in the slums weren't actively against education. But the hill people . . . some of them went to jail rather than send their kids to school, where they might learn about other religions or read stories about wizards or participate in mixed sports. I couldn't teach them.

But even if none of her daughters stayed to help, Mother had never given up her mission to maintain Wakefield as an outpost of culture and civility here in the unforgiving mountains.

Her house—our house—sat there at the top of the road, a great brown toad of a house, shingled and sprawling in a dour Victorian way. I pulled in to the circular drive and taking a deep breath, grabbed my shopping bag luggage and walked up the stone steps. I didn't bother to knock—no one locked the door in Wakefield—but as I entered the foyer I called out, "Mother?"

My voice echoed in the stairwell. It was dark there, under the stairs, but I could smell the furniture polish and figured Merilee's ethics hadn't allowed her to leave a job with dust on the banister.

I dropped the shopping bag on the lowest step and went through the hallway to the kitchen, set back over the garden. In the sink was the first sign of life after Merilee—an unwashed cereal bowl and spoon. And then, through the wide back window, I saw my mother, still as straight-backed as the days when she showed horses, there on the flower-pot bordered terrace with a middle-aged man in a tan suit. His neat little beard typed him as "college" better than leather elbow patches would. Between them was a white wrought-iron table with two coffee cups on a silver tray.

The young boyfriend, I presumed. I was relieved he turned out to be far beyond student-age. And they weren't holding hands.

They both looked up as I emerged. Mother looked surprised. The college man looked intrigued, probably because he'd never seen Mother look surprised before. But it didn't last. She rose and then, hastily, so did he.

"Ellen, this is Dr. Urich, the new president at the college. My daughter Ellen. Her daughter Sarah is considering Loudon."

President Urich stepped forward, his face alight, his hand out. "How wonderful! Another generation of Wakefields at Loudon—that would be a great honor."

I took his hand. "Sarah is an O'Connor, actually."

"Oh, yes," Mother amended. "Her father is Thomas O'Connor, the special correspondent on CNN."

It was, perhaps, the first time I'd heard my mother boast about Tom. It would have pleased me a week ago, but now I just wanted to change the subject. "It's nice to meet you, Dr. Urich. I'm sorry to intrude."

"No intrusion!" he exclaimed, picking up his file folder from the table. "I'm always glad to meet a prospective student's parent. I hope you can bring your daughter for a campus visit soon." He made a graceful exit, not through the house but out the garden gate to the side drive— he'd been here before.

Mother watched him go, a smile lingering on her face, and then bent to pick up the coffee cups. "Hold the door, will you, dear? I wasn't expecting you today."

"I—" I don't like to lie. I never did, and since I was ordained, it had only gotten harder to justify. So to explain my appearance, I gave her a fraction of the truth—but that fraction was all mostly true. "I had a couple days off, and thought I'd run over and we'd have that talk you mentioned. I want to go through some of the books and papers I stored in the attic, and this seemed like a good time for that."

"I hope you'll stay long enough to come to church with me Sunday."

And that was it. She accepted my presence and my muddle of motives without question.

When we got into the kitchen, she set the cups in the sink next to the used cereal bowl. I ran water for washing, but as I reached out for the coffee cups, she stilled me with a hand on my wrist. "There's a chip on the lip of that cup. I'm going to throw it away before someone gets cut."

I shrugged and washed the cereal bowl and the spoon, while Mother found a bread bag in a drawer—like so many children of the war period, she saved bags and aluminum foil and margarine cups—and carefully bagged up the cup. She was always so thorough about such things.

Finally I brought up the other reason for my visit. "About Merilee, Mother, would you like me to talk to her?"

"There's nothing to talk about," she said, with that eternal cool of hers. "If she would have just admitted what she'd done, I might feel differently. But stealing and lying about it . . . "

"But the cameo was buried with Cathy," I insisted.

It did no good. "You've never had a reliable memory, dear. Now don't you worry. I put an ad in the paper for a new housekeeper, and I have a couple applicants coming this morning."

For just a moment, I wished we'd abided by that morbid 19th Century custom and taken a photo of Cathy in her coffin. That would prove me right. But there was no use arguing. "I'll sit in on the interviews with you, and give you my impressions," I said firmly.

She shook her head, smiling. "Whatever you say, Ellen, but I don't know that I need help. You are, after all, trained to look for the best in people, which is praiseworthy, but not a great aid in looking for household help."

I was almost forty, deep into my second profession, and she persisted in thinking I was unworldly. It had never annoyed me as much as today, when I was sleep-deprived and preoccupied. After all, I'd lived all over the world, and she'd lived only in one town in West Virginia. I snapped, "I've looked for household help in six countries so far, including three where the national sport is ripping off your employers. I'm not in the least naïve about human nature."

With a level look, she said, "But Merilee, you trust. That doesn't indicate much discernment, unfortunately."

I took a deep breath and reminded myself that Mother wasn't just being her usual patronizing self, that there was something wrong. So I said only, "I'll tell you what I think of the candidates."

After that confrontation, the actual meetings in the front parlor with the two housekeeper wannabes were something of an anticlimax. They were both clearly unsuitable—in fact, that's what my mother called each afterwards. "Clearly unsuitable." The first was too old and arthritic to manage dusting, much less vacuuming. Probably none of her previous employer had paid social security taxes for her, so here she was, older than my mother and twice as infirm, wanting to clean her house. I wanted to go after her and give her a list of social services—but I was a daughter here, not a minister.

The second was a middle-aged woman whose dark eyes were rimmed with red. She used to work in the mines, she whispered in a tubercularly hoarse voice. "But I'm good at cleaning," she promised, before she was seized by a fit of coughing.

Mother rose, the grand and compassionate lady. "Thank you for coming, Mrs. Price. I'll call if I decide I need another interview with you."

The woman glanced up at the name, but then only said her thanks in a subdued voice and departed.

As the door closed behind her, I said, "You called her Mrs. Price."

Mother glanced down at the application she was holding. "I did not. I called her Mrs. Peterson."

I was going to have to start taping our conversations. "It's an understandable mistake. She obviously had a touch of black lung, like Mr. Price. And she's a housekeeper like Mrs. Price."

"I called her Mrs. Peterson. I would never call her Mrs. Price."

And Mother crumpled the application into a ball, dropped it into the grate, and stalked out.

Gathering my courage, I followed her into the kitchen. "Perhaps just a quick checkup would be in order, Mother. Dr. Weaver could—"

"Dr. Weaver?" She shoved the faucet on with a harsh motion and watched as the sink started to fill. "He was probably the one who put Merilee up to her theft. I wouldn't doubt it. She's gone over to work for him now."

I swallowed a sigh. I wasn't uncertain any longer. Something was wrong when both our long-time housekeeper and our family doctor were suddenly objects of suspicion. And the Mrs. Price mistake—"There are other doctors in town. Just a checkup."

"I had a checkup last November. I was fine. And I'm fine now."

She jammed off the faucet and turned to face me. Just like that the anger flowed out of her face, and she said, "Now what did you think of President Urich? A well-spoken man, don't you think? I don't know if you remember him from his earlier teaching appointment here, but we were lucky that he came back to be president. And he's so appreciative of the house. And the garden! He was head of the botany department at a college in Maryland, you know, and he gave me several organic solutions to the slug problem."

She chatted, in her steely brook-no-interruption way, about slugs and aphids and other pests, and then announced she had weeding to do.

I gave up, but only for the moment. Retreating to the dark study—there was no phone line in my 70's-era bedroom—I hooked up my laptop. How bad was it, I asked myself as I plugged in the modem cord. Just a slip of the tongue.

But it was this particular slip that worried me.

Mrs. Price had been our housekeeper before Merilee, indeed, for much of my childhood, until around the time my father died. And . . . well, she was Theresa's mother. Birthmother, that is. When she and her husband moved out of town—he had black lung disease, we were told, and couldn't breathe here in the mountains—they left Theresa with us, and Mother adopted her. It had always been the most awkward of subjects around the house, because Theresa had been, for the first six years of her life, the housekeeper's daughter, and only after that our sister. We were all careful not to remind her of that earlier status or suggest that she hadn't always been one of us. At least I was. I didn't know about Laura, my younger sister, who always seemed to resent Theresa's arrival.

No, in ordinary circumstances, Mother wouldn't mention Mrs. Price. All the more reason to believe something was wrong. And it was my duty to try and help her, even if she didn't want help.

I dreaded this. It was hard enough helping my mother when she asked for help.

I'd never quite gotten used to being the eldest. Second children, the psychologists say, mold their identities around what the older sibling isn't, and I was certainly evidence of that. Cathy, almost four years older, was the leader. I was the one who followed, making meek little suggestions whenever I could. I was quiet where Cathy was outgoing, conscientious where she was adventurous. And while I was definitely "the responsible one," all through our childhood I deferred to her when it was time to make a decision. She was positive and decisive and always knew what to do, and so even if it wasn't the decision I would have made, I usually went along.

Now I was the eldest, and I had to be decisive. I had to think like Cathy.

But a few minutes of thinking like Cathy made me very nervous. I couldn't stride into Mother's room and insist that she listen to me and obey me. Cathy could do that, but I was, alas, still myself, certain that direct confrontation led to direct destruction.

And I decided that I wasn't going to make this decision or take this action without my remaining sisters sharing the heat.

So I wrote a long email about Mother's condition and her refusal to go to the doctor, stressing the seriousness of it all, and, in an aside, mentioning the college president and his apparent interest in the estate we'd had every expectation of inheriting, and cc'ed the whole tome to Laura and Theresa.

Thank God for email. No matter where Theresa had been posted, or where Laura was on location, they could pick up their email. In fact, last year Laura had been doing a film in one of the remotest places on earth, Tonga, and she sent me a photo attachment of her with the chubby, rattan-skirted Tongan king.

And even in her cloister outside of Pittsburgh, Theresa had email. Or at least the mother superior did. I presumed she'd pass on the message.

We were a rootless globetrotting set of sisters—a natural reaction, I supposed, to parents who, like Laura's Tongan king, were rulers of their small region and uncomfortable anywhere else.

While I was at it, I called into my office and told Jill that my mother wasn't well, and that I'd had to come home to help her. I felt guilty about this, even though it was true enough. Jill made the appropriate sympathetic noises and reminded me about the wedding on Saturday and the two services on Sunday. "Terry?" she asked delicately.

Terry was our youth minister, an energetic young man just out of seminary. He was wonderful with kids, but froze when he was in front of an adult group. "I don't think he's ready for primetime yet. I'll call the presbytery and see who's on call this weekend to fill in."

"Chuck would be glad to do it, I'm sure."

Jill had a carefully calibrated voice, a real asset in a church secretary. This time her tone was telling me that calling the presbytery first would offend the Second Church's former minister, Chuck, and that in turn would offend all the Seconders. And Chuck, though long retired to the golf course, was an experienced and accomplished preacher, and did a good wedding too. My only objection, and it was a selfish one, was that every week he sat in the third row and took notes on my sermons, not the gratifying notes of someone struck by my wisdom and spirituality, you understand, but notes which he'd expand on in an email that I'd receive Monday morning: I paused too long at the conclusion of the reading, and I made the same point about the prodigal son's older brother twice, and that prop I used, the dragon beanie baby, was really a bit undignified for the later, more traditional service.

But Chuck got away with that because he knew what he was talking about, and so, reluctantly, I got his number from Jill and called him. Don't worry, he assured me, he happened to have six new sermons in reserve, just in case, so I shouldn't hurry back.

Oh, well, I thought as I hung up. At least the Seconders would be happy for a couple weeks. Sometimes I thought they saw me as a usurper, though I hadn't replaced Chuck. Between his retirement, just after the church merger, and my hiring, another minister tried to meld the two congregations. He failed utterly, poor man, becoming a victim of the crossfire between the conservative congregation with more money, and the liberal one with the better building. The Seconders made a formal motion to fire him after a sermon on the Eye of the Needle, which seemed to imply rich people were less likely to impress God than the rest of His children. Two interim for different ailments, and if each doctor prescribed even one drug, the medications could counteract each other. Some might even cause memory loss and what looked like dementia, but could be corrected with medication-management.

That sounded promising. Mother's lapses weren't so very noticeable, I told myself, nothing like the ones profiled in the articles about Alzheimers. She didn't lose her way walking home from downtown, and she didn't think it was 1978. She just had a couple missing memories, and a verbal lapse or two—and a sudden interest in giving her money away. It was probably just a medication problem.

Now all I had to do was somehow get hold of her list of prescriptions. Simple.

Just had to call up her pharmacist and pretend to be Mother, right?

I couldn't do that. And I didn't think I could bring myself check Mother's medicine cabinet.

I glanced out the study door towards the staircase. Maybe I'd wait till Laura came, and let her do it. Laura had always been more curious, not to mention more . . . more *bad* than I. Besides, she once played a real estate agent who snooped through the houses she was listing, looking for blackmail potential. She could just flash back to that role and slip into Mother's bathroom and get a quick glimpse inside the medicine cabinet.

I bet Laura never thought I'd be asking her to use her underground talents for my own purposes.

I copied the list of suspect medications from the Web article to an email form and sent it to myself. And while I was online, I told myself, I might as well do some research into that other conundrum that nagged at my consciousness. Brian. Adam. Tom's son.

There were all sorts of adoption registries online. That's probably how he tracked me down in the first place. I remembered his birthdate, his birthplace. Maybe that would be all I'd need to track down the identity of his true mother . . .

But I don't want to find out.

The little voice in my head interrupted my thoughts. I hushed it—so craven, so cowardly. But I couldn't hide from it. I didn't want to investigate.

I took a steely therapist attitude and asked myself what I did want. *I want it to go away,* my inner coward said. *Failing that, I want Tom to tell me himself.*

It was too pathetic to dwell on.

The doorbell shrilled, startling me. It was that college president again, smiling.

He had a surprise! For Mother! A student-recruitment video! Just completed! Soon to be available on the Web! And it mentioned her husband and father-in-law and showed the plaques dedicated to them!

Mother, excited as a girl on her first date, got her sweater and purse and headed out, calling back over her shoulder, "There's a housekeeper candidate coming in twenty minutes, dear— please interview her and report back to me."

I chose to take this as a sign of confidence in my abilities, but then again, she probably just didn't want to stand up President Urich.

As the presidential car—a subdued BMW—sped off down the hill, I had a dread thought. What if—no, he was so much younger. He couldn't be more than . . . fifty-five? And Mother was sixty-nine. And she hadn't even considered another man after Daddy died. Not once—as far as I knew.

I had no time to contemplate this, as the housekeeper candidate was at the door. She spent most of the next ten minutes gazing around her, I assumed, mentally cataloguing Mother's possessions and totting up the total they'd bring on eBay. I cut the interview short and ushered her out when she admitted she was not bonded.

It looked like Mother and I would have to clean the house ourselves.

I looked up at the broad expanse of staircase and remembered having to polish every balustrade after that first time—the only time—I skipped school. There were eighty-two. The little twists in the oak made them all the more challenging.

The Yellow Pages yielded the name of a maid service, bonded and licensed and insured. Mother would disapprove, of course, as contract maids would lack the personal touch, and wouldn't do windows or dishes or dinner. But at least they'd keep the place dusted until Mother came to her senses and hired Merilee back.

The next morning, when the doorbell rang, I hoped it was the service come to say they had a cancellation and could fit us in. But it was Theresa. She was standing there under the noon sun in a heavy brown suit, her face miraculously free of sweat, her hand holding, incongruously, a black nylon Nike sports bag.

I started towards her, to embrace her, but she'd pulled the Nike bag up to her chest, and I ended up awkwardly putting my arm around her shoulder. The fabric of her jacket was starchy and stiff under my hand. It looked like the sort of suit slightly liberal nuns wore instead of a habit. "How did you get here?" I exclaimed, letting her in.

"I took the bus from Pittsburgh. It let me off at the bottom of the hill." Theresa had a low voice, gentle in tone. But she didn't look at me as she spoke. "It didn't take long."

"The bus?" I could just imagine what it would be like taking the mountain roads in a Greyhound. But I guess nuns didn't rent cars, and that vow of poverty probably precluded an airline ticket. "You must be exhausted."

"No." She set the Nike bag on the floor and looked around the entry hall, her gaze pensive. It must have been a couple years since she'd been home. "Everything looks the same. Now what is this about Mother?"

"I'm not sure," I said, glancing up the stairs to make sure we weren't being overheard. "Maybe you should see for yourself, and form your own judgment. With your nursing training, maybe you'll know more. Did you have trouble getting away?"

"No. I was given permission."

It was a laconic statement of fact, one that hinted at real conflict. "I appreciate your coming when you didn't really have to."

"Of course I had to come. She's my mother too."

Now that sounded like a rebuke. And she might be right—maybe I was guilty of thinking Theresa of a little bit different than Laura and me, a little less responsible, not because she was adopted, but because she was adopted so late—she was six when she came to live with us. So — well, yes, our mother was her mother, but she had another mother somewhere who had nurtured her long before she became one of us.

I didn't want to think about adoption or mothers giving up babies. "See what you think, then, if she—"

She was coming down the stairs, in fact. "Theresa!" Mother was smiling—not that social smile I was so accustomed to, the one that had so many uses, but a real smile. She was happy. Happy to see Theresa. I felt a little poignant twist in my chest, to see her genuine pleasure. And then my sister, so distant with me, opened her arms for our mother's embrace.

Maybe I'd done the right thing after all, asking Theresa to come home.

"Isn't this a nice surprise, Mother?" I said, in a rush to get this out before she got suspicious. "I told Theresa and Laura about what you're wanting to talk to us all about, your will, and they both agreed to visit."

Some of the pleasure left Mother's eyes, replaced by wariness. "Laura too? My word. How long has it been since she favored us with a homecoming? But it is nice of all of you, to help me with this estate-planning."

I held my breath, willing Theresa not to contradict me. It was a half-truth at worst—that is, entirely true, just not the entire truth—but Theresa tended to be more of an absolutist than I was. But she didn't say anything about the other reason she had come home, and anyway, Mother was bustling her up the stairs, chastising her for not calling for a ride, asking, "When must you get back to the convent?"

I barely heard Theresa's reply as they rounded the landing. "I don't have to be back any particular time."

That sounded . . . suspicious. She'd been at the cloister for a year, after six years in a nursing order. And in that year, she'd never left the monastery outside of Pittsburgh.

But she'd also never taken her vows.

It was hard to believe the mother superior hadn't given her a return date.

My suspicions increased when she came into the kitchen a half hour later, not in the pseudo-habit, but a gray cotton dress of Mother's that was too big and too long for her. The stockings were too large too, drooping at her narrow, unshaven ankles. On her feet were the clunky black shoes she'd arrived in. Her light brown hair was cropped short, no style, just straight across the back.

"I think I need some other clothes," she said, yanking the cloth belt tighter around her narrow waist.

I wanted to ask if this meant she were leaving the convent, if this was the end, but I just didn't feel comfortable being so direct with Theresa. It would be like asking—well, if I were planning on leaving my husband. Too personal. Too provocative.

I was, I knew, too sensitive to nuance, too delicate in my awareness of other people's boundaries. My counseling professor used to warn me that too much respect for privacy meant that I'd never learn enough to help those I was counseling.

But Theresa wasn't coming to me for advice. And anyway, we'd never had the sort of relationship where we confided in each other. Cathy and I did, and since Cathy's death, Laura and I had shared a secret or two. Theresa— she did not welcome that sort of camaraderie. She seemed to cherish her solitude and self-sufficiency, and I respected that even now, when I worried that she was on the brink of changing her life.

Join the party, I told myself.

"I could probably use a few tops myself." I tried to sound casual as I dried the last coffee cup and put it away in the cupboard. "I can drive you to a store."

But Mother, coming up behind her, said, "No, I'll take her to the mall in Buckhannon. There's no variety here in town, really. And I'll pick up a couple blouses for you, Ellen. Just something casual, a light knit. I know what you like."

I didn't object. It had been a year since Mother had seen Theresa except through the filter of a rice-paper screen. I didn't blame her for wanting a little time alone with her now. So I just said casually, "Can you get me a pair of khaki shorts too?"

"I'm sure they'll have some at Lukens." She opened the refrigerator and brought out a carton of milk—Theresa had always been a big milk drinker. "While we're gone, dear, you might think about replenishing our larder. President Urich wants to take us all out tonight—so kind of him—but if Laura is arriving, we'll need to begin planning meals for the rest of the week."

I didn't actually mind this duty, or the self-assigned task of tidying up the house after Mother took Theresa off in the car. There was some serenity, or at least mind-fog, that came from the familiar rhythms of housework. By noon, I was at Odom's Market, trying to remember my mother's brand of soap and my sisters' favorite foods.

In the narrow, box-lined aisles, I ran into several old classmates and exchanged the usual homecoming pleasantries—no, I wasn't staying long; no, my husband wasn't along; yes, I'd pass on my best wishes to my mother. It was back at the butcher's freezer that I saw one person I'd never expected to see again here in town. Jackson—

Jackson something—I'd forgotten his surname, but I remembered him. When I worked summers in the library, he used to come in, a most unlikely patron of literature. He'd looked like a hood with his tangle of dark blonde hair and torn t-shirt, but he was unfailingly polite whenever he asked to see the motorcycle magazines we kept behind the circulation desk. Once he asked me to direct him to a book on criminal law, and from the tense, conscientious way he took notes, I gathered it wasn't because he was planning to go to law school.

Naturally, this was the boy my little sister Laura chose for her secret rebellious high school passion. I only knew because she called me at college and swore me to secrecy—"I have to tell *someone*," she whispered. "And he's nothing like you'd think—he's a really evolved person inside."

And now I guessed, looking at him in the crisp blue uniform there in Odom's Market, that maybe Laura had seen some otherwise unrecognized potential in him, because apparently, sometime after his entire family was escorted to the state line, he'd evolved right over to the right side of the law.

He looked . . . very masculine.

Maybe it was the uniform. Maybe it was the aura of simultaneous safety and danger that seemed to surround cops, even in small towns like Wakefield. Maybe it was the gun on his hip, though I was, of course, a pacifist who didn't believe in violence. I don't know. But rather suddenly I realized how attractive he was—not with that abstract appreciation of male appeal that was all I used to allow myself, but with . . . well, real appreciation. His hair was shorter and darker now, but still a little tangled, and the smile he gave me wasn't so shy, and he called me Ellen, not ma'am—he looked all too good to me.

I reminded myself that he was younger—four years younger, just like Laura. Not that at our age that was much of a difference. But he was Laura's old boyfriend, which put him off-limits for life. And, oh, yeah, I was married.

So I didn't proposition him right there in the meat department.

All I did was pick up the chicken breasts that were right next to the steak he was getting, so that our hands were in close proximity if not quite touching. There was no ring on his hand . . . and there was one on mine. It was truly sad, I thought, how little it took to make me feel illicit.

To divert myself from my own weakness, I said, "Oh, did you know Laura is coming back to town? She's driving down from New York. She should be here tomorrow."

His hand stilled, just for a moment, then he set the steak package down in his cart. "I thought she lived out west. In LA."

"She summers on Long Island. Anyway, she's coming for a visit." Well, that was close enough to the truth. I wasn't going to tell him that she was coming to help me assess whether our mother was going batty.

As if he could read my mind, he said, "Your mother doing well?"

It was casual enough, the sort of thing an ambitious young police chief might say about the town matriarch, whose favor was politically important. But he'd spoken it as a question, and as I assured him Mother was just fine, thank you, I felt my anxiety index rise. Surely Mother hadn't called him and tried to report that Merilee had committed a theft. "Have you, uh, spoken to my mother recently?"

He started to answer, but just then the butcher in his blood-stained apron looked up from his cutting and said, "Hey, Chief! Hear you're going to be a TV star."

Jackson turned to grin at him. "Yep, me and Katie Couric. Or the local equivalent." He glanced over at me. "Not very impressive, comparatively. Your husband is on CNN, isn't he?"

I didn't want to talk about Tom, so I answered shortly, "Special correspondent. But he's mostly teaching now. So what show are you going to be on? And when?"

"Tomorrow. The evening news on Channel 8. All about the new city lockup, and how to protect your kids against predators, you know, that sort of thing. Not CNN, so don't expect too much."

"I'll watch for it," I promised. And maybe Laura would be watching with me. Of course, maybe she wouldn't want him now that he was on this side of the law.

Laura arrived as scheduled the next afternoon—with a heavy duffel trunk, but without a car. "Lady Porsche," she said, unpacking the trunk in her old room, the long narrow space off the back staircase, "couldn't take the mountain air. She gave out up on the Gorge. You know where I mean— where Daddy used to paint." She pulled out a crop top of the sort my teenage daughter might wear, regarded it regretfully, and laid it back in the suitcase. Not in the Wakefield wardrobe, I agreed.

We settled almost without volition into our usual camaraderie. Laura and I shared little but our looks and a common set of parents and the dubious honor of growing up Wakefields of Wakefield, but we'd always been friends as well as sisters. It was sometimes a bit dim, growing up in the shadow cast by our charismatic older sister, but there was safety there too, and a special access to the parent we both preferred (me secretly, Laura openly) in those years before his death Cathy got most of Mother's attention, and they often went off to riding competitions, a mother-and-daughter team of equestriennes. So for weeks, and once an entire summer, we were left with Daddy, the most gentle of guardians.

Now it was a relief, after the tense and artificial encounters with my mother and Theresa, just to be with Laura, who understood when I was had yanked it right out of the modem card, and I needed that, as there was no wi-fi in this old house..

She was hovering at my shoulder. "Is that a problem?"

"Just a minor one," I said. Actually, it meant I was going to have to replace the modem. That would be an adventure. I wasn't sure if I'd be able to find a compatible one here in Wakefield, and besides, I'd never opened up a laptop before. But I couldn't live without email, not with Sarah off at camp with her own little notebook. I forced a smile. "Really, Mother, it's nothing to worry about."

"Can we still get on the Internet?" she asked.

"Well, no, not until I get one little part installed. But I'll get that tomorrow."

"Oh, I'm glad. I was just beginning to get the knack of it." Mother smiled and added, "Now what was that you were saying about meeting with my attorney?"

CHAPTER FIVE

The attorney's office was on the second floor of the bank building, which meant he got most of the town's trust and estate work. He greeted us with a pleasant reserve that didn't quite conceal how eager he was to get more work on this important estate.

It was an old-fashioned office, with worn leather chairs grouped in an arc around the desk. It looked just the same as it had many years ago, when Mother brought us here and signed the papers that made the six-year-old Theresa our sister.

I glanced over at Theresa, wondering if she remembered that day. Just like then, she was sitting in the last chair, her hands clasped in her lap, her gaze steady on our mother. The last two days must have been hard for her—all that worldly stimulation after so long in a place of quiet and peace. I could almost feel her tension radiating across the room. Impulsively I crossed to the seat next to her, sat down, and reached over to touch her cold hands.

Her fingers curled. Just for a second our eyes met, and I could see the effort it was taking her not to pull away. Had she always been so resistant to touch? Or was that the result of her year in the cloister? I didn't know. And that meant I didn't know her.

"Mrs. Wakefield." The attorney came out from behind his desk, a folder in his hands. "Here is your latest will. You'll remember you updated it just last year."

Mother took the folder and opened it on her lap. "Well, I'm likely to make some changes in it, now that my daughters are all here."

"What sort of changes?" I asked, trying to sound only mildly interested. "I know you and Daddy set up some trusts."

Mr. Wampler's eyes lighted up. "Yes, the family trusts are key to the estate planning." He went off on a long lecture about taxes and generation-skipping and probate, while I fought the urge to reach over and take the will from Mother's restless hands.

"So you're saying," Laura interposed smoothly, "that the trusts might need to be modified in light of the estate tax changes."

"And because of family circumstances," Mother added. "There is a trust for grandchildren, but I've only been blessed with one grandchild, so—"

"Don't count me out yet as a grandbaby-maker, Mother," Laura said coldly. "I'm only thirty-five." She glanced over at Theresa, sitting there with utter stillness, her shoulders slightly hunched. She didn't add that Theresa wasn't even thirty.

We had touched, if only for that moment. She knew I cared. And I knew—what? That she was thinking of the distant past, of what she had lost when she became one of us.

All that dust dried my throat, and I went down the backstairs into the kitchen for a glass of iced tea. Laura was already in there, talking on the phone, and as soon as I saw her face, I knew something was wrong.

She hung up and turned to me. "That was Jackson. He said one of his men found Mother sitting in her car out by the highway. The car had gone off the road and hit the guardrail. Mother didn't seem hurt, but she was dazed, so they took her to the hospital."

CHAPTER SEVEN

"I need a drink."

It wasn't the sort of thing I usually said. In fact, I'm sure I got the line from some sitcom. But it seemed perfectly appropriate when we walked back into the kitchen that evening. I did need a drink, maybe more than one.

"I need ice cream," Laura said, opening the freezer door. "This is making me regress to childhood."

I regressed only as far as college, using Laura's ice cream and Mother's liqueurs and blender to create the sorority house version of a cocktail. "Just try it," I urged Theresa. "It tastes just like a milkshake. Only with a kick."

"And we won't count the carbs." Laura took a slurp of the grasshopper shake (crème de cacao and crème de menthe, plus Haagen Das) and then tasted the pina colada. "You know, we could open a milk-shake tavern. These are really good."

Theresa looked dubiously down at her glass. "That's a lot of liquor."

"The ice cream coats the alcohol and nullifies the effects," I said positively. I gave the blender jar a quick rinse and then sat down at the kitchen table, suddenly exhausted. "Do you think Mother is really sick?"

Theresa took a seat across from me. "I don't know. The doctor gave her the standard treatment for a stroke, a clot buster, but he didn't seem very worried if he's waiting till tomorrow to schedule a CAT scan. And Mother seemed perfectly lucid when we got to the hospital."

"All a mistake—she wasn't in an accident." Involuntarily, I was mimicking Mother's dismissive diction. "She was just pulled over for a moment, daydreaming." I thought about that. "Mother doesn't daydream, could she?"

"It doesn't sound like her," Laura agreed. "But she sure seemed alert enough when we saw her. I loved the look on your face when she asked you to bring your laptop in so she could check her chatrooms."

"I am *not* taking the laptop to her. I refuse. She can just wait until tomorrow." I could feel Theresa's gaze on me, and I flushed. I sounded something less than Christian, I knew, but—but I really liked my little laptop, and Mother had already broken it once. Leaving it alone with her would be like, well, leaving an infant alone with a four-year-old. I decided to change the subject back to something important. "Theresa, have you had any experience with those mini-strokes the doctor was talking about?"

"We have five very old nuns at the convent, so I've seen the mini-strokes before, and the big ones too," Theresa said. "I don't know. That

CHAPTER EIGHT

LAURA

Maybe it's true you can't go home again. But if you try, it's best to do it in a Porsche.

That's what I decided when Ellen told me about our aging mother and her new enthusiasm for revising her will. I didn't want to go back to that dull little town, but if I didn't, my old neighbors would assume I cared nothing about my own mother. And we couldn't have that rumor getting into People magazine. So I'd make my return in my fancy sports car, and give them the eyeful they wanted. I even stopped at a K-Mart in Harrisonburg and bought a long flowing chiffon scarf, in a shade of yellow that matched the Porsche. As I sped down the highway, I caught sight of my image in the sideview mirror. I looked like Isadora Duncan just moments before her dramatic scarf-death.

I was driving in from Long Island, where I had a summer home. It was a good time for me to leave. All my fellow Hollywooders were arriving, and the line at Starbucks of a morning was on the edge of insupportable.

The action was getting uncomfortably hot on another front too. My cottage was being renovated, and the architect, a gentle man named Alex, had started lingering over coffee after our blueprint consultations, musing that he hoped to be marrying and starting a family before he turned forty, and didn't I think the cottage's third bedroom would make a good nursery. I knew just a single word from me and he would ask me for something significant—a date, a wedding perhaps. But I couldn't say the word . . .

Coward, I told myself, but I couldn't help it. My sister's email gave me the excuse I needed to escape, just for a week or so, the push-pull of attraction and resistance.

After I crossed the Canaan Valley, the narrow road started climbing and twisting, and the Porsche started coughing. It had always been as temperamental as any starlet, and the clear mountain air infected it more than the worst Los Angeles smog. I managed to limp to the top of the mountain before it sputtered out, leaving me only enough momentum to coast into the scenic cut-out over the river gorge as an old pickup roared past me in the passing lane.

My cell phone was handy, but I didn't pick it up. Instead I climbed out of the car onto the gravel shoulder, slamming the door behind me. The noise echoed through the gorge and came back to me a moment later as I leaned over the guardrail to look down into the abyss.

I hadn't seen the gorge from this angle for many years, but I remembered it sharply as I stood there—the cragged stone face on the other side, the distant rush of the water below, the cool mist that rose in transparent billows into my face.

This was one of those family spots. My daredevil sister Cathy had rappelled down this one cliff one summer while Ellen and I watched, transfixed with fear, both of us begging her not to do it. She had to use three ropes, anchoring the first on the oak tree at the edge of the road—she said it was very uncool to anchor a rope on something manmade like a guardrail—then dropping to the ledge about a hundred feet below, fixing another rope to the stone face, and descending to another ledge. When she finally reached the floor of the gorge, she was just a tiny stick figure against the river, one stick arm waving up at us. She hiked out of the canyon and met us back where the river entered the valley east of town.

That's how she died—not here, thank goodness. On the next mountain over, rappelling one afternoon, she fell a couple hundred feet to the canyon floor. Same river, however, just a few miles west.

Cathy had gotten all the risk-taking genes, I guess. All I ever did here at the gorge was sit quietly for hours with my back against the big boulder, quiet and attentive while my father painted the view. "You're a good watcher," he told me. He meant that as a compliment, as something we shared.

Daddy and I were the observers in a family full of do-ers. Mother founded and ordered and organized; Cathy experienced and conquered; Ellen strived and achieved. Daddy and I just watched. And Daddy painted what we saw.

The gorge, he told me, happened when one of the oldest rivers in the world started to eat away at one of the oldest mountains. He had to show me what he meant, and he painted it for me, a series of watercolors—a hundred-million years in the life of the gorge. The first in the series showed a little stream, running placidly down a mountain far more jagged and fierce than worn-out old Aidan here, as a brontosaurus bent its long neck to drink along the bank. And then another watercolor, elaborately detailed, with the stream gouging a channel through the mountain, a pterodactyl soaring overhead. And then another seven watercolors, on through the epochs, the gorge getting deeper and deeper and the mountain softening under the effects of time and erosion. The last showed a serious little girl in a baseball shirt, sitting on the boulder and looking down at the rushing river, hundreds of feet below.

They were just the sort of whimsy to delight an imaginative child. And they were mine. Once they had hung in a diagonal line across the back wall of my room. But the night I left home almost twenty years ago, I'd taken them down and hidden them in the attic.

Now might be a good time to retrieve them, to hang in my renovated by how many scurrilous articles she garnered. I was that more common breed, the character actress, the supporting actress, the heroine's best friend, the hero's ex-wife, the witness who wasn't guarded by Ice T and so dies in the season finale. I was good at the job, and never lacked for work, but I wasn't beautiful and didn't get paid to be glamorous and scandalous. Rather I succeeded because of my wry tone and quick wit and everywoman appeal, or so the reviews told me. The producers told me it was because I showed up on time, knew my lines, and didn't insist on two personal assistants and a bowl of cocaine. That is, I was no diva.

Only divas benefited from negative press. That's because TV series were built around them, and the more complicated their existence, the more complexity it lent their performances. (Most weren't, I'm afraid, capable of complexity in acting, but in performing, yes.) Their roles were amplified by their reputations, so that some star playing the mother of a dying child took on additional resonance for all those who might have read an article about her mother or her son— she could be the role, plus herself.

But I wasn't supposed to be plus myself in my roles. No producer wanted a supporting character amplified by real life. Any nasty little scandal attached to my name might be forgotten quickly, but the taint would remain when the casting director thought about calling my agent. "Didn't she—what was it? Drugs? Something. Never mind. Let's not take the chance. Kelli Williams might be available."

I had a good life. A good career. A popular series just renewed for the third season, and a contract worth more per episode than most people earned in five years. Bi-coastal housing, money in the bank, the yellow Porsche, pretty clothes, hardback books, two good friends and twelve more I could enjoy without trusting. And the shelf-life of a character actress being considerably longer than that of a diva, I could conceivably work for another couple decades, maybe even into old age, as long as I stayed on the right side of the reputation meter. So I strived to be as boring as possible, and for the most part, I'd succeeded. I was under the radar of the tabloids, except once, and fortunately Jack Nicholson broke up with his young girlfriend that week, so there was no space for any of those celebrity date photos or breathless speculations about an engagement.

I lived discreetly, and it paid off now as it had paid off those years after my father died and Theresa came to live with us, when Mother told me I had three sisters now, and that I was to be especially nice to the newest one, who wanted so badly to be a part of our family.

Three sisters. It was just a Chekhov play to me. In my mind, I had only two sisters, the ones I was born with. My father's other daughters. Cathy and Ellen.

Not that I had anything against Theresa. But she came to us after Dad died, and so she wasn't really my sister. She'd never known him, except as her mother's employer, I supposed. Yes, my mother adopted her, but my father had no part in who she was or who she became.

I could think of her as my half-sister. That I could do.

So call it two-and-a-half sisters. Two point five sisters. I don't know what Chekhov would make of that.

I didn't blame Theresa for this. It wasn't her fault she'd never known my father. It wasn't her fault that Mother chose her specially. It wasn't her fault that I'd been the youngest and then suddenly she was. It wasn't her fault that Cathy died and left me with only one point five sisters.

Except the once, Theresa made no trouble for me. Another girl, one less scrupulous and careful, might have scored a few points with Mother by passing on the information that I was secretly seeing Jackson, but Theresa had kept quiet. All she did was study me with those big suspicious eyes, and I waited for her to present me with a blackmail demand. She never did, but just in case, I left money on her dresser, a few dollars every couple days. She had to know who it was from, because the bills smelled like popcorn from my weekend job at the Resource Cinema downtown. And she had to know what it was for, because, well, what else would it be for?

But we never spoke of it, and I learned later that St. Theresa couldn't be bought.

She was, I came to realize, loyal only to my mother. But maybe not— after all, she left too, left Wakefield and this house and all of Mother's many plans behind.

I wondered if Ellen's summons would be reason enough for Theresa to emerge from her cloister for the first time in a year.

I know. What a collection. A minister, an actress, and a nun. It sounds like one of those jokes where St. Peter awaits at the pearly gates.

Ooh. Shiver. The pearly gates. And the lost sister. Involuntarily, my mind's camera framed that shot. (Like most character actors, I thought I'd make a good director.) Open on marzipan archway into a blue sky. Cue the harps. Zoom into . . . lovely lost Cathy, all strong cheekbones and angel wings, amidst pillows of joy.

She would be bored to death.

Enough nostalgia. I raised the knocker and let it drop.

Mistake. This was my childhood home. I'd run in and out of this door a thousand times. The symbolism of knocking was all wrong.

I was about to twist the knob when the door opened, and Ellen stood there. "Laura!" Her sudden smile warmed me, and I remembered how easy Ellen was. No complications, no secrets, no blackmail, just a big sister who always remembered my birthday and bequeathed me her Narnia books the day she left for college.

We hugged there in the doorway, and then, laughing, she grabbed one handle of my suitcase and dragged it in. Together we managed to get it up the stairs, past the old family portraits, and, without any conscious thought, I tugged the case in the direction of my old room.

how much money my mother actually had. (It was idle speculation, nothing personal. I didn't need her money and didn't expect that she'd leave me more than a token amount, if that.) There were the shares in the bank that Daddy once ran, and I presumed some safe old-money investments and insurance policies, and this house, of course.

Anywhere else, this old monster house with its three acres of gardens would be worth more than a million. But this was West Virginia. No one around here had a million to spend on a house. I felt a moment's pity for whichever of my sisters got stuck with the place and had to pay to heat it during the long winters. "So ask to see a copy of her will."

She laughed, a short, unamused laugh. "You first."

"You're older."

"I'm not old enough for that." For a moment, she was quiet enough that I could hear the bees buzzing in the rose bush under the window. Then she said, "I'm glad you both could come."

"How did you explain about us all coming home? I mean, she's got to figure that's an unusual event." Like the first time this century, and only once in the last century too.

"I let her think it was her doing. She kept talking about the college president, and about bequests, and I suggested that maybe we could all help her make the decision."

"Oh, I get it. She's supposed to think we're so greedy that we'll come back to insure our inheritance, if not to actually visit her."

"Well, I didn't know how else to justify it," Ellen shot back. "Was I supposed to say that I was calling a family meeting because she's losing her marbles?"

"I don't know. But I would like to make it clear to her somehow that I have no expectations. I don't want the house and I don't need the money." This was Ellen, I told myself. I could trust her, at least a little bit. "All I want is a few mementos of Daddy, maybe—" Yes, I trusted her. But I didn't want to remind anyone of the watercolors. "Maybe his desk."

She shook her head, smiling again. She never could stay mad very long. "Yeah, that big old heavy desk will fit right in with all that pretty white Euro furniture of yours. You're welcome to it. It'll cost a thousand just to ship it."

I glanced behind me, worried that somehow Mother might hear. I didn't think she'd wiretap her own house, but you never knew. "It's so weird, talking like this. Like she's going to die soon, and we have to divide up the possessions."

"She's not going to die soon. But we don't want her giving away all her money before she does. I don't know about you, but I really would prefer that she didn't move in with me."

I had to laugh at this. "I can just see the look on Tom's face when you announce that he's got to make room for his mother-in-law."

As soon as I mentioned her husband, she glanced away, and her hand went nervously to the gold cross at her throat. I wondered if already he'd made it very clear that Mother would be moving in over his dead body. Not that I blamed him, but I didn't like to see my sister anxious like this. I tried to reassure her. "She's really very strong, remember."

Ellen nodded. "I know. But something feels different. When she gets back, you see what you think. Maybe I'm overreacting. She seems fine physically. She walks down the hill every day to the store, and back up again. It's just—"

She didn't have to say it aloud. We were both thinking the same word. Alzheimers. But I didn't have time to explain how utterly foreign this concept was—our formidable mother with a weakened mind—when the matriarch herself returned with a wary but appropriately dressed Theresa, all spare body and straight cropped light hair and taupe crepe, still a nun, even without the wimple.

In the hall, I kissed my mother without a hint of awkwardness, one of those patented moves I'd learned from Joan Crawford—taking the hand (so that we didn't have to embrace), leaning forward, pressing lips to cheek, and murmuring, "Mother." But when I did, I faltered just for a moment, breathing in the fragrance that lingered on her powdered cheek. Chanel #19. I'd sent her a bottle last Christmas.

"Welcome home, Laura," she said, drawing back. Her tone was so perfect, so admonitory, so courteous and reproving in reminding me how long I'd been gone, that I shot a glance at Ellen. At this moment, Mother seemed entirely Mother to me.

I turned to Theresa, and took a step towards her. She took a step back. It wasn't an insult, I knew, but an involuntary response. She wasn't used to being approached like that. I reminded myself that she had been in a cloister for a year, and moved to the side, as if all along I'd been planning to go pick up her shopping bag. "Hi, Theresa," I said casually, as if we'd seen each other last week. "Did you bring home anything for me?"

Deliberately, she reached for the shopping bag and removed it from my hand. "Just some new clothes. For me."

I smiled. She hadn't changed either.

Ellen, of course, took over and made everything nice. She sensed that Theresa didn't want to be asked about the clothes, and drew Mother towards the sun porch. "I made some iced tea. You sit down and I'll get you both a glass."

But Theresa chose to disappear up the stairs, so I was left with my mother. I inquired politely about the drive to Buckhannon, explained that my car was in the shop, and was tempted to mention Jackson. Instead, as casually as I could, I asked for local news.

Mother had a catalog of harmless and trivial news, about the garden club benefit and a new addition to the library. At first, she was making eye contact, and then her gaze drifted over my shoulder and over the garden, and a little after that, her recitation just sort of faded out. She was no longer paying attention to me.

Okay. That was weird.

I was about to say something when Ellen returned with a tray and a glass with ice and tea and lemon and spoon arranged just as we'd been taught. The bustle brought Mother back, and she focused her gaze on me. "So do you find the town much changed?"

I mentioned the commercial strip, and all the landscaping, and then, unable to help myself, I said, "And I see the police have some snazzy squad cars. Chargers, it looks like. That's pretty racy for Wakefield."

"Yes, that's true." Mother stirred her iced tea. She was a tough one—no lemon, no sugar, no Sweet and Low. Just tea and ice. "We had to bring in a new police chief, and he made some demands before agreeing. New squad cars, a new building."

My heart started beating faster, but I kept my tone casual. "That must be one expensive police chief."

She nodded, still stirring. "A young man out of Bristol. He's used to a bigger city, with better facilities. But he came highly recommended, and we did need to upgrade our facilities. We don't have a lot of crime here, but he was right that we couldn't keep the city lockup in the basement of a house."

I felt Ellen's gaze on me. She knew who the new police chief was, and she knew who he was to me. Oh, not that we'd eloped, as Mother had gone to some pains to cover that. But she knew that we'd dated and that Mother had disapproved. And she knew what I was thinking. Mother knew the provenance of everyone in town: who was an aunt of whom by marriage, who had a cousin-in-law on the planning board, which derelict was connected to which founding family. Even without the personal connection, she should have known exactly who Jackson was, one of those worthless McCains who arrived from Charleston in 1984 and scattered out of town, one step ahead of the gambling commission, in 1992.

"Okay," I whispered to Ellen as we went upstairs to change for dinner. "Maybe you're right. But—" I stopped outside of the door to her room, looking around for eavesdroppers. I still didn't trust Theresa. "But what can we do about it?"

Ellen sighed as we stopped outside my door. "She told me that nice young president from the college is taking us all out to dinner. So we can't say anything then. And—here's my thought—sometimes medications elderly people take can interact in weird ways. Maybe Theresa can go through Mother's prescriptions."

Before she entered the cloister, Theresa had been with a nursing order doing mission work in Romania. I wasn't sure if experience with cholera and polio would help her interpret Mother's pharmacology, but I supposed it couldn't hurt.

Besides, it would make Theresa a party to our conspiracy, and thus equally culpable.

Was I paranoid? Maybe. But I had reason to know that Theresa's first loyalty was to the woman who adopted her and gave her a life of relative luxury, not to the sort-of sisters who shared her home for a few years.

At the Farmhouse restaurant, the nice young president from the college fawned nicely over Mother, but in off-moments turned his charm on me. He wasn't actually young—fifty-five at least—but he was as handsome and as blow-dried as any LA entertainment attorney. Merely a botany professor, he told us modestly, elevated to this leadership position because no one else would take it.

"I was very surprised they chose me," he confessed, "because I'm definitely one of those outside-the-box thinkers. I'm all for tradition, but this is a new century, and the ivy on those walls is getting dusty!" He leaned forward confidentially. "Do you know, I'm hoping to make Technology Week's list of top-ten wired colleges this year. Small college division, but still . . . every student is given a laptop, and all the dorms have wi-fi access. And I particularly like to do online recruiting chats with interested high school students. That way we make sure that we're getting a good crop of techno-savvy freshmen. Do you have a website?"

I had to admit my publicist had set one of those up, which so far had mostly led to a lot of creepy emails from techno-savvy prison inmates.

"I'll be sure and visit it. Perhaps you could link to the Loudon College site? Since you are an alum?"

This was news to me. "I am?"

"Didn't you attend our summer science camps when you were in high school?"

Now that was thinking outside the box as far as alumni categories went. Summer campers. "Yes, maybe one summer." Don't get the wrong idea. I only did it to be near Jackson—he had to go to make up the credits he'd missed while in reform school. "But I didn't even graduate from high school. My sister Cathy was the Loudon alum."

"Ah, yes, I remember your sister. One of our athletic stars. On the ski team, wasn't she? Forgive me for bumbling around like that." He bowed his head as if to acknowledge our family tragedy, then looked up with a smile. "We'd love to award you an honorary degree," he assured me. "You could give the commencement address."

I was tickled in spite of myself. Yet was another example of his outside-the-box thinking. There I would be, an utterly uneducated actress, known primarily as "Uma's best friend in *Casework*, the one who steals Uma's boyfriend and then tries to commit suicide" (I was brilliant, sawing away at my wrists like that with a penknife), telling these little college graduates how fortunate they were to have coasted through Lit 102. But then, when I thought more about it, his offer stung a bit too. I resolved there and then that if I wanted to get a college degree, or high school diploma even, it wouldn't worry about me anymore."

"I—you know. It kind of overwhelmed me, to hear you were better, and that you'd thought to call him, and that—And so I broke down some, which was sort of embarrassing, but he understood. He and his wife applied to have me come stay with them a couple weekends. And then, when I turned eighteen, I got out. And he helped me get the record expunged so I could join the Bristol force." After a minute, he added, "He's the one I wanted for chief, who got forced to retire instead. "

"He was kind to us. He didn't have to be."

"Yeah. Christ. Can you believe how young we were? And we got married. It was crazy."

"It was romantic. Daring."

"Just like in the movies." He glanced at his watch, and turned back to the car. "Look, I got to get back to town. They're dedicating the new police building this weekend, and we got a lot of boxes to move first."

I was both disappointed and relieved that our interlude was over. Once back in the car, I said, "Oh, yes. I heard you made extortionate demands to the town board. Chargers as squad cars, a new building."

"We needed one. The old building never had a lockup. They just put a cell in the old house the police chief used to live in. And that's cruel and unusual punishment, to be locked up in somebody's basement."

I caught his grin and realized he knew this from experience. "So do you live out there in the house over the lockup?"

"No way. It's over on 21, halfway out of town, and falling apart. Besides, the last chief, he used to store the heroin in the garage. I was worried if I lived there, a packet he left behind would show up, and they'd figure I was in on the business too." He turned back onto Main Street and shot me a glance. "And it was no sort of house for a kid, anyway."

I felt a pain in my chest, a sudden seizing. Stupid, I told myself. Stop it. Nothing showed in my voice, however. "I know what you mean. A child could get locked into the cell. Especially if there was more than one child. A few times I would have liked to lock my sisters behind bars." The barest pause, as I gathered my composure. "Do you have just the one?"

"Yeah. Carrie. She's twelve."

Twelve. So he probably waited years before he married again. That at least was some comfort. "Is she going to be at the dedication?"

"No. She lives with her mother back in Bristol. We got divorced last year, before I took this job."

The seizing in my chest stopped as suddenly as it started. I shouldn't care. It wasn't like anything would happen between us. I didn't want anything to happen between us. I wanted something to happen with the architect back in Long Island, that good-looking and sensitive artistic guy. He would be just right for me, I knew it, just the right sort of man for me—if I could bring myself to touch him.

CHAPTER ELEVEN

We parted at the garage, Jackson speeding off in his squad car, I following at a more tentative pace, unwilling to push the Porsche's goodwill. I stopped at the grocery store to pick up a packing box and a roll of strapping tape. Then I returned to the ugly old house, retreated to my room, packed up my father's watercolors, and addressed the box to Grady, the architect in Southhampton. Just in case—just in case.

On the way to the post office, I called Grady on my cell phone to let him know the package would be arriving, and that I'd like the pictures arrayed on the walls of my new breakfast nook. He accepted this without demur, though I wondered if he'd be so tolerant when he saw the dinosaurs. The construction was going well, he assured me. "I miss—" and then, quickly, he added, "I miss your insights on the design. The contractor—well, he just follows directions."

"A good thing in a contractor, isn't it?"

"Yes, but dull. So will you be returning soon?"

I replied vaguely something about next week, wondering why two relatively experienced adults had reverted to a junior high school way of relating. He could just ask me out for a date, after all—or, for that matter, this being a new millennium, I supposed I could ask him out. But instead we traded innocuous comments that we meant to be heavy with significance, and neither of us took the risk of direct speech. When I got back, I promised myself, I'd just do it—take him out to dinner, take him dancing, take him to bed . . .

My chest tightened. I wasn't ready. I just . . . wasn't ready.

It wasn't Grady's fault. An intuitive man, he wouldn't press me if I resisted.

I needed to know him better, I told myself. That was all. I needed to know him well enough to be absolutely sure that he would be kind and gentle, that he wouldn't turn into a monster. I had to trust him.

Rationally, I knew he wasn't a monster. I knew he would be kind to me. But my body didn't know that. And I needed my body's cooperation, if I were to resume a normal love life.

That night I crawled into my old bed, and dreamed of making love again—and for the first time in a long time, the dream didn't become a nightmare. But the man in my dream, the man who took me past my fear, wasn't Grady, the artistic, sensitive architect. It was Jackson McCain, the bad-boy turned cop.

I was suddenly reminded that Theresa was somewhere out there, with my lemonade. Alone in this crowd. She probably didn't like being in a crowd. So as the mayor droned on, I pushed my way back through the summer-sweaty bodies to the open area near the statue. I still couldn't see her, so I clambered up on the low lip of Alexander Hamilton's pedestal and craned my neck to look for her over the heads of the crowd. Then I saw her, standing under a spreading tree, both hands closed around plastic cups.

I filed this picture away as I jumped back to the ground. Someday, maybe, I would write a screenplay—yes, yes, we character actors don't just fancy ourselves as future directors, we want to write all the lines too, and make sure they can be said by actual humans—about growing up in a small town, and I'd build the story line around such significant small town events—the fire department's christening of the new ambulance, the Lion's club fish-fry benefit for the boy with leukemia, the high school play. And maybe an almost-former nun, released from the cloister and alone in a crowd.

But as I made my way over to her, I saw a boy approach her from the sidewalk. He said something to her, a question, I thought from his posture. And as an answer she walked over to a trash barrel and dropped the plastic cups, the lemonade splashing up and then down again. Then she gestured to him to follow.

She was giving him directions. That was all, I realized with some relief, as she stopped at the corner and gestured across the street towards the old brick county office building. But then she stepped off the curb and into the crosswalk and he followed, sprinting a bit to catch up to her, talking all the while.

I watched, amazed. Theresa talking to a stranger. A male stranger. Well, he was hardly more than a boy, nothing wicked there, but—

But now the mayor's ringing tones were fading, and I looked back at the stage, and there was Jackson taking the mike. And when I heard his cool voice, always with the laugh hiding underneath, I forgot about Theresa and her mysterious young man.

He didn't talk long, just welcomed everyone and thanked them for the bake sales and the benefit concert and the support. And then the mayor trooped down the steps and over to the big red ribbon in front of the new annex. An aide handed him a big pair of pinking shears, and he snipped the ribbon in half. A cheer went up. The band started playing that old John Denver song about West Virginia, and that was all there was to the great historical moment for our town.

Without conscious choice, I lingered there by the statue, waiting. Waiting for Theresa to come back. Waiting for Jackson to detach himself from the ones who tugged at his uniform sleeve and the ones who declared their loyalty to the law. Waiting.

Finally I turned to look again for my sister. But instead, across the heads of the crowd, I thought I saw my brother-in-law. Ellen hadn't said anything about him showing up, but that was Tom, wasn't it? Leaning against the black Jeep in front of the library?

I liked Tom. He was a good man, and good to my sister, and when he got drunk, he lapsed into the most delicious Irish accent. And I supposed I should go over there and welcome him to town. But Jackson was walking away, towards the police station, and—and I'd see Tom back at the house.

Just as well. In the time that I'd glanced over at Jackson, Tom had gotten back into his car and was starting to drive away.

I tried not to make it too obvious that I was, well, pursuing Jackson. After all, I told myself, my tax dollars, or at least my mother's tax dollars, partly paid for that fancy new jail lockup, and it was practically my civic duty to inspect it. This got my shoulders straight and my head high, and I walked down the old sidewalk regally, my mother's representative. Her ambassador. I entered the old police headquarters just a few yards behind Jackson, and, as my heels clicked on the marble floor, he turned and saw me.

He made it easy. "Come for a tour?"

I nodded. My civic duty. "The mayor made it sound like quite a commodious place."

Jackson nodded to the sergeant manning the desk. "I'll just be showing Wakefield's most famous citizen the lockup."

"Sure, Chief, whatever you say." The desk sergeant's expression indicated he had no idea who I was or why I was famous.

Not everyone we passed in the narrow hallway to the annex was similarly clueless. I felt the gaze of a policewoman on me and wondered if she thought I was poaching on her territory.

But then we burst into a light-filled room with windows high along the ceiling and walls painted a soothing blue-green. No doubt this was meant to calm down the angry patrons. Along the wall, near a battleship-gray armored door, was a bank of TV monitors and an empty desk.

"No guests yet." Jackson punched a code into the keypad by the door. "But the day is young." The door opened with a whisper, and Jackson gestured for me to enter.

I hesitated, gazing into the dim space beyond. "You first."

With a grin he pushed through the door, and stood on the other side of the threshold, holding it open for me. "I told you—the cells are empty."

He was right, of course. The four little cells were virginal—as clean and shiny as a new car. Even so, the bars gave me a chill.

Jackson was regarding me with a slight, challenging smile. He opened one cell door, and walked in. I remembered a dozen times when we were teenaged lovers, when he would look at me that way, challenging me to ride his motorcycle, to sneak out with him, to run away . . .

I responded as I did all those other times. Took him up on it. I stepped across the threshold into the little cell. "Hmm, vinyl tiling. I was expecting concrete floors," I said, as if I were all-too-familiar with the dreary decorating

Alicia Rasley

of most jails.

"On concrete, it's too easy for an inmate to bash his cellmate's head open like a cantaloupe." Jackson pointed to the cot. "Try the bed. It's bolted down, but it's got a five-inch mattress."

"Also bolted down," I observed, gingerly testing it with my hand. It wouldn't come away from the bed frame. "Don't tell me. That's so the inmate can't use it to smother his cellmate."

"You're catching on. Notice all the video."

I looked up to the ceiling outside the bars. Three tiny videocams were poised, one on each cell. I was used to cameras, to say the least, but it gave me a shiver. I supposed they would record anything, even the inmate's use of the steel toilet in the corner. "Are they recording now?"

"Nope. So I guess I'm in trouble, huh?"

It wasn't quite flirting. But it was enough like it to give me hope. And we were alone, and no one was spying through those little cameras. I could tell—there were no red lights. And, of course, I trusted Jackson to tell me the truth.

So I sat down on the bed and patted the bare but fortunately pristine mattress beside me. After a pause, he sat down a few inches away. "Ready to move in?"

"Absolutely. At least it's finished. My cottage is still in the midst of reconstruction. And my room here in Wakefield— the walls are now maroon. Classy and depressing."

"Your mother must have found the graffiti."

I remembered it suddenly, that night he climbed up the oak tree and into my window, and with Theresa only a few yards away, we had to made love in absolute silence. At dawn I woke to find him gone, and on the wall a red heart with our initials drawn in permanent marker. I had to move the dresser to hide this evidence of our forbidden love.

Just the memory quickened me. This was an odd place to mount a seduction. But we were alone now. And we could move the actual act elsewhere.

I reached out. I felt strong, for a change. I took his hand.

He looked startled. Not a good sign. I realized that his thoughts hadn't been going along the same path as mine. But—but I was strong. I didn't let go.

And then he smiled and gripped my hand. "It's good to see you again, Laurie."

That was better. I looked down at our clasped hands and took a deep breath. "Me too. I've never forgotten."

"I know." He gave my hand a last quick grip and rose. "Let me show you—"

He was going to get away. "Jack, wait."

He turned, his hand on the cell door.

"I have a favor to ask."
Jack hesitated only an instant. "Anything, babe."
"Sleep with me."

body and a few hours of your time.

But I didn't say any of that. He looked so honestly anguished about it all. I let that soothe my wounded ego. At least he seemed to *want* to help me.

And I wanted him. Even if that desire seemed destined to go unfulfilled, it felt good just to feel again, to want to touch a man . . .

I didn't want to tempt him. I didn't want to tempt me to tempt him. I got up. "Okay. Sorry. Never mind."

He let me past him, through the cell door, back out through the armored door. "If it weren't for this, Laurie, you know—"

I managed a smile. "I understand. I'm glad you're still . . . you. Still, you know. Stalwart."

He shook his head. "Wish I weren't."

Well, that was humiliating. I managed to walk out of the police station without looking back. Back straight. Head held high. Marie Antoinette going to the guillotine.

I'm being melodramatic. It wasn't that bad. But beyond the embarrassment, there was also the disappointment. I really . . . wanted him. It wasn't just that I could see him as the key to restoring my poor lost desire. I really desired him. All of him. The lean body I remembered so well. The mouth that smiled as it kissed. The simple truth of him. The caring.

Just as well that I didn't get all that. Because I'm not sure I would have had as easy a time giving it up as I'd hoped. Just seduce him and go back to Grady ready to commit, I'd told myself. Now, as I walked, head not so high, up the hill to the old house, I thought maybe that would have been a painful exit—more painful than this one.

And it was *good* that I'd told him. About what happened. What I'd never told anyone. It was . . . healthy. It would help me recover. He was gratifyingly protective. Such a . . . guy. He wanted to beat the man up. Of course, he didn't know who it was, but just knowing he was willing to break his own laws to avenge me—well, it helped.

I just sort of wished he'd break his vows and heal me.

But it was for the best. No complications now.

I'd about talked myself into this scenario, that I was better off without his kisses. Then a couple hours later, when I was home, the phone rang, and I heard his voice, and my knees gave out and I had to sit down on the little bench next to the phone table. "Jackson." My voice came out a whisper.

But his voice wasn't soft. It was clipped and professional. His police chief voice. "Laurie, it's about your mom. She's okay, but she's been taken to the hospital."

My fingers tightened on the receiver. It was starting. Ellen was right. "What happened?"

"One of my officers found her sitting in her car over near the caves off 51. The car was safe on the shoulder, but the bumper was right up against the guardrail. No damage, and he didn't see any sign she was injured. But she was just sitting there, like she was dazed. So he called for an ambulance."

I managed to thank him, and hung up and immediately called the hospital. The nurse I reached was reassuring—no obvious injury, but still a bit out of it. A night under observation, a check by the neurologist in the morning . . . maybe a CAT scan.

Mother looked strangely diminished in the big hospital bed, her hair still perfect against the white pillow, but her arms hooked up to IV bottles. She had to be hating what the fluorescent light did to her complexion—if you think I'm vain, at least I came by it honestly—so as soon as I could, I opened the curtains to let in the late afternoon sun. I almost regretted it, because she perked up right away and began issuing orders.

She wanted out. Failing that, she wanted to check her email. Ellen should go home and return with the newly repaired laptop.

That had us exchanging glances. Check her email? Ellen muttered as we left that she'd never seen such a rapid descent into email addiction, and she was not going to enable it by bringing her laptop to the hospital.

I had to agree. Mother should be worried about her prognosis, not her inbox. Besides, the doctor had prescribed a sleeping pill and an early night, and Ellen wouldn't want to keep her up.

So we left her seething there in her hospital bed, her fists gripping the coverlet. I glanced back once, then ducked out the door. It was embarrassing how intimidating I found that glare of hers, even at my advanced age, even after decades of defiance, even knowing she was trapped there, tethered to the IV poles.

Ellen, to her credit, didn't say I told you so. She didn't say anything until we were out in the parking lot and she reaching into her bag for her keys. Then she said, "I wonder if it's about Cathy. All of this. You know, forgetting that the cameo was buried with her and blaming it on Merilee. Bequeathing the house to Cathy's alma mater." She aimed the key at the car door and clicked. "Maybe she's been thinking about Cathy's death. Wondering about it. Feeling guilty about it."

I climbed into the passenger seat. When Ellen and Theresa were both settled, I asked, "But why? It's not like her to feel any guilt. And, well, it was hardly her fault. Cathy was always doing dangerous things."

"Not always as bad as during that last year." Ellen shoved the car into gear and peeled out of the parking lot like a teenage boy in a Firebird. Her knuckles were white against the tan steering wheel. "Before that, Cathy did crazy things, but she was careful. That last day, she didn't even have the harness fastened right. She must have been distracted."

Or had a death wish. But I didn't say that aloud. "Well, that happens to the best of us, doesn't it? One little lapse of concentration, and disaster. But,

CHAPTER THIRTEEN

Mother's CAT scan the next day proved to be normal, and, emergency over, she reverted to her usual manner. I rather admired that, though I thought it would go over better with a Joan Plowright accent. But after less than a week in her presence, I'd run through my patience and just about exhausted my acting skill. Another few days, and I'd be snapping back at her, and all my careful armed-truce-building work of the last decade would be ruined.

I decided to go back to Long Island. There was nothing keeping me here. I couldn't face Jackson again, that I knew. He'd done a wonderful job rejecting me gently, but it was still a rejection, and I felt both hurt and humiliated. I was afraid if I saw him again, I'd try to tempt him away from his resolve, just to make myself feel better. And that wasn't fair to him or his ex-wife and daughter. I'd never been the home wrecker type, and didn't want to start with Jackson.

Maybe if I went back to Southhampton, seized the bull by the horns, and—Okay. No bull. No horns. No seizing. I'd just ask Grady out. Or, if my nerve failed, I'd send him the non-verbal signals that he could ask me out. And surely convention and nature would take their course. I'd grit my teeth and let him touch me, and after that, it would have to be easier, wouldn't it?

I wouldn't have to grit my teeth, if I were with Jackson.

Enough of that. Sunday night, I started packing my clothes. Monday morning, I started packing Daddy's things.

I heard Mother's measured treads outside my bedroom door, and quickly shoved the box of photographs into my carry-on bag and zipped it shut. As the footsteps retreated down the stairs, I taped up the box of Daddy's sketch books. Hefting the package, I wondered grimly how much it would cost to ship it. I just couldn't fit any more into my trunk, and too much luggage stowed in the passenger seat would excite Mother's suspicion.

I stashed the box under the bed, and with a bright smile, went down to breakfast with my mother.

She sat with Ellen, in the sunlight streaming over the breakfast nook. She was impeccably attired in casualwear from the Talbot's catalog, a soft pink scarf highlighting her still smooth complexion. "Dr. Urich is hosting the Garden Club today, giving us a tour of the botany department's greenhouses," she announced as she cut the crusts off her toast.

"I think I'll go along," Ellen said, pushing her coffee cup aside and getting up from the table. "I need some landscaping ideas for my back terrace."

I was sitting across from Mother, and saw the protest rise to her lips. But it came out gently. "Now, dear, you don't have to."

"I want to. I feel the need of some communing with nature."

"It's a greenhouse, Ellen," Mother pointed out. "Not quite natural."

"I'll drive," Ellen said, in a tone that brooked no dissent. If she wasn't careful, she was going to end up sounding like Mother some day.

As she went off to collect her purse, I said carefully, "How long do you think this greenhouse tour will take, Mother? Should I make lunch for you and Ellen?"

Mother had been looking abstractedly after Ellen, but turned her focus on me now. "Thank you, but no. I think we'll be several hours. I might take Ellen to that new teashop on Third Street." After a moment, she added politely, "Perhaps you and Theresa would like to join us."

Theresa had left the house early this morning— I'd heard her getting ready in our common bathroom at seven. "I think Theresa walked downtown," I replied. "I'll see if I can find her. Why don't you call and tell us when to meet you?"

For just a second, I saw something in Mother's eyes, a flash of something sweet, longing, as if I'd somehow managed, for the first time in recorded memory, to say something that pleased her—but then it was gone. "Yes, I'll try to call. But don't wait if you have other plans."

My plans consisted of raiding the house for more of Daddy's work and personal items, but I couldn't tell her that. "Oh, I don't mind waiting," I said airily. "Just be sure and call, say, an hour before we should meet you, so I can collect Theresa." That would give me plenty of time to hide my booty, maybe even get to the UPS outlet to ship some more of it back to Grady for safekeeping.

I was on the lookout for Theresa all morning, glancing out the window whenever I heard a noise, certain that she would catch me out. She had a knack for figuring out whenever I was doing something that could incur Mother's disapproval, and storing the knowledge away like a nut in a squirrel's cheek.

But at eleven she called, sounding, for Theresa, excited and breathless. "I've got something to do. I won't be home tonight. Maybe not tomorrow night either." And then she said, "Goodbye," very quickly and hung up before I could ask any questions.

I replaced the hallway receiver thoughtfully, and returned to my room to finish boxing. If it were anyone but Sister Theresa, I'd think she met some guy and was going off with him. But . . . but it couldn't be that. Still . . . she didn't have a car. I don't even know if she had a driver's license. And without

"Don't bother. It was doomed anyway. I think this is just an excuse. We were getting to the one of us has to move issue, and that looked to be unsolvable." He laughed shortly. "You know, it's like 'I'd die for you, but I won't relocate for you.' Modern romance."

Now I understood why he'd called me. Or I thought I understood. "So . . . you're saying you're free."

"Is that what I'm saying?"

I wanted to throw something at him. "You tell me, how about?"

His eyes were still closed. "Look, babe, the truth is, I broke up with Michelle yesterday, left my daughter in tears yet again, drove most of the night, worked all day. I'm tired and depressed and—"

It didn't sound good. "And?"

"And if you want anything from me, you're going to have to do all the work."

"All the work?" Oh. Boy. "You mean—"

"I mean the spirit is willing but the flesh is weak." He opened his eyes and looked at me. "Or maybe the flesh is willing and the spirit is weak. I can't tell. But you want it bad enough, you make it happen."

I was outraged. Who the hell did he think he was, lying there like some sybarite, telling me that if I wanted him, I'd have to come and get him? I wouldn't have taken that kind of attitude from the biggest Hollywood star.

But . . . I did want him. His shirt had fallen open and I stared at that hard tan chest of his, and I wanted to touch it. It felt so different, wanting again. Dangerous. I took a step towards the couch. He'd closed his eyes again, and I thought maybe he would fall asleep if I didn't do something. So I took another step. And then I was standing by his side, looking down at his face, the weary set of his mouth. "What do you want me to do?"

He wasn't asleep. He opened his eyes, just for a second. "Do whatever you want."

Damn him.

What did I want?

I wanted to get that stupid shirt off him. It wasn't doing anything worthwhile, as his chest was bare and only his upper arms and shoulders were covered. Useless shirt. So I let my hand drop to the collar—I only had to bend a bit to grab it—and I tugged. With a murmur of protest, he lifted his head and let me tug the shirt off one arm, and then the other.

Then he dropped back down with a sigh. "I guess that's a start."

I was getting a bit irritated. Wasn't he even going to touch me?

Apparently not. I stood there indecisive for a moment, and then sank down on my knees beside him. I put my hand on the drawstring waist of his pants, and got an immediate and amazing response—suddenly, under my fingers, under the cloth, stirring . . . emergence.

I almost drew back. This was where I'd always drawn back, this past year. The undoubted evidence of a man's lust, a man's aggression—I waited for the panic to overcome me.

But there was no panic. It seemed pointless to be afraid now. After all, he didn't even seem to notice, in his drowsy state, that he had a lovely big hard-on.

I noticed, of course. I could hardly ignore it, close as it was to my hand.

Grimly I untied the drawstring and pulled at the waistband. Another muttered protest from him, but he let me slide the cargo pants off, down past his knees. I yanked them free of his feet and sank back on my heels with a sigh of satisfaction.

Nothing underneath. He was naked now. And completely vulnerable. I'd never really seen that before, how a man could be so vulnerable and yet still so powerful, but that is what nakedness did to Jackson. No protective covering, no shield, no defenses. Just the tan skin and the rigid muscles and the hard-on and the . . . trust.

Of course, I still had my defenses. I was fully clothed.

I did slide off my sandals. Then I touched him. I just let my fingers do what they wanted to do— they brushed his chest, just below the collarbone, then darted to his jaw. My thumb found its way to his mouth, tracing his lower lip.

"Mmm," he said, and I felt something on my thumb. His tongue. Fire shot right through me, right down to that poor neglected erogenous zone of mine. Wow. If he kissed me—kissed me on the mouth, maybe . . . I could almost imagine.

I bent a bit lower, so that our mouths were only inches apart. He opened his eyes, but didn't move. "Aren't you going to kiss me?" I said, in my lowest, sultriest, Marlene Dietrich voice.

"You're in charge. Do what you want."

I wanted to hit him. Instead I lowered my head and kissed him. He responded slowly, as if he weren't sure about this. But when I slid my hand behind his neck and deepened my kiss, I felt him move under me. I was having an effect, whether he was going to admit it or not.

With my free hand, I undid my blouse, because it was apparent he wasn't going to bother with that task. I fumbled my bra open, and drew back so I could bare myself to him. I cupped my hand under my breast and let my fingers roam to the nipple.

Now he was watching, a light flickering in those dark eyes. Now, finally, I had him interested.

He raised his hand towards my breast, then, as if it were too much for him, let it drop back down to his side. "Pretty," was all he said, but as I watched, his hand closed on the fringe of the afghan. I could see white on his knuckles.

I took his hand and tugged it free of the fringe, then pulled it to my breast. His fingers curled over it, and my nipple hardened instantly against his palm. Then, reluctantly, he reached out with the other hand, sliding it behind my back and pulling me closer. He slid his hand under my breast to bare the nipple, and even raised his head a crucial inch or so, and kissed me there, a slow, sweet kiss.

It ended, too soon, as he lay back against the cushions again. He was obviously too tired to follow up, and here I was, burning.

I yanked off my skirt and my panties. But while his eyes widened and his erection pulsed, he didn't move until, impatient, I touched myself where the burning was. Then, his voice a bit annoyed, as if I were making too much trouble for him, he said, "I guess I can do that." And he slid his hand over mine, his fingers sliding into the spaces between my fingers. "Oh," he whispered. And "Kiss me again."

I obeyed him. I was supposed to be in charge, but I wasn't sure anymore what that meant. All I knew was his touch, and his kiss, and the sweetness of the feelings inside me.

"Laurie," he murmured against my mouth. "Baby."

Gently he pushed me back, so I was kneeling again. He sat up and slid down to the floor, ended up sitting with his back against the couch. He opened his arms. An invitation. And I accepted. I slid over him, slid onto him, and those arms closed around me. I was safe again, with him, next to him, in my own body again.

Sometime that night we got into his bed, into the cool clean sheets, and for the first time in a long time—maybe in twenty years—I slept securely in a man's arms. At some point, I felt Jackson's hand slipping down my body, and felt no instinctive protest. It was his idea this time, and that didn't frighten me. I was right to trust him, to trust in the magic of our shared past. He restored myself to me.

We woke at the same time, when the first light slipped through the drawn drapes. It was dark still, but I saw in his eyes that momentary disorientation when he realized that he was holding me. And then, there was the sadness. He was remembering, not me, but Michelle, the final loss of that dream of reconciliation.

"It wasn't really my fault, was it?" I asked.

He didn't have to ask what I meant. "No. I think we just couldn't put the pieces back together. And there's a limit to the number of times we can put Carrie through our experiments."

"What are you going to do?"

He shrugged. "What I've been doing. I'll go down there every week. I'm not going to make Carrie do the traveling just to make it more convenient for me. I'll get an apartment down there or something." Burrowing his head into my shoulder, he said, "Tell me she'll be okay."

"She'll be okay. She'll see more of you than a lot of kids see of the dads who supposedly live right there." I added, "My dad died when I was twelve. I turned out okay. I knew he loved me, and that helped."

"Great. So Carrie will run off with some biker when she's sixteen, like you did."

"She should be so lucky." I stroked his hair. "You were clever last night, weren't you? Making me come to you. You knew that would disarm me, make me feel in control. You were . . . intuitive."

"I was lazy." Then he moved back a couple crucial inches, and the sheet fell in between us, and we weren't touching anymore. "So . . . now what?" His voice went a little hard. "You got more use for me, or are we done for the—"

Before he could finish, or I could come up with an answer, the phone rang and he grabbed it. During the brief conversation, he disengaged himself from the bedclothes and sat up. "I'll be there in a few minutes."

He hung up and headed for the bathroom. I heard the shower running. I felt him leaving me in more ways than just that one. And I couldn't stand it. Bolder than I'd ever been, even before the problem started, I slipped past the shower curtain and slid up against his wet back. He hesitated for a moment, then turned, sliding against me, and held me hard against him as the water beat down on us. "I have to go, babe," he said. "And you do too."

"I do?"

"Yeah. It looked like something weird happened out at the Super-8. Someone heard the sounds of a struggle inside a room, and when the manager got to the room, the door was open." He climbed out of the shower and toweled off. "He smelled fumes that made him dizzy, so he called the fire department."

I followed, dripping water, as he headed for his closet. "What do you need me for?"

"I need you to go be with your sister." He yanked on a uniform shirt and grabbed his gun belt from a hook behind the door. "It was your brother-in-law's room, and there's no sign of him. And the fumes—they came from a cloth on the floor—soaked with chloroform."

CHAPTER FOURTEEN

In his squad car, I fought through my shock and remembered what had been nagging at me. "Tom. He's been through this before. He was kidnapped and held hostage for more than a year in the Middle East. He finally escaped. You don't think that they came after him again?"

He gave me a skeptical glance. "To Wakefield? I think someone would have noticed if a bunch of Middle Eastern types came into town. Not the most tolerant and open-minded group of people, our citizens. But," he added thoughtfully, "he's a journalist, right? Maybe there's some story he was working on?"

I shook my head. "I doubt it. He's mostly just teaching now, from what Ellen said. I don't know anyone who would have it in for him." Except, perhaps, Ellen. I wasn't clear what happened between them, but they were at odds, with him hanging out at the Super-8 and her at our mother's house. I wasn't to mention that to Jackson, however. I trusted him—especially this morning—but one starry night wasn't enough to overcome my instinctive wariness.

Or my loyalty to my sister. Something was going on with Ellen, and I was going to make her tell me what— and what it had to do with this crime against her husband.

Ellen was scared. But not scared enough.

I sat beside her on the brocade couch in the front parlor when Jackson showed up later, flanked by two patrol officers. In his hand was a transparent plastic evidence bag containing a running shoe. An old one, beat up and worn down at the heel.

Ellen rose to take the bag from him and then just held it. "Yes, it's Tom's. Where did you find it?"

"Outside Harriman's Caverns. Right there by the guardrail."

"The caverns." I took the shoe from Ellen and gave it back to Jackson. "They go back—"

"For miles. Yeah. We're getting some experienced cavers to lead a search party. And searching the woods above there too. But . . . it could just be a diversion, you know. To get us to concentrate over there, when he's being held somewhere else. So I want to make sure we're covering all the bases. It'll be easier to find him if we have some idea of who might want to do something like this."

"She's gone. She called earlier and said she would be gone all night, and maybe tomorrow too." Personally, I thought it made it all easier—Mother gone, Theresa gone. We wouldn't have to explain to them or deal with their objections. We could just figure out what to do and do it. "Do you think he told her? About Tom?"

Ellen puzzled over this as she paced around the edge of the rug. "I don't think so. I can't see her knowing that and not showing it somehow."

"She can be very secretive, you know." But even I couldn't imagine Theresa would knowingly conceal her contact with a kidnapper. "Wait. This boy. Tom's . . . son. What did he look like?"

"Medium height. Buzz cut. Army-navy surplus."

It was an efficient description of the boy I'd seen with Theresa in the county square. "I think I actually saw him approach Theresa Friday, at the jail opening. Looked like she didn't know him then. He came up to her and asked her something, maybe for directions. And then she led him across the street to the recorder's office. You don't think she—"

"No." Ellen's voice was firm. "I think he might have used her to find more about our family, maybe. Or where Tom was. But I can't believe she'd help him do anything like this."

"Me neither." I went to the window and looked out. A single patrol car was parked down at the bottom of the hill, gleaming in the late afternoon sun. But as I watched, it pulled away from the curb. Wakefield PD wouldn't have enough resources to mount a search and guard our house round the clock too. "But she did walk with him right to the recorder's office. What's there?"

"Property deeds. Birth and death certificates."

"So he was looking for his birth certificate? But you said he already had it."

"Yes, and it wasn't from here." Ellen stopped pacing by the phone table. She picked up the receiver, listened to the dial phone, and then set it back down. "He was born in Pennsylvania, across the state line."

"So what would he be looking for? *Your* birth certificate?"

"Why? I'm not his mother. And Tom was born in Ireland."

"Maybe he wants to see what this house is assessed at, wants a cut of the inheritance. We just need to tell him that the college gets it all, and maybe he'll go away."

I knew Ellen was really worried when she took my facetious comment seriously. "He has no claim on anything Wakefield. I'm *not* his mother. And I might not be Tom's wife much longer, so he can just forget about—"

"Ellen." I went to her and put my arms around her. "You need to stay calm and just focus on the essentials. What does he want from Tom?"

"His mother's name. As far as I know."

"And Tom won't tell him?"

"Tom says he doesn't know. But obviously neither the boy nor I believe

Great. I would never make a good detective, not when my only witness was a nun who had never owned a car. "Old? New? Four door? A mini-van, a sedan?"

"Just a regular car. Sort of old, but not banged up. Four doors. He had blankets in the back. That's why I think he was sleeping there."

I wasn't likely to get much else from her. "I've got to go. If you hear from Brian, call me."

After that phone call, I was full of suppressed tension. But I couldn't leave—someone else could call. And I couldn't wake Ellen up, because she needed the rest. So I grabbed a rag and some Windex from the pantry and started cleaning the dirty window in the parlor. Windows— or any other kind of housecleaning—isn't something I've done since I became a regular on the series, so I was almost enjoying the novelty. We used to have to wash these big windows every week, Cathy and Ellen and I. Oh, I was too little to do much more than rub away at the lower part of the pane on the inside. But outside, Cathy used to prop me up on the porch rail and hold my legs so I could stretch up to the fanlight at the very top.

Today, as I swiped away at the streaks, I watched the street at the bottom of the hill—for Tom's black jeep, for Jackson's patrol car, for Mother's anonymous sedan, for some unknown car bearing a boy with a grudge. But the cars just passed by, none turning up into our long driveway.

I was putting away the cleaning supplies when Ellen finally emerged. She'd showered and washed her hair, and it was drying in soft waves around her face. She looked weary but composed. "Any news?"

I filled her in on what Theresa said. "There could be a thousand reasons why he was talking about Highway 21," I pointed out. "But it's all we have to go on at this point." I added, "The police could search along there."

"No. Not today. Maybe tomorrow."

"Ellen . . ." But there was no changing her mind. She was so seldom stubborn, I didn't know how to counteract this attitude. "Well, I think maybe before sundown I'll drive out that way, just see what's there." And look for bodies in the ditches, I thought grimly.

"As long as you're not followed."

A cell phone rang from the pile on the chair we'd made of our purses. It wasn't mine— mine was a gift from my series producer, and played the *For What It's Worth* series theme song. Ellen stared at her purse for just a moment, then ran across the room to grab it.

I could tell from her expression that it was the boy. The kidnapper. She listened hard for a moment, and then demanded to talk to Tom. There followed a marital argument I really wished I didn't have to hear. Ellen's voice was hard as she said, "No, I won't tell the police about the boy. You know why. I'm not going to have him arrested of a felony when you can make this right with a single name."

When it was over, I grabbed the phone out of her hand, located a pen and pad from my purse, and jotted down the incoming number. "What's that?" I said, showing her what I'd written.

"Tom's cell phone. So no help at all. He probably had it in his pocket when he was taken." She didn't sound too upset about it.

I pressed call-back, but got immediately transferred to Tom's voice mail. The kidnapper must have turned off the phone. I contemplated leaving Tom a message— but what? Tell? Please? Before I go crazy with guilt? "Is he all right?"

"Yes. Angry. But the boy hasn't hurt him."

"What did he say? The boy? What's his demand?"

"Just what I thought. He'll let Tom go in return for the name of the mother." Ellen shook her head. "Tom—he couldn't believe I hadn't told the police."

"I can't believe it either," I confessed. "I can't believe *I* haven't told the police. So did he give you any indication where he is?"

"Tom said there were bars. Like a jail cell." She sighed meditatively. "He hates being confined, you know. Always has to have a window open. The bars will drive him mad."

"Ellen, please stop sounding like a sadist. What are we going to do?"

"Wait and see what Tom does, I guess."

"Ellen . . ." It was, I had to admit, a wail. "Please. Listen to me."

"No. Not if you're going to talk about turning that boy over to the police."

I didn't see how we were going to avoid it. Jackson wasn't just going to quit asking questions once Tom was freed. And it sounded like Tom was angry enough to tell him the whole thing. What that meant for me and Jackson, I didn't want to imagine.

I contemplated telling Ellen that Jackson and I were, well, together. In whatever capacity we were together. But I was afraid she'd stop trusting me. And she needed someone to trust, someone who might be able to rein her in if necessary. Hmm. "Tom said there were bars? Like a jail cell?"

"Yes. Maybe he's in some underground site of the water company, inside the dam."

"Oh, well, that's comforting. Millions of gallons of water right there with him." I remembered something . . . . "Ellen, Jackson said before they opened this new lockup, they used to hold people in the basement of the chief's house. There was a cell there. It sounded so creepy. They hadn't used it for years, because they were leasing a cell from the county jail. But I remember he said it was abandoned now, scheduled to be demolished. Out on Route 21."

"I know where it is," Ellen said. She grabbed up her purse, and before I could protest, she was out the door.

feel for you to keep me in the dark."

It was true, and yet it wasn't. What I wanted to do with him, I'd want to do anyway . . . but I could hardly deny, to myself anyway, that I'd taken advantage of the moment to distract him from his suspicions. But it backfired. He was more suspicious than ever, and angry at me besides. "I feel the same way you do. Don't you know that?"

"No. I know you wanted me last night because you thought you could trust me not to hurt you. And you were right. But that was using me too, only you were honest about it. Making yourself whole again, maybe for someone else. I went along with it. Don't ask me why." He walked past me towards his car, but stopped a few feet away. The evening sun was golden on his hair, but shadowed his eyes. "I'm not going along with this. You owe me the truth, and you know it. Call me when you're ready to be honest. Or maybe once again your family is going to keep up from being together."

He waited, but I couldn't respond. So I watched him drive away, and had to fight back the urge to cry. We almost had it back . . . and now this. He blamed my family for breaking us up before, when Mother had taken me away and annulled our marriage. And once again, I was blaming my own weakness, the loyalty that made me support my sister even when I didn't agree with her, the sympathy for that poor boy who considered himself abandoned by those who should have loved him most. And I blamed my own fear of trusting Jackson, no matter how worthy of trust he was. To trust him would be . . . to love him. And that scared me most of all.

Ellen paced across the kitchen as she told me about seeing her husband tense and unharmed in a dusty cell, the boy Brian hovering defiantly in the outer chamber. He couldn't believe that she had come alone, without the police. Tom couldn't believe it either. "He was so angry."

"Well, you had to expect that. What did Brian say?"

"That Tom just had to tell him the truth. That's all. And he'd let him go."

"Did he threaten you? Did he say he'd hurt Tom if you went to the police?"

Ellen shook her head. "I don't think he's violent. I *can't* think he's violent."

That didn't comfort me. "Ellen, is Tom going to forgive you?"

"I don't know." She drifted up the stairs, looking back at me, her eyes troubled. "There has to be a reason, something terrible, that he won't tell the truth. And whatever it is—maybe I won't forgive him."

I gave Ellen a couple valium and got her settled in her bed. When I checked on her a half hour later, she was sleeping fitfully. But at least her eyes were closed and her hands were still. I couldn't sleep yet, so I roamed about the big old house, finally settling in again at Daddy's desk, looking through the drawers for comforting little treasures—his old fountain pen, now dried beyond repair; a magnifying glass; a sketching charcoal, worn to an inch-long nub.

Finally I fell asleep on the couch with Letterman on softly, and woke up when the sunlight drifted in and Ellen came down.

"We have to figure out who the mother is," she said, standing in the doorway. "Help me think this through. It has to be someone I know, or Tom wouldn't be so resistant to telling me."

So over coffee and toast, the cordless phone between us on the oak table, we sifted through the memories of that year long ago, when Tom and Ellen broke up and then married, and Tom's two children were conceived.

"So who knew about you and Tom? That you'd married?"

She shook her head. "Everyone who cared. I mean, it was in the paper, the alumni magazine. It wasn't a secret. But whoever it was, she and Tom were together the summer before we married. While we were broken up. So if she found out later that Tom had married, I suppose she could have done some research. She didn't have to know me before, well, before the boy was born."

"What about that summer before then? Who knew you were broken up? Not me—I was off at theater camp."

"Mother guessed. She didn't say anything, but she guessed. She was pleased about the breakup. Cathy too, I told her as soon as I got home. She kept introducing me to her rock-climbing friends, the male ones, I mean. She said I should jump back into dating right away, as the best sort of revenge. But I couldn't do it. My friends here knew too—Janie and Linda mostly. I cried on their shoulders often enough."

I shook my head. Janie and Linda were great gal pal types, but not likely candidates to tempt a man like Tom into folly. "Okay, let's think this through. It must have been someone who knew about you to put your name on the birth certificate. Someone who knew your name and where you were born and that you and Tom had married."

"I know. I've already figured that out. Maybe an old girlfriend of Tom's went after him that summer. He grew up in Washington, and I know he went steady with a couple girls in high school. And he could have met one of them again, or she could have kept in touch with his father, and learned about me." She shook her head despairingly. "But why would he bother to keep that from me? I mean, the child would be a complication, but he could have told me."

Sternly I said, "Let's not worry about the why now. Concentrate on the who. Who else would have known about your marriage?"

"Some of my sorority sisters were there. And a couple were pretty jealous of me for wrapping Tom up like that for so long and not giving them a chance. Everyone in the sorority house knew we'd broken up about an hour after it happened. You can't keep news like that secret for long." She frowned. "They'd all know where I was born and all that, because we were quizzed on each other's background during rush. And you know how much you get to know each other living together for four years."

I didn't know, actually. I'd lived with my sisters for a lot more than four years, and never got to be able to predict what they'd do. I'd never have imagined, for example, that Ellen, the devoted wife and mother, would let her husband be held captive like this and not turn over all she knew to the police. "Any one of them in particular? Maybe one Tom fancied?"

She considered this without the jealousy I would have expected. Maybe she was beyond that. "Oh, one liked him very well, but Tom didn't notice her, as far as I could tell. He wasn't interested in the typical sorority girl. And I don't think he'd be so resistant to telling me if it were just a sorority sister." She glanced at the phone, then back at me. "I think it must be someone he has to protect. Someone who shouldn't have had a baby then. Maybe someone famous. I don't know."

"Could be," I replied. "The press loves to get hold of such stories. But who could it be? Who did you known then who now has to be protected from scandal in the tabloids?"

She gave a short laugh. "You, I guess. You're the only one I can think of."

"And here I confessed to a hankering for Tom's Irish lullabies. But it couldn't have been me. I think I'd remember. Besides, I was marooned in Yellowstone that summer, wasn't I? Wearing fake deerskin and Indian beads in that summer-stock play." I picked up a pen and wrote *1990* at the top. "Come on. Tell me everything you can remember about that year. There's got to be some clue."

She talked slowly through the chronology, and I took notes on the back of an electric bill. *July 1990.* The child would have been conceived then. And in late July, Tom had called suddenly and proposed. Two weeks later, they were married, so quickly that none of us had time to come. Except Mother—she managed to get there, no doubt with a fixed smile and four place settings of silver wrapped up in pretty paper. A couple months later, Ellen was pregnant with Sarah.

"I wonder if subconsciously, I knew something, knew that something had happened to him. That I had to bind him to me quickly or I might lose him."

"He didn't want a baby so soon?"

"Oh, no, he did. We both did. We thought we'd do it while we were young and had plenty of energy, and we'd get the wanderlust out, do the foreign assignments early, when she was still too young for school. Then Tom would have paid his dues and gotten a good post covering the Defense Department, or something like that, just in time for Sarah to start first grade." She was silent for a moment, then said, "It didn't work out that way. He liked the foreign assignments more. Didn't want to come home. So Sarah ended

CHAPTER SIXTEEN

TOM

So I lied.

I stood there in my front room and looked at the boy standing next to my wife, holding a birth certificate with her name on it, and I lied.

Of course I remembered who the boy's mother was, which of the one-night stands she had been during that summer of my discontent. For one thing, she wasn't a one-night stand, and for another, I was a good Irish boy, which meant I would never sin without the skin— that is, I always had condoms handy, even in pre-disease days, and used them. Except with her, except that once, when we were back deep in the mountains and fifty miles from the nearest Walgreens, and anyway, we were wet-slick with rain and I could hardly manage to get her clothes off, much less a condom on.

Eventually I knew about the boy too, at least in theory. I wasn't sure I ever believed it, and I certainly never figured on him finding me if he existed. I thought she was the sort who would cover her tracks better than this. But then, from the very first, I misunderstood, misjudged, misapprehended her . . . in other words, she knew what she was doing every minute, and I never knew that at all.

She was a real education.

I sound cynical, and—well, I am, from this vantage point, having hit forty with a daughter not much younger than that girl that day. (Best not follow that thought, or wonder what my daughter is doing those nights after her campers go to sleep . . . this is how men like me are punished, you know. We are granted the great boon of daughters, for whom we would gladly die, and instead, we must watch them walk away with the most unworthy of our youthful counterparts. Poetic justice.)

I am a journalist, dedicated to truth. I spent a year and more in hell, defending the truth, or at least that's what I told myself as I huddled there in a dank cell—I was the light-bringer, the one who dispelled the darkness.

But when it came time to focus the light on that little bit of darkness in my own life, well, all I could hear was my dad's voice, "Time to be careful, lad. Don't go pulling at that thread, or the whole wall could come tumbling down."

My father, mixed metaphors aside, was a wise man when it came to protecting one's own interests. He balanced his whole life, and mine too for a time, on the precarious formality of a marriage a woman he hadn't seen for years. He would have lied.

But I had a better reason than self-protection. Or so I thought, when I saw Ellen's face and that boy beside her—a younger, meaner version of myself. The truth was too volatile. It would destroy her. Or it would destroy us.

And the boy didn't want to know it anyway. I could tell. He looked at the birth certificate and back at Ellen and I know what he was thinking—that he wanted her as his mother, this compassionate cautious woman with the graceful soothing voice. I couldn't blame him. Everyone should have a mother like Ellen. I never stopped regretting that we couldn't have more children after Sarah, because I knew (my Catholic boyhood meant somewhere within me I believed these things) up there in Limbo there floated a half-dozen sad children who were meant to be Ellen's.

I don't know any who would grasp at the chance to be mine, and this boy was no different. By the time he realized what Ellen meant by her introduction of me, he'd already connected with her, and regarded me with suspicion. He was already feeling protective of her, moving closer to her when he thought I might be threatening somehow—as I were some threat to my own wife. But maybe he sensed what I couldn't say, that there was a threat there, and he was the embodiment of it—

The curse of the Irish (besides the drink, that is) is that we never escape our past. Never. We might go along thinking that we got away with it, but that's an illusion borne of intoxication. There is no doubt. We will be punished for our own sins, not to mention the sins of our fathers and grandfathers before them.

It hardly seems fair. The English don't worry about their crimes coming to pick like vultures on their flesh. Only the Irish.

The hell with it all. That was my thought as I watched the boy walk away. It was hot in the house, and the walls seemed too close, and Ellen was waiting for an answer. And there was none. There was nothing I could say to explain it all away.

When I came back from running, she was gone. I knew a moment of panic, then got hold of myself and checked the calendar on the refrigerator. Session meeting. That would last into the evening, and I'd meet her afterwards, and then we could talk. Only, of course, talking was exactly what I didn't want to do.

I'd figured out a few options by the time I got to the church and approached her car. I could invent a woman, or apply a new name, an untraceable one, to a woman who had actually shared a bed with me that long ago summer. I could also, legitimately, point out that what happened before we were married, when we weren't together, wasn't grounds for—well, for whatever I thought I might have seen in her eyes that afternoon.

But she didn't stay to listen. She drove off. Almost twenty years of marriage, and she'd never done that, just left me like that. Once, she refused to come with me on an assignment, because she had a new job, and Sarah had just started middle school. So I went off alone, and when I returned, a very long time later, she was still there in the same house. I'd always been the one to leave, and she the one to stay.

Now she was leaving.

I waited another couple days. Well, I wasn't waiting—I had the journalism review to get to bed. Through war and famine and riots, I'd never missed a deadline. I wasn't going to let a spot of marital trouble screw up my record.

As I finished a few last-minute edits, and approved the cover revision, I gave a thought to the boy. Where did he live? Where did he go after he left our house? Back to his own family, his real family? Would he try to contact Ellen again?

He didn't try to contact me, that's all I knew.

But then, neither did Ellen.

I spared a few minutes to go online and punch in his name and his approximate birthdate. He showed up in a two-year-old list of honor roll students at a high school in Williamsport, PA.

He didn't look like an honor roll student. He looked like a disaffected young thug.

Williamsport. Home of the Little League World Series. (Journalists' minds are full of such useless connections.) I wondered if he'd played Little League baseball. Sarah never had, because we spent her childhood mostly in Europe, where everyone played soccer. She was a great forward—took after me. We hoped she'd get an athletic scholarship next year and save us the college tuition.

The boy could have played soccer, I supposed. He looked light on his feet. And athleticism was in his genes too, I guessed.

I didn't want to pursue that thought, and logged off.

Forty-eight hours later, the journalism review was at the printer, and the only signal from Ellen was a singularly unrevealing email. I'd called every hotel in town, and spent a stupid hour driving around all the bed-and-breakfasts, scouting for her car in the parking lot. We'd been investigating doing a B&B ourselves, to help pay for our ever-ambitious renovations, so the owners of the small inns and private houses all knew us. I had to be circumspect. I didn't much care for myself, but Ellen's job was ever-precarious, balancing as it did on the mutual antipathy of two warring religious tribes. Any suggestion of instability at home, and one or the other group could use it against her and get her removed from the pulpit.

I could make some comment about these good religious folk, but I won't bother. Hypocrisy should come as no surprise from that quarter.

That's why I held off calling her at work. Neither of us was the sort to conduct loud shouting battles on the phone, but I didn't want her breaking down there in her office. Still I was getting worried. So, making my voice as cheerful as I could, I greeted the church secretary and identified myself, and then waited. My instinct for silence proved correct. If I'd asked for her, Jill would have been taken aback, as it turned out that Ellen wasn't there, hadn't been there, since the session meeting.

"Oh, hi, Tom," Jill said. "If this is about the wedding, Chuck has already spoken with the bride and groom, and it's all going fine. So tell Ellen that she can forget about that and just concentrate on getting her mom well."

Her mom. Ellen would never refer to her formidable mother that way, but it was all the clue I needed. I thanked Jill, promised to pass on the word to my wife, and hung up.

I hesitated there in my office, my hand on the receiver. It could be that her mother's was only a cover story, and Ellen had headed off to the Caribbean for some restorative reggae and ganja. But she wasn't one to lie, even when it didn't matter.

She'd gone back to Wakefield.

Funny. I'd never imagined Ellen running back to her mother after an argument. But apparently that's what she'd done now.

I settled the receiver back in the cradle and got up from my desk. No need to call. It was Friday, and with Sarah away at camp, I had nothing much to do till my summer seminar started in ten days. I'd just track Ellen down and make her understand that I'd done what was best for the both of us.

That's the problem with marriage. You end up so tightly bound that doing the selfish thing feels like doing the right thing, because anything that hurts you hurts the marriage.

And hurting the marriage—one way or another, I'd done enough of that already. So, with the best intentions in the world, I went to tell my wife more lies.

Ellen was from the best family in West Virginia. She used to say that with a laugh, adding that it meant their trailer was mounted on cement blocks, not old railway ties. But even the poorest state had its aristocracy, and the Wakefields were the West Virginia version— connected to the Randolphs of Virginia and the Beauchamps of North Carolina and all those other forefather slave-owners. (It was okay, Ellen assured me earnestly early in our relationship, because West Virginia, alone of all states, was born of abolition—it broke off from Virginia after secession.)

It wouldn't do to be obviously rich in a state that mingled the worst of industrial pollution with the direst of rural poverty. So the Wakefields were modest compared to their counterparts in Virginia. They lived quietly for generations in the biggest house in the town named after old General Wakefield (one of those many Union generals who never won a battle), endowing the local college, setting up genteel associations, donating books to the library.

I don't mean to make light of the family. It's a worthy task for a century or so, to build a town and make it work. If the Wakefields had done it on a larger scale, for an entire country, perhaps, I'd have covered it admiringly in some front-page analysis. After a decade reporting on nations ruled by evil despots or incompetent socialists, I had a sneaking appreciation for an effectual benevolent dictator, and so, I suspected, did the town of Wakefield. Hence the ascendancy of Mrs. Wakefield, who ruled with the sort of noblesse oblige generally unknown in America.

I wasn't really an American. My dad brought me over from Kerry— western Ireland—when I was twelve. My mother was supposed to follow with my younger brother, but in the end she just couldn't leave her family and her home, and so she never came. She and Dad kept saying she'd be coming to Washington, but she never did. I think she was afraid even of visiting, that she'd get caught here somehow if she stepped on American soil. The Irish of that generation still lived in the 19th Century, when family members emigrated and were never seen again. You can show them all the ads for $399 round-trip six-hour flights between Shannon and Dulles, and it makes no difference. They know once America's got hold of them, they'll lose Ireland forever.

And I guess there's some truth to it. Dad and I never went back either, except for short visits. It was too lucrative to be Irish in America to ever settle for being Irish in Ireland again. Dad cashed in on his fine tenor and his intimate knowledge of beer and ales to manage and finally buy a pub in the District, where he held court, pouring out the Guinness, telling Irish jokes, singing maudlin ballads, deepening his brogue till his own grandmother would have had to ask for a translation into English.

He did well enough to send me off to a good college, where I wandered among the careless children of minor Virginia aristocracy, too alien to be intimidated by them. I'd been raised in a tavern, and nothing impressed me— until I met Ellen. She was soft and shy until she decided to be sharp and imperious, and I appreciated her in both modes, maybe not as much as she deserved, but more than the other fools at that college.

Ellen was the perfect college girlfriend, dependable, helpful, fun in bed. I knew she wouldn't pick a fight right before finals, or seduce my advisor or my roommate or my roommate's sister. Sometimes I was amazed at her sweetness, her smile, her kindness. I wasn't really used to that.

And of course there was that indefinable class aspect. Sleeping with the daughter of the best family in a state, even if the state is West Virginia, had its illicit pleasures for an Irish boy who grew up over the pub. Not that she was a snob of any sort—in fact, she was very much the opposite—but there was something unerring in her knowledge of The Correct Way that gave her an aura of confidence. She had her insecurities—a thousand of them, last count—but I doubt she ever worried that she wasn't dressed right or might pick up the wrong fork or say the wrong thing in a social situation. If she dressed that way, picked up that fork, or said that sentence, it was, perforce, correct.

This was the 80's, and that kind of confidence was out of fashion. None of the girls wore white gloves or even dresses, and as for the right fork, well, most were lucky to have one fork apiece in the minimal college kitchens. But without being the least bit arrogant, or "stuck up," as the sorority girls would call it, Ellen had an ease about her that made everyone take her a bit more seriously than they might otherwise.

She was an intriguing mix of the poetic and the pragmatic. She could recite great swaths of verse, with a sincere melodrama that even my father would have appreciated. One spring day, she did the entire Ode to a Nightingale as we sprawled out on the quads beside the dogwood tree. I told her, "Sure, and you must have some Irish in you."

She replied, seriously, "My mother was a MacDonald, but that's Scots."

"No, sweetheart, the Scots haven't a drop of poetry in them. I'd say some young Dublin boy came over to the MacDonald clan to train the horses, and stayed to seduce the lady of the house, and generations later, there's your poetry."

But in an instant, her practical side emerged. "Nonsense. I don't believe genetics plays that much of a role. My forebears are as solid as could be, from a long line of bankers, and I don't think any of us girls are remotely like that. Cathy likes to climb mountains, and I write poetry, and Laura—well, Laura's got at least three different distinct personalities, not one of them solid. And Theresa—well, she hasn't any of our blood, as she's adopted, but she's probably the most like Mother—serious and responsible and with a strong sense of mission."

"Perhaps your mother writes romantic poetry, and hides it," I suggested, and Ellen looked horrified at the idea.

"God, I hope not. Then I'd have to stop doing it. It's my only rebellion."

"What about me?" And I drew her down beside me on the grass. "Aren't I a rebellion? Surely Mother wouldn't approve of me."

She kissed me quick, light, three, four times, her eyes sparkling. "She better not. Or you're history."

I believed her. Oh, she was in love with me, of that I had no doubt, from the very first. But the question was why. I'd like to think it was my charm and innate goodness that did the trick, but likely the poor Irish shebeen-owner's son designation had more to do with it. If I'd been a blond scion of an insurance executive, a Phi Delt or a Sigma Chi, would she have been so intrigued?

It wasn't the first time a good girl had fallen from grace for me, but it was, perhaps, the first time any girl had ever been so analytical about it. I was Ellen's education, as much as her History of Theater class and her research paper on images of lions in children's literature. She'd come to college to broaden her horizons, to experiment, to learn new ways, and I was on the syllabus.

I know—this is America, not Ireland. Good girls date bad boys all the time. Upper class and working class co-mingle freely. It's true. Certainly none of our friends thought we were a mismatch. We were a glamour couple there at Jefferson, in fact, Ellen with her gentle grace and her drive to collect books for the poor children in town, I with the glib editorials in the student newspaper. Unlike the typical Greek-house good time kids, we were quietly confident about being different and knowing that different was better.

Anyway, it's hardly as if once we married, I was some poor adjunct to my wealthy wife (not that she was wealthy yet, or maybe ever, if her mother proved to be as manipulative with her last testament as she'd been with every other gift she made). This is America. I made a success of myself. I ended up relatively rich, at least by Irish standards, and famous in a minor way, though not for the right reason, and the glamour that comes from being on TV dusted me with glitter, and glitter counts for more than anything else in America.

But Ellen couldn't have known at the time that I'd turn out acceptable— and she must have counted on my earning her mother's automatic disapproval.

I was young enough then not to care too much why a woman wanted to come to my bed, as long as she came. And I had no illusions about the gulf between us. She liked to pretend this was nothing new, visiting with my da in the pub, helping pull a few drafts while he told stories of the potato famine and the Easter Rebellion and a dozen other atrocities he knew only from the history books. But I overheard her a couple times on the phone, telling one sister or another or even once her mother about "Mr. O'Connor, the pub owner" and his adorable brogue, and there was that proud challenge in her voice. She was, in her polite way, spoiling for a family fight about this.

Her mother was too smart to give her one, no doubt thinking that there was no percentage in making a fuss over a temporary college relationship.

She was right, as it happened. It didn't last, our romance. I called it quits the week before graduation, to give us both time to get used to it. It wasn't as if we'd made any plans to be together. I knew I was going to Washington to work for the *Post*, and she was looking for a teaching job. I could have just let the relationship fade into nothing, but that didn't seem fair. I knew Ellen and her sense of ethics, and I knew as long as she thought we were still a couple, she'd never date another. So as nicely as I could, I cut us apart and headed off to my new life alone.

I used to be nostalgic about that first summer at the *Post*. For a long time, all I could remember was hanging out with the other new reporters, drinking and talking politics, chasing down leads and writing stories that occasionally even got into the morning edition. And the girls, of course, the ones who thought every young male reporter had to be the next Woodward, were ever a cherished memory.

But now I remember all the disorientation, the uncertainty, the constant recognition that I was in over my head and sinking fast. I drank more that summer than I ever did in college, and it wasn't just for fun. I was scared. The *Post* in those years after the great Watergate triumph was a place of long hours and cutthroat competition. If I did well that first year, the world was open to me. If not, I'd live the rest of my life knowing that I'd blown my big chance.

It's easier to accept that now that I've arrived somehow on the other side—grownup and recognized as an authority. Now I'm the kind of person who made the younger me feel inadequate and desperate to catch up. Back then, all I knew was that I was on a constant jag, hardly able to take a deep breath. It felt like excitement, but it was mostly fear.

Ironically, I'd gotten the job because of my father. His pub was just down the street from the *Post* building, and a favorite hangout for political reporters because of the Guinness and Irish music . . . and because of my dad, who could spin a better sob story than most of the *Post*'s high-paid feature writers. I helped him tend bar on my college breaks, and he introduced me to the right people, and in the end, that counted more than the degree and the editorship of the college newspaper and the clutch of writing awards.

So that summer sometimes I hung out there with my new colleagues after work, coming in after the last deadline, long after the happy-hour folks had gone home to the suburbs, drinking and talking about serious journalistic issues—noble ethics and ignoble editors and scoring the best assignments. One night, Dad waited till after they all left to tell me thought I was drinking too much, even for an O'Connor. He waved away my explanation that I was just stressed out from working hard. He'd never worked too hard, and he'd never stressed out from anything to do with a job, even when it wasn't clear he could make payroll. The only reason he could accept for drinking this much was a woman. He attributed it to Ellen, or rather, my break-up with Ellen. "You're missing her, aren't you?"

I was in a martyred mood, because the unworthy colleague at the next desk had gotten promoted to the State Department beat, the one that came with invitations to embassy parties and a silver spoon for the caviar bowls. So as soon as Dad said her name, I thought maybe he was right. Ellen—Ellen would know how to soothe me. Ellen would tell me I was the best writer in the history of the *Post*, that the other young wolf should be writing obituaries at the *Ottumwa Gazette* . . . Ellen would make me feel better.

But that only made me feel worse. I drained the last drop of Guinness and held my glass out for more. Dad ignored it. "You should have stuck with her," he said, polishing the bar with a pristine cloth. "She might not have been exciting, but she was reliable. She'd stick with you."

I supposed this was an implied rebuke to my mother, neither exciting nor particularly reliable. She just never could get herself quite stuck to Dad, and still lived with my little brother Pat in Kerry. And that made it all the more sad. Only twenty-two, and I was like my old man, bereft of the love of my woman.

But then I remembered all the good points I'd made when I set her free. "Ellen deserves better than that. She deserves a man who thinks she's better than just reliable, who thinks she's the center of the universe and all that." I meant it then, but thinking of her all alone made me feel even worse. She did deserve better than me, but the poor girl loved me, and so probably she would never open her heart to another man.

It was hard, I told myself, being irresistible.

"You need a woman." That was Dad's second-favorite prescription. "Not one of those silly tarts you keep bringing here, more hair than wit. You need someone who can make you forget the girl you left behind. A real woman."

He packed me off down the street to my apartment, and I was as sad as only an Irish boy drunk on ale and fiddle music can be. If it hadn't been three a.m. and my address book lost somewhere in the depths of my closet, I would have made a miserable penitential drunken call to Ellen, and very likely none of what transpired would have transpired.

But it was more dignified to fall into bed fully clothed and sleep off the drink and the despair.

And the next evening, Dad brought over the woman who was going to erase my sad memories and infuse me with new life, or whatever it was he thought a night of meaningful sex with a woman who knew what she was doing would do for me.

Every man should have a father like mine.

He'd come up with the perfect antidote—a dark-gold-haired beauty queen in hiking boots. It was June, and all the other women at the bar wore strappy sandals, at least the ones who weren't wearing power pumps. But Dad's choice was wearing a khaki shirt, khaki shorts, and hiking boots. I couldn't help but look down that long expanse of tanned bare leg and focus on the little rim of red sock above the ankle of the boot, the only spot of color in all that tawny tan and brown. Delicious. I fell in love.

"She's going to hike the Appalachian Trail," he told me. And he told her, "My lad Tom here went to Jefferson University. That's right off the trail." He was holding her hand, all paternal benevolence, and she glanced at him with a wry little smile, showing that she saw right through him but appreciated his performance.

That impressed me more than the Appalachian Trail information, that she recognized my father for what he was, a professional Irishman. Now that

shaping up in the South Carolina primary. Three well-funded candidates appealing to disparate factions of the party.")

Finally I turned the room key in and headed north. Time to kill, might as well.

I reached Williamsport around dinnertime, and stopped at an old Victorian mansion turned restaurant for a steak. The town was pretty in that *It's a Wonderful Life* stage-set sort of way— wide streets and big old robber-baron mansions in one part of town, and little brick and frame bungalows across the tracks. The Little League stadium was an absurdly large monument to pushy parenthood. Not enough for kids to play stickball in the street—no, they had to be organized and coached and trained into teams and leagues and tournament champions. (Okay, so my plans for my daughter's soccer scholarship started back when she first smashed a ball at the age of two-and-a-half . . . but seeing an institution devoted to such ambition made me question my motivation.)

There was a game going on under the overcast evening sky, two teams of fourth- or fifth-graders dwarfed by the big field, their parents scattered in the stands. I got out of my car and walked to the fence, watching the pitcher wind up. She was a little girl with a ponytail sticking out of the back of her cap and a fierce look on her face. Sarah always looked like that before she laid into a penalty kick, her little face scrunched up in a scowl.

In the distant hills, there was a rumble of thunder, and the coach in the dugout looked up. "Game called!" the umpire shouted. The parents rose like good soldiers and started packing up their picnic baskets and folding their blankets. A few of the kids protested, but trooped off after their coach, heading home to beat the storm.

I went back to the car and sat in the driver's seat, my legs out the open door, my feet planted on the gravel parking lot. I waited until all the cars pulled away and the first big drops of rain came down, splashing on my knees. Then I opened the envelope again and withdrew a single sheet— the scan of the boy's tiny footprints. In the corner was an indistinct copy of a photo— the birth photo, the black mark of a paperclip visible at the top.

Ellen said he looked like me.

I didn't see it. But then, Sarah looked like Ellen, and Ellen never saw it. She'd say, "No, Sarah looks like *Laura*," which pleased Sarah no end, to be compared to her famous aunt. Laura and Ellen looked like sisters, of course, but still Ellen couldn't see herself in Sarah.

I stared down at the picture. This baby looked like a baby. He also looked a bit like my little brother Patrick when he was a baby.

Okay. Patrick and I had always looked alike. Perforce, this baby looked like me.

There was none of *her* there I could see, and that was a relief.

I shoved it all back into the envelope and started up the car.

It took a moment to connect the laptop to my cell phone and start up the browser, but soon I had the boy's address and a helpful little map. He lived over on the robber-baron side of town, but in a new development, in a big brick house on a small lot, squeezed in between two equally imposing demi-mansions. Through the rain-drenched windshield, I could see a Mercedes in the driveway. A husky boy in shorts and no shirt was out in the rain, hauling in the porch furniture. From the disgruntled look on his face, I imagined he was cursing the absent brother who wasn't there to help.

He wasn't poor then, this Brian. His father was probably an attorney or an accountant, his mother some similar profession, nice stable people in a nice stable town.

He should count himself lucky. Sarah had never lived in a brand-new house in a brand-new development with a pool and tennis courts.

I put the car back in gear and drove to a liquor store, got a fifth of Bushmills, and took a room in some anonymous motel off the highway. I could not envision how this could turn out to be anything but a disaster. Even once I'd finished a quarter of the bottle, I couldn't come up with any plan. What did I know? That the medical records were available to anyone with a clever line. That the boy was persistent and unpleasant. That Ellen was regarding my withholding of information as a flat-out lifelong lie. That Sarah's life was going to change, one way or another, along with her belief in me . . .

I could make separate peace with Brian. Swear him to silence, then tell him the truth. But he wouldn't be able to keep that promise. He was nineteen. He wanted more than a name. He wanted an identity. He was longing for life meaning just as I was, my eighteenth summer, when I decided I was Irish, goddamnit, and went back to Kerry to live with my mother and brother and . . . well, be Irish. A month in the poorest nation in Western Europe, a month with no McDonalds, only two radio stations (one all religious music, the other Gaelic-language), two TV stations with no MTV, and a mother who expected me to kneel and say the rosary every night, taught me that my identity was that of an urban American teenager. I came home to DC and promptly filed for US citizenship.

Somehow I thought that lesson would be lost on this kid.

So maybe I could confess all to all. Shut the kid up, shut everyone up. But that looked to be even worse a disaster. The truth would hurt Ellen more than the lie did.

No way to make it work. I'd never learned patience, but I'd picked up the art of resignation. And so in the morning I got in my car and drove back to Wakefield, resigned to seeing it through.

I drove back the next day, checked into the same room at the Wakefield Super 8— still didn't feel like home, thank God— and went out for a run in the evening cool, working the old kinks out of my knees. I spent a long time under the shower, then gave myself over to an evening of answering emails. I used to spend my work evenings in exotic bars, drinking with other correspondents, talking shop about bloody revolutions and evil dictators and wicked assignment editors. Now I typed noncommittal answers to students who didn't like their spring semester grade.

I ought to get back to real reporting. Away from this teaching trap.

Better choose now. Pretty soon, I might not have a choice.

I was watching CNN with half my attention—Mongolia was heating up again. I'd spent a miserable month there a few years ago, trying and repeatedly failing to send dispatches by satellite in that place where electricity was a rarity. So I was rooting a bit for the rebels when someone knocked at the door.

It was the boy. Brian. He stood in the doorway, his shoulders hunched, his shorn head outlined by the floodlight in the parking lot. There was ultimatum in his eyes. I sighed and stepped back to let him in, wondering if I could get away with half the truth, the safe half.

I turned to douse the TV, and he clipped me one good with some blunt weapon. I was fighting for consciousness when something covered my mouth and nose, and I gasped in the sweet sick stench, and descended into darkness.

CHAPTER EIGHTEEN

I woke raging. With a raging headache, anyway, and a tension in my chest that felt like danger.

I opened my eyes to darkness. Breathed in, slowly, to decrease the pressure on my head. There was something cold and rough under my cheek— concrete— and the smell of dirt and underground must, and for a moment I thought I was back in Tehran, still a prisoner.

No. That was in the past. I closed my eyes again and sorted through a mix of memory and dream until I assembled something resembling a reality. Wakefield. The Super-8. Sarah safe at camp. Ellen . . . no. Don't worry about that now.

I'd read the Sunday paper recently. Seen the Secretary of Defense squinting and gesturing on a Sunday morning talk show.

It felt like a Monday. Very early.

Graduate seminar starting . . . Tuesday. Some Tuesday. Next Tuesday? The one after that?

Better not be this Tuesday, or I would probably have to cancel.

I tested my body. Rolled over onto my back. Opened my eyes and turned my head to the pinpoint of light. In a few moments, I was able to distinguish a few shapes, darker than the darkness— vertical lines breaking into the faint light.

I reached out a hand towards the lines. Felt cold metal. Closed my fist around it. A bar.

Jesus Christ. I was in a cell.

Again.

I used the bar to pull myself to a sitting position. My head protested. I ignored it. I felt around me until I got some sense of the proportions of the cell. Six by eight, maybe. No window, just a slab concrete wall, cold and damp under my fingers.

It all came back to me—Ellen, the fight, Brian at the motel. I raised a hand to the back of my head, felt the sticky hair, the bump. He'd attacked me. Drugged me. Brought me here.

I was about to put up a yell. Then stopped. Better not to let him know I was conscious. Reconnoiter first.

I'd been a foreign correspondent for fifteen years. I was always entering some new city, scrambling to learn a few words of a new language, scanning every room for evildoers and exits and escape hatches. So, though my head was splitting and my mouth was sore and fuzzy—the son of a bitch must have chloroformed me as well as clocked me—I yanked myself up and felt along the bars until I found the lock holding the cell door shut.

It was a padlock, closed around a substantial chain. My eyes were adjusting to the darkness now, and I could make out a large room outside the bars, empty except for something ominous and hulking in the corner—a big furnace or boiler. Beyond that was that sliver of light, coming down, I thought, from a door at the top of a bare wood staircase.

I closed my eyes and listened. I could hear movement upstairs. The hum of traffic outside. A highway. A rooster crowing nearby. I wasn't in the middle of town, but not isolated either. Get out of this cell somehow, and I'd be okay.

Cell. My cell phone. Clipped to my . . .

No belt. No wallet. No watch. No handy Bic pen to stab into his eye. No shoelaces. No shoes, for that matter.

There was a clatter on the steps, and I dropped back onto the floor, facing out, almost closing my eyes. I could see through the slits of my eyelids the pool of light from a flashlight, moving closer, almost to the door of the cell. A pair of battered Doc Martens, the ragged cuffs of jeans, a bottle of whiskey dangling from a hand—

The little fucker stole my $50 bottle of Bushmills.

Insult to injury. Too much to bear.

I stood up, grabbed through the bars at him. He stumbled away, fell backwards, dropping the flashlight, stumbling back into a metal pole. "You're—"

"Yeah. Let me out of here."

The boy retrieved his flashlight and staggered back towards me. "Not until you tell me what I need to know."

Just a kid, a malevolent kid with a drunk-ugly sneer and a grievance against the world. And especially against me. "What do you think you're doing?" I was genuinely puzzled as well as angry. "You got a life, don't you? College coming up in the fall? Friends back home? And you're doing this?"

"You don't understand." He slumped back against the metal pole. He really was drunk. I tried to decide whether this was good for me or bad.

"I understand you're on the verge of screwing up your life, for nothing. Let me go now, and—"

Brian focused the flashlight on me, aimed the glare right into my eyes. "I'm not going to let you go till you tell me what I need to know. My—my whole identity is at stake. I need to know who I am."

I was getting really tired of that demand. "You don't need to know anything. You know who you are, and it doesn't have anything to do with me. You understand what adoption is? It means all ties are severed. You don't have to like it, but it's true."

"Not fair."

The eternal adolescent lament. It would be amusing if I wasn't the one behind the padlock. "Yeah, well, life's not fair. And you're going to make it worse you keep this up. What's your family going to think when they hear about this?"

He set the flashlight carefully on a pile of boxes, so its glow illuminated this half of the room. Then, exhausted from the effort, he took a big swig from the bottle. "I don't care."

I watched him sway there in the wavering light. "Let me have a drink."

He just stared at me.

"Come on. I paid for it. And I'm getting thirsty here."

Slowly he came forward, the bottle dangling from his fingers. When he was a couple feet from the bars, he held the Bushmills out.

I grabbed at his wrist, yanked him forward, got hold of his collar, mashed his face against the bars. "Give me the goddamn key."

He was too drunk to be surprised by this change in his circumstance. He just grimaced, his face stretched tight against the cell door, and said, "Can't. Not stupid. I hid the key somewhere else."

Roughly I used my free hand to search his pockets, pulling out a mesh wallet and a Chapstick, but no key. I kept tight hold of his collar, cutting off his breath, contemplating. I could—but I couldn't. Of course I couldn't. I shoved him away, and he fell back, protecting the bottle with his arms.

Then he was up on his feet, backing away to the staircase, reaching his free hand, coming up with a handgun. I'd seen a lot of guns in my travels through terrorism, and this one looked real. So I backed away, into the shadows in the corner of the cell, and held my hands up, palms out. "Easy now. You're not going to get anywhere with that."

He waved it around, sighted down the barrel, grunted. "I can scare you with it."

"Not when we both know if you shoot me, you'll never get what you want." I had no intention of giving him what he wanted anyway, but best to remind him of the reality. "Instead you'll get jail time and a wrecked life. Where'd you put the key?"

"Somewhere else."

"And if there's a fire, are you planning on retrieving it and letting me out of here before I burn up?" That had been one of my preoccupations when I was imprisoned in Tehran. I was feeling the dread creep into me now, though I hoped it was beyond unlikely I'd be unlucky enough to face a fire. Unlucky, however, seemed to be my mode this last week.

He was frowning, considering this. "I'll make sure you get out."

"Big of you." I grabbed for something to hold onto in all this disorientation. "What time is it? I can't even tell if it's day or night down here."

"Six a.m. Dawn."

As soon as he said it, I could feel it, the sunrise. I needed this, needed the anchor to the reality beyond that wall. Needed to envision a world waking up, noticing I was gone . . .

The boy took another swig from the bottle and then sat down heavily, his back against the pole, his legs stretched out ahead of him. In the uncertain light, his face looked green. He leaned his head back and let the gun clatter to the floor. Too far for me to reach. Then his eyes closed, and he groaned, and passed out.

If he thought he was going to be an O'Connor, he better learn to hold his liquor better than that.

My head ached and my nerves jangled, but I forced myself to get back under control. Now that I had some light, I explored the small confines of my cell. The kid had tossed a Boy Scout sleeping bag on the steel cot. No pillow. There was a steel sink and toilet in the corner, both bolted down. Neither had any parts that might pry the lock or chain loose.

I sat down on the sleeping bag and studied the rest of the basement. There were windows, actually, but they were boarded up. If I squinted, I could see faint slivers of light coming in through the chinks, and I felt relief course through me. Sunrise. There would be light, at least a little, even when the flashlight's batteries died.

There was no way out.

He woke up after a few hours, picked up his gun, and left, and I got to lie there trying to sleep while thinking about fires and mudslides and insanity and Ellen and Sarah . . .

And him getting hit by a car and me gradually dying of thirst. (No water came out of the sink taps. I would die before I'd resort to the rusty stuff in the toilet bowl.)

It seemed like afternoon when he returned. The flashlight had died, but there was enough light through the window boards to illuminate the bag in his hand. He'd learned his lesson. He stood several feet from the cell door and told me to hold out my hands. He set the bag and a plastic cup a few inches to the right and stepped back.

It was just fast food, but tasted like the first McDonalds meal I had after escaping from Tehran. I could do commercials for them, you know? Tasted like freedom and home.

He was replacing the flashlight batteries when I finished. "You wouldn't happen to have bought a newspaper."

He glanced over at me, skepticism in his eyes. "No. Why?"

"News junkie here. Also I want to see if they've figured out what you've done."

This hadn't occurred to him, that the police might have been alerted. The kid was a good planner, up to a point, but I got the idea he wasn't so adept at figuring out consequences. Or he just didn't care. "They won't know who did it."

"Ellen will."

This stopped him. Then he smiled. "Let's make sure of that."

He drew a phone from one of his pockets— a small silver phone. Mine. "I found your wife's cell phone number in your wallet. If I call that, I won't have to worry about phone taps."

Okay, so he did have the occasional rational thought. Within the overall insanity, that is. (I didn't tell him they could triangulate a cell phone call pretty quick.) I found I didn't want him to talk to Ellen. I didn't want him to worry her if she didn't know. I didn't want Sarah to know either. I just wanted to get out of here and go back to my life.

The last time it took thirteen months to escape. But my captors were an entire guerilla organization, not a single American teenager.

Then again, I had no qualms about killing my captors in Iran. I knew I wasn't going to kill this one.

He was already dialing, and I imagined Ellen hearing the ring and having to search for her phone—

She found it. And the boy succinctly summed up the situation for her, and then he smiled and took the phone away from his ear. He punched a button and held it up. "Go ahead. It's on speaker."

I'd had a hope he'd let me take the phone and I could call 911. But he'd thought this much through. "Ellen," I said loudly. "Call the police. He's got me in a cell, with bars, and a padlock."

I could hear her voice coming faintly through the tiny speaker. "No, I won't tell the police about the boy. You know why. I'm not going to have him arrested of a felony when you can make this right with a single name."

"For Christ's sake, Ellen, he's got a—"

And the boy punched the speaker button off, and put the phone to his ear and said, "If you know the truth, call this number and tell me."

And then he rang off, and stood there grinning, and ceremoniously pushed the END button until the familiar "goodbye" tones told me he'd turned off the phone. "You got voice mail, I suppose? I'll check that later."

Not without my password, I thought, but didn't bother to say it out loud.

He left again, taking the flashlight with him. Nice kid. Maybe I'd manage to kill him during my escape after all.

There were a couple fries left in the McDonalds bag, so I decided to let him live.

Ellen—she was with him. Oh, I knew she hadn't planned this, hadn't known of it beforehand. But she was on his side. Allying with him against me.

A half hour later, they came down the basement steps together.

Ellen's face showed some shock when she saw me, standing there, my hands gripping the bars. But she recovered quickly enough. She crossed the room, the boy at her heels, and pushed a plastic bag through the cell door at me. I took it, brushing her fingers with mine, trying to remind her—

There was bottled water in the bag, and aspirin, and protein bars, a newspaper and other necessities, but not a single bolt cutter. The boy was watching carefully, studying her, and so was I. Neither of us could quite figure out what she was about.

"Did you call the police?" I asked in a low voice, but he heard, of course, and instinctively glanced behind him.

"No. I just came to make sure you were all right."

"Does it look like I'm all right?"

She nodded, but her eyes were indecisive. "You're not hurt."

"Except for the knot on my head. He hit me with a gun, you know."

I expected shock, anger, outrage. I should give up expecting anything at all. She looked at the boy, giving him her admonitory third-grade-teacher gaze. "Give me the gun."

He turned into a third-grader, just like that, sheepishly reaching into his pocket and withdrawing the handgun and handing it over. I was treated to another anomalous sight, my pacifist wife efficiently removing the clip—she must have seen that on TV—and sticking the gun in one pocket of her purse and the bullets in the other. She said, "You will just get yourself in trouble that way. I understand why you're upset, but don't be stupid."

I understand why you're upset. I pushed away from the bars and retreated to the corner, pressing back against the stone wall. "Ellen," I whispered, and found my stronger voice. "Walk out of here and call the police and get me the fuck out of this cell."

Ellen didn't react. She just stood there, one hand on the crossbar of the door, looking at the boy. He turned to me, looking scandalized that I would swear like that in front of her. I wanted to rip his face off, but —

"I can't, Tom. I told you. He needs an answer, and so do I."

"Why?" This came from deep in me. Why? Why do it? Why tear us apart for a stupid name that would fix nothing and change everything? What did she think it signified, that name? What would it give her that she needed badly enough to leave me here?

A way out.

That was what she wanted. It came to me then. She wanted out of our marriage, some excuse to escape. The mere fact of the woman wasn't enough to ease her conscience—she hoped the identity would provide additional incentive.

And of course she was right. The name would give her all the reason she needed.

The boy had been speaking for some time, but I was just now starting to hear him. He thought Ellen was an ally, and his voice was plaintive, his face open and boyish. "I've always known that I was adopted. Always known that this wasn't my real family. I always wanted to find where I came from— who I came from. What's wrong with wanting to know my real family? That's not so crazy, is it?"

I waited for Ellen to say something sensible, like *What's crazy is kidnapping someone*, but she only tilted her head, as if she wanted to hear more before making a decision. Well, I didn't want to hear more. This kid and his whiny little quest for meaning — I might have had some sympathy yesterday, but not today.

"I don't know why you think you are due some extra serving of parents," I said. "Most of us are stuck with the ones who reared us. Some of us don't even get that much. Ellen there, her father died when she was a mere seventeen. Do you think she went out looking for a replacement? And me— yes, I still have a mother. A *biological* mother. Back in Mother Ireland. Let's see. I saw her three times between the ages of twelve and twenty-two. She didn't even come to our wedding, because she's afraid to fly."

"But she's blood," the boy whispered.

"So what? What does that mean?"

"Genetics. You're alike. You look like them. Like your father."

I was silent for a moment. I did look like my father, or at least as he had been before the cirrhosis bloated him. Then I shrugged. "A bit. But what does that do for me? I get to worry that I'll succumb to the curse too and end up a drunk all yellow with liver problems."

He said, "I'm not like them. My parents. They're jolly. Do you know what I mean? They like to watch football on TV. They're always wanting to go camping. They don't understand . . . And my brother. He's just like them. He's their real son, and it shows, and we all know it."

I remembered what Ellen had said so long ago about children and parents and the misfit that can happen even with blood. "You know what? I have a brother. A one-hundred-percent blood brother. And he's jolly too and he likes to watch football on TV, only it's Irish football, which is worse. I made my life as a writer, but I don't think he's ever read anything I've written. Not because he doesn't like me, but because he never reads anything. We share the genes, but I've got more in common with— " with you, I almost said— "with the Italian I once shared an office with."

"At least you know. You know who your father is. You know who your mother is."

"I'll tell you who your mother is."

This came from Ellen. For just a second, I thought, she knows the truth. Somehow.

But she didn't. Or she knew the real truth, just not the one the boy wanted. "You know her too. You've known her all your life. Your mother was the one who woke up at night to give you a bottle or take your temperature. Your mother was the one who put you on the bus that first day of kindergarten and then followed it all the way to school to make sure you got there safely. No matter who gave you life, the one that kept you alive is your mother."

He nodded, nodded, as if it was only politically correct to agree with this analysis. But he repeated, "I have to know. And maybe you can help me find out."

Helpful Ellen. She said, "That birth certificate. Do you still have it?"

"Upstairs."

"Go get it."

He trotted off obediently enough, looking back only once from the stairs, probably wondering if Ellen was just sending him away so she could slip me the gun. No need to worry about that. Ellen was adamant. Ellen was implacable. That tag-team act of ours a minute ago was just for show. She wasn't my partner anymore.

She waited until the door closed above and said, coldly, "He's not buying it. Not entirely. And neither am I. He's not going to let you go."

I sank back on to the cot.

"So get me out of here. For Christ's sake. You just need to call the police and—"

"And the boy will be prosecuted for kidnapping? No."

"I won't prosecute."

"You won't have to. The prosecutor can bring charges without you. This is assault and kidnapping, and if that doesn't stick because you won't testify, there's still criminal trespass. And I'm not going to do that to him. He hasn't hurt you."

I closed my eyes and breathed in the damp from the stone walls.

"And all you have to do is say the name. And the only reason you're not doing that is because it's too dangerous. And you better tell me why."

"There is no why." That sounded good—it sounded existential. Zen. Something. It sounded true. There was no why. There was only the emptiness that lurched along after the truth.

"You're protecting her, aren't you? That's why you won't tell us. Because she's someone who could get in trouble if this is known."

"No."

"Who is she? The lieutenant governor?" She was baiting me. Our lieutenant governor was a proud lesbian.

"I don't think so."

"The president's wife. The president's mother."

"There's no one famous involved."

Bitter now. "Then it's because you still care. You don't want to ruin her life. She's still that important to you."

I closed my eyes. It made me feel even dizzier. I recalled the passion, that pure, extreme, dangerous passion, that I'd only experienced the once. I never wanted to experience it again. "No. When it was over, it was over."

"Then what? Maybe she's been blackmailing you?"

"No." I laughed. It hurt my lungs. "Yes. Something like that. That's where he got his criminal nature. Not from me."

I heard her get up. Panic seized me. "Where are you going?"

"I'm leaving. I'll tell him that I won't talk to the police, and that he needs me to find the answer for him, but I'll only do that if he promises not to hurt you."

Tell him to let me go then, I thought. But it revealed too much weakness. I wasn't going to do that anymore. Wasn't going to show weakness to her. I didn't want her saying, in that sad way, that I *needed* her. That she had to stay because of my *need*. She wanted out and I wasn't going to keep her with my need.

"He's got another gun," I said conversationally. "Maybe you better go back up those steps and get out of range."

Laura looked ready to comply, but Ellen just fixed the boy with that look. "Another gun? Give it to me."

Brian handed it over readily enough, muttering something conciliatory as she put it into her purse.

I didn't trust him. Well, yeah, but I *really* didn't trust him. "He's probably got another stashed. Card-carrying member of the NRA too."

Ellen very much disapproved of the NRA. But she seemed to disapprove of me more, because she wouldn't even look at me. She kept her gaze on the boy. "Laura and I figured it out. So you can unlock that door."

I resigned myself to it. She knew now. I didn't care about anyone else.

He was silent for a moment, then took a deep breath. "Tell me first."

Ellen didn't even bother to argue. In a voice that managed to sound both gentle and firm, she said, "It's not good news. Your mother is dead."

That dashed any hope I had that she had the wrong answer. Involuntarily, I glanced over at the boy. He was staring, his eyes glassy. "Who?"

Ellen glanced at Laura, then said quietly, "Our older sister. Cathy. She died in 1992."

"That's—" He took a breath. "A year after I was born?"

"Yes," Ellen said quietly. "She was a mountain climber. She died in an accident east of town."

"So you're like . . . my aunt?"

"Yes." Ellen took Laura's hand and pulled her closer. "This is Laura. She's another sister. Of Cathy's."

"And you've already met Theresa," Laura said.

She gave him a level look, and he ducked his head. I didn't know what this was about— didn't care. I was watching Ellen not watching me.

It was lost. I didn't care about anything anymore. Just wanted out. Just wanted away. Just wanted to talk to Ellen alone, explain.

She and Laura answered a few stuttering questions from him, but he ran out of things to say. Probably never expected what he'd heard—that his birthmother had been dead most of his life.

"Ellen," I said finally. She turned to me, her gray eyes opaque in the dim light, and I added, "When I'm out of here, I'll explain."

"What's to explain?" she said in a brittle voice. "That you were young? That she was beautiful? That when she came and visited us and sat in our living room and held Sarah on her lap, the two of you were still keeping this a secret? That you had this little inside joke? That you were laughing at me?"

I felt them all around, all the others. This should have been done in private, in our bedroom maybe, or some solitary glade in the woods behind our house. This was just us, just our marriage, not public property—but there we were, out front, all our terrors and dreads and intimate secrets shared now not just with each other, but the world. I think I realized then that it was over. We weren't one anymore. We weren't even two anymore.

"No. That's not it. I never laughed at you. I didn't even know who she was."

I couldn't finish my defense. At that moment a man came down the stairs, a gun in hand. It was the new police chief—I'd seen him before, at the jail opening last week. He took one comprehensive glance around the basement, then pointed the gun right at the boy. "Get down on the floor. Face first. Now."

Brian took a quick hard breath and dropped to the floor. The cop—he wasn't in uniform; he was in a t-shirt and jeans, but there was a gold shield clipped to his belt—bent down beside him and put his knee right in the small of the back.

"Jackson," Laura whispered. I guessed she knew him. And to judge from the hard glance he gave her, they weren't on the best of terms anymore.

"Yeah. I followed you." He roughly frisked the kid, finding a Swiss army knife in a back pocket. "I got backup outside. You okay?" he asked me.

"Yeah. I just want out of here."

The boy coughed, and the cop eased up pressure on his back just a bit. "Where's the key?"

"I hid it," Brian muttered. "Let me up, and I'll get it."

"Okay. Just the key," the cop said, rising. "And don't forget the gun, because I sure won't."

But as the boy started off towards the space under cellar stairs, Ellen got in between him and the cop. I knew what she was doing. I guessed I deserved it.

"No, Jackson," she said in her firm schoolteacher voice. "No key until we all agree there is going to be no prosecution. No arrest."

The cop looked honestly baffled. I can't blame him. He was probably more used to crime victim's spouses wanting revenge, not mercy for the criminal. But his gun never wavered. He just pointed it past her arm at the kid's belly instead of his head, presumably so if he had to shoot the kid, he wouldn't splatter Ellen with too much brain material. I owed this guy a beer.

"It doesn't work that way, Ellen. He gets the key. Your husband presses charges. If your husband doesn't, I can still arrest the kid because I witnessed a crime."

"Then you'll have to arrest me too," Ellen said firmly. "For obstruction of justice."

The cop glanced back at me. I started laughing. It trailed off because I was too tired to keep it up. "I just want out of here. I don't give a shit about pressing charges. He's not really dangerous. He's just . . . I don't know what. Ruthless. Ellen knows where he got that from. Her side of the family." She didn't move, and I added, "Look, she means it. She might make you shoot her. Can we just forget all about this and go home?"

He finally holstered his gun. "You know, Laurie," he said conversationally to my sister-in-law, "I think your whole goddamn family is crazy."

It took a couple minutes for the kid to locate the key, but finally there he was, coming towards me. "Let me do it," I said, thrusting my hand between the bars. He was chastened now, and didn't protest as I took the key from him and unlocked that goddamned padlock and pushed open the door and walked a few feet into the open basement.

Ellen put her hand on my arm. "You can come on back to the house."

I looked down at her hand. I didn't know anymore what to feel. I should feel gratitude, I supposed, that she was offering this refuge. But she was just being nice, and I didn't want that. I shook my head. "I'll be okay. I just need to get cleaned up, and I'll head on home. I have—" it seemed so strange, but it was true—"I have to prepare for that seminar. Starts . . . " I couldn't remember what day today was. "Next Tuesday. Hey, chief, can you give me a ride back to the hotel?"

The cop shook his head. He didn't mean "no," he meant I was crazy. "Sure." He fixed the kid with a sharp look. "I got my eye on you, boy. You better make this right, or I'm going to remember my sworn duty and pack you in that cell to see how you like it."

The boy muttered something conciliatory and looked down at his boots. He was probably trying to figure out what it meant to "make this right," and I was sorry I couldn't help him there. I was a lot older and presumably a lot wiser, and I didn't know myself. Nothing, probably, would make this right. I knew I had to deal with him somehow, reassure him, be a father, something. But I felt nothing at all for him. Nothing. No kinship, no hatred.

So I grabbed him around the neck, flung him into the cell, slammed the door, closed the lock, and pocketed the key. Then I said, "So what about that ride?"

The cop smiled. "Sure. Let's go."

A minute later I was standing out in the sunlight, feeling the breeze coming down from the mountains on my face. There are ways to feel pleasure even at the broken moments of life, and that's what I felt. I had to remember this, because I had the idea I was in for more brokenness ahead.

Sticking my hand in my pocket, I found the key, and looked around for a worthy target. The mailbox, out by the end of the driveway. I sighted, and threw the key over there, and heard the clink of metal against metal.

"Good shot," the chief said.

"I grew up in a pub. Played a lot of darts."

I looked back at the porch, and Ellen was standing there. She was looking at me, not the key lying in the gravel. As I climbed into the cop's Charger, she turned and went back into the house.

"You didn't have any backup, did you?" I said as we backed out of the driveway.

"Nah. Figured I could handle it more . . . discreetly by myself." He looked over at me. "Your wife was worried about your daughter finding out."

He didn't need to say it out loud—that if Ellen hadn't protected the boy, there would be no reason to worry about Sarah finding out.

"Well. Thanks for showing. And the ride back."

He dropped me at the motel. No recriminations. No questions. Small town. No bureaucracy, no rules that couldn't be broken. I supposed I should be relieved. There would be no story about me on the wire services, no speculations about the kidnapper, no sidebar about the last time I was trapped in a cell. It was all over.

CHAPTER TWENTY

The hotel had kept the room for me. I yanked off the yellow police tape across the door and went in, my stomach clenching at the faint smell of chloroform clinging to the carpet.

First I took a long shower. Then I got out and pulled on some shorts and went for a run. The high school track was deserted. Just me and the open air and the mountains all around.

I ran back to the motel and took another shower. I thought maybe I should keep that up forever—shower and then run and then shower . . . stay in there forever. No need to face what was ahead of me.

Instead I got dressed and called for a pizza to be delivered and fired up the laptop and checked my email. Two days worth of newsletters from various news sites, some jokes from friends, a couple more queries from students too worried about their grades to wait for the report to appear in the mail. And an email from Sarah. She hated the camp. She hated her boss. The kids were obnoxious and didn't obey. And she was homesick.

That was code for missing her boyfriend Josh, a slight red-faced boy who never spoke above a whisper when I was around. That could have been because the first time he took Sarah out, I took him aside and told him if he treated her with less than respect, I'd break every bone in his scrawny body.

Sometimes being a father was really rewarding.

But it also had its responsibilities. I sent off a quick reply, telling her to hang on for another week, and if she still hated it, her mom and I would come pick her up and she could get a job at the mall for the rest of the summer. I figured that she'd be happier in a week and I wouldn't have to make the drive. I read it over and then backspaced and deleted "your mom." I doubted I'd be going anywhere with Ellen for a long time.

By evening I was okay. I started going through my notes for the journalistic ethics seminar, noting down examples from my experience to illustrate each ethical point. I was amused now at how often reality defied the black-and-white dictates of the ethics textbook. Then again, life was always more complicated than any textbook writer could describe.

I was getting better at this, this getting over being held hostage. Last time, as Ellen so kindly reminded me, it took years. This time—hell, four hours and I was back to normal.

There was a knock on the door, and my pen froze on the page. I forced myself to put it down, get up, go to the door, and look through the peephole. Ellen was standing there, her face distorted by the fish-eye lens, surrounded by the glare of the floodlight. Probably her partner, the kid, lingered just outside of viewing range, mace in hand.

I let her in. She was my wife, after all. For the time being, anyway.

And she was alone.

"Where's the kid?"

She glanced back through the open door, as if worried I meant it. "You shouldn't call him the kid. He has a name."

"Two, in fact. What's up?"

It was all very casual, considering the circumstances. That is, until she came to me and, her expression purposeful, began unbuttoning my shirt.

I gripped her hands and they stilled.

"I'm a little old to be eager for a pity fuck."

She looked up at me. Her eyes were usually a clear gray, but now I couldn't read them. Her hands closed into fists within mine. "Let go of my hands, or I'm leaving and going straight to an attorney's office."

"I don't know that you'd find one open this time of night." I relaxed my grip, and let her resume her unbuttoning. "Another ultimatum. Whatever happened to my generous, giving Ellen?" I meant it ironically, but it didn't come out that way.

"I decided I'd get more respect if I became the demanding, difficult Ellen."

"So," I said, as if I didn't already know, "what's your demand?"

She wasn't nearly as difficult as she'd claimed, and for at least a little while it seemed like all was well again. It had been a week or so since we'd last shared a bed, and everything had changed— but the magical thing about marriage was that you could in good conscience keep making love even so.

I told her, just to get it on the record, "I don't *need* this."

"But we do."

I didn't want to think about how much that composed wisdom of hers was concealing. She was hurt. She was confused. I knew that, even if she didn't show it. I summoned up some courage, and, lying there in the dark, her head on my shoulder, I said, "Ask me. I'll tell you."

But she said nothing. I suppose, with all the mystery there was between, she couldn't begin to choose a single question. So I started with a single answer. "You're the only one I love. The only one I ever loved. That's why I couldn't tell you. I didn't want to lose you." After a moment, I added, "And I couldn't figure out how to explain it anyway."

"You really didn't know she was my sister."

"No. How could I know? I'd never met her. There are a million Cathy's out there. It never occurred to me."

"You didn't ask why she came after you that way."

"I was 22. She came up to me in my father's pub and wanted to take me

182

to bed. You think I asked why? I thought I knew."

"And you never guessed? All that time afterwards?"

"You know," I said with some exasperation, "First I put it out of my mind because I was ashamed of the whole episode. And second—come on. Never in a million years would I have imagined your sister would do that. You always talked about how wonderful she was." Ellen was silent. I didn't like the sound of that, so I added, "And I didn't meet her again. We got married so quickly she didn't come to the wedding, thank God. And then we were posted to Europe."

"But she knew from the first. That's what you're saying. She knew who you were and came and found you. Deliberately."

"Yeah. I don't know how she tracked me down—"

"Oh, I told her. I cried on her shoulder for weeks. She had all the salient details. Your name, what you looked like, your father's pub. She didn't have to be a Sherlock to find you." Ellen said this with an edge of bitterness, then added, "I'm not sure why she did it."

"Revenge. That's what she told me, anyway. She got me back for hurting you."

"When did she say that?"

"In Belgium. You remember. She stopped there on her way to climb the Matterhorn blindfolded, or some fool stunt."

"At night. She climbed it in one night."

"Right. I came home from work, and there she was, sitting with you. I was too stunned to make any sense of it, but then you left to shop for dinner, and she told me all about her desire for revenge." I added, "I thought she was nuts. Crazy. I thought she was going to tell you."

"Did you know about the boy? Brian?"

"Not till then. And I didn't believe her. I thought she just wanted to cause maximum pain. And she was jealous of Sarah. That was clear to me. She didn't think it was fair that we had Sarah. So I thought she invented another baby, just to get back at me. And at you."

"You hate her," she said wonderingly.

"Oh, yeah." I stopped and took a deep breath. "I did. It took me a long time to stop. It was so willful. She was trying to hurt me—that I could understand—but she hurt you too, even if she wouldn't let you know because she wanted you to go on loving her. And so, after that, she was always there somehow with us, even if I didn't think of her for years on end."

"Sarah was still a baby then. So . . . 1992?" Ellen paused, then whispered, "That was the last time I saw Cathy. She did her climb and went home and then she was dead a month later."

Neither of us could follow that thought any further. Finally Ellen said, "Laura knew, see. Oh, not about you. But she saw Cathy that winter. She was pregnant then. And Cathy told her she would have an abortion. But Laura told her I was pregnant with Sarah. She must have changed her mind then."

She whispered, "I don't know how to feel about her anymore."

I slid my hand up her bare arm to her shoulder. Remembered her sister, the fierce woman who took over my life for a little bit, and changed it and never stopped changing it, even after she was gone. Felt within for some compassion. "She wanted revenge for something. That's what it felt like. I thought it was because I broke up with you, and maybe it was. But . . . but people break up. I know it hurt you, and I'm sorry I did that, but it wasn't something that needed revenge."

Ellen stirred against me, her hand clenching into a fist on my chest. "I never even noticed. I mean, she was always so tough and so strong. That summer—it was all about me. I was depressed, and she was my cheerleader, and she must have been so much more hurt and frightened than I was."

"Or angry." I covered her fist with my hand. "She was just striking out. At men, I suppose. And I'd hurt you, so she could tell herself it was for you."

Ellen said wonderingly, "No. She meant to hurt me. I see that now. I don't understand. It's like she hated me."

I wanted to disagree, but I couldn't. "I thought she was trying to teach me a lesson. That I should appreciate you better. And it worked. But that day in Bruges—the way she looked at you. And Sarah. Like you'd cheated her. Like you got to be happy and so she couldn't. I told her—" That I would kill her if she hurt my family. But I couldn't say that now, though I said it then, and meant it then. "To leave you alone."

"But why? I loved her. I mean, we were sisters. We were friends too. She didn't have any reason to want to hurt me."

"She was messed up. She must have been. More than the usual young mistake mess-up. That's why she did it. Not really to hurt you. But because she was so screwed up."

She sighed, pressed into me. "I hate this—hate all the disorientation. All week I've been looking at you, and can't figure out what's you and what's my illusion of you. Now I have to look back at Cathy and wonder who she really was and how I could have deceived myself so much about her and what she felt for me."

I didn't say it, but I thought it—*and I had to look at my wife and know how far she could go away from me.*

She sensed my thoughts. "Are you still mad?"

"Yeah."

"Me too." She sighed. "Maybe we'll forgive each other."

"Maybe. I suppose it helps that we're equally angry."

"Makes it harder to abjectly apologize, however."

"I don't think," I said, "that I'm going to be able to let go of this. I don't believe in . . . in us anymore."

"Neither do I."

We were talking about two different things. She was talking, I assumed—I didn't want to ask—about my keeping this big secret all those it, that we could work it out, that we could find some way past the past— but not here, where the past was all around.

Her eyes were bleak. "Not if you leave."

If it was a test of my devotion, I chose to fail. She could stay here, or come with me. But she'd chosen once already to ally against me, and I wasn't going to wait for another betrayal.

I walked down the hall in time to hear Laura now channeling what's-her-name, the coat hanger one— Joan Crawford. Silky venom-dipped voice. Absolute hauteur. Laura was, in my experience, a pleasant young woman, unassuming despite her fame. But now she sounded every bit a match for her mother. And it was her mother she was taking on again. "You can stop lying, Mother. I know why you hid that letter from Brian. And I know why you waited until Daddy died to adopt Theresa."

As I went out the door, I looked back to see Ellen's stricken face. I must still be furious— surely two weeks ago I would have turned around and gone back to her, stood with her as she took on this family crisis. But I just kept walking till I got my car, and then I kept driving till I got to the top of old Croak Mountain. I wasn't going to hang around here waiting for one of us to give in and forgive the other.

CHAPTER TWENTY-ONE

THERESA

I lived most of my childhood in sin.

My childhood sin was uncertainty. That's why I ended up, almost thirty years old, in a cloister where every move, every moment, was prescribed. There was nothing ambivalent about cloistered life.

And that's why I found myself in the prioress's office lifting up my humble head and asking if I could leave the cloister for a few weeks to visit my mother. I knew what to expect— cloistered nuns weren't let out for family visits. You renounced those earthly ties when the doors closed behind you.

But she smiled gently. "My dear, of course you may go."

I stared at her. "But I assumed that—"

"You haven't taken any vows here," she said. "This year as a lay associate is meant as a time of exploration and consideration. The sort of commitment professed nuns offer isn't expected of the lay associate."

She wasn't putting emphasis on that word *lay*, but I felt it anyway. For six years, I'd been a novice sister, under simple vows to a nursing order. I had sought dispensation from these vows only so that I could join a cloistered order. But the prioress insisted on an exploratory year, and so for the last few months, I was not "Sister" and not bound by vows ... and I had never gotten used to it.

Nervously I fingered the rosary in the pocket of my plain skirt. I wasn't allowed yet to wear the habit of the order, but I tried to appear inconspicuous here in the house, in a modest outfit of the same brown color. I didn't want to stand out, though of course I did. All the sisters knew me as the convent nurse, the one they consulted when they needed treatment.

I'd always suspected the prioress would have turned me away entirely except for my nursing skills.

"I don't need to go," I said. "My mother has two other daughters—"

The prioress tilted her head to the side. "Why do you not call them your sisters?"

This stopped me. I didn't like personal questions—that was one reason I was a lay associate instead of a novice right now, because in the interview I hadn't demonstrated sufficient humility. I was trying, however, so I humbly said, "The word *sister* means something else to me now."

application for confirmation class at the Presbyterian Church, I didn't take it. "I'm—" I was going to say something positive, something strong, something St. Stephen would have said before the Romans skewered him. But at the last moment, as I gazed at the only mother I had left, I mumbled, "I don't know if I want to be confirmed," I said.

My voice was so weak, I wasn't surprised when she looked blank and asked me to repeat what I had said. When she finally understood, she regarded me with confusion. "You don't?"

At least I saw no anger in her eyes, no denial of me for this defiance. "I … I don't think so."

She sighed and shook her head. "It is your decision, Theresa. But . . . I do wish you'd think this through. Sunday after church, you must talk this over with the minister."

I didn't have to make good on that pledge. When Sunday came around, Mother was gone. When I finally got up, nervous about the coming confrontation, I found only Merilee downstairs in the kitchen, making a pot of soup. "Your mother had to leave town," was all she said as she ruthlessly chopped the celery into little cubes.

I was too relieved to puzzle long over my mother's unprecedented absence, and dutifully did my homework, sat alone in the dining room to eat Merilee's soup, and helped her with the dishes. At five, I put on my coat and said I was going down the hill to my friend Katie's house to study for a test.

Merilee glanced up from the classifieds at the old grandfather clock and sighed. "No word from your mother. I guess I'll be here for the night."

"You don't have to stay," I said, hesitating at the door. "Laura and I will be fine for one night by ourselves."

"Laura?"

Merilee looked disconcerted, and I realized that I hadn't seen my older sister all day. That wasn't so unusual; Laura was almost seventeen, and we hadn't ever been close in the five years since I came to live here.

Looking back from adulthood, I could hardly blame her—she'd been the baby of the family before I came along and dethroned her. Now I realize that I was adopted soon after her father died, and she very likely associated the two events.

Back when I was a little girl, accompanying my mother to work—my other mother, the housekeeper before Merilee—Laura kind of liked having me to boss around in a genial big-girl way. She was an entertaining playmate, with an extensive set of Barbies and endless imagination at making them move around the Barbie Townhouse and Barbie Office Building. She'd enact great melodramas that would alternately terrify and thrill me. I still recall the one where a beautiful blonde Barbie went under the hairdryer at the Barbie Hair Salon, and then (Laura performing some sleight of hand and replacing this Barbie with one she'd altered) emerging with her hair a sickly green and broken off on one side. "And she is to be married tomorrow! But she can't let Ken see her this way! So she jilts him at the altar! And doesn't tell him why! And Ken—" Ken, I'm afraid, got into his low-slung pink roadster and brokenheartedly drove off a cliff; quite a common means of suicide in the mountains around Wakefield, as a matter of fact.

All that stopped once I came to live with them. Laura and her expressive face and her graceful hands and thrilling voice withdrew. She wasn't the sort to practice open hostility, but after a few rebuffs when I asked to play Barbies with her, I got the message. And if I didn't, I got it when, on my eighth birthday, she packed up every last little bit of Barbie paraphernalia into a cardboard box and left it on my bed with a note, "You can have them all now, if you want to play with them so bad."

I never did. I never even took them out of the box. I could be stubborn too.

And so we'd lived for four years in adjacent rooms, sharing a bathroom, sharing a mother, sharing a pair of sisters, and never touched. I think, by the end of it, I hated her.

"Where is Laura?" I asked Merilee, pulling my gloves on and glancing out the window. I should take a flashlight. It would be dark before I got home from Mass.

"She—she went with your mother, I think. So I have to stay tonight. Can't let you be alone."

I walked on down the hill and across the bridge to the church, but my responses to the prayers during Mass were automatic and mumbled, as I worried over Merilee's revelation. If Laura didn't much like me, I thought she very likely hated our mother. She hid it quite skillfully, and I'm not sure Mother recognized it. But I was an intuitive child and, besides, I'd already felt the Laura brand of alienation. Laura played a certain part whenever Mother was near, the composed, self-contained, self-sufficient girl that I suspected she'd cribbed from repeated viewings of early Grace Kelly films. It wasn't an unusual type among upper-class girls, and in fact was rather prized as an effective way to be elite without seeming snobbish. But it wasn't Laura, not the Laura who once created tragedies with Barbies and now whispered on the phone with her secret boyfriend, the bad boy from reform school with the old Indian motorcycle.

I knew about that boy because of our shared bathroom. Each of us had a door into the bathroom, and sometimes, if both doors were open, I could hear Laura moving about in her room and talking on the phone Ellen had given her for her sixteenth birthday. And whenever she talked to that boy, her voice got low and sexy and much more like Marlene Dietrich than Grace Kelly. Not to mention that once, on my way home from confession, I saw Laura behind him on the motorcycle, her dark hair flying back like a pennant. Her face was alight in a way I'd never seen.

I took some comfort in that. I wasn't the only one in the household living a secret life.

But Laura . . . I was struck yet again, watching her, with the odd notion that inside we were somehow similar. She might smile brightly and speak lightly and pretend to be a social animal, but I remembered her as a girl, playing her parts, putting on her costumes, speaking her lines. She did that to hide herself. I didn't have her ability— I couldn't disguise who I was. But I knew that quiet need to withdraw, to hide, to stay safe within.

I didn't want to look at her and see that commonality. So I told myself we weren't all that much alike, after all. Touch of any kind was odd to me, alien. But it was just men's touches she didn't like, I realized as she and Ellen walked arm in arm up the porch steps to the house, their dark heads almost brushing as they talked—just like sisters.

As soon as we got inside, I went off to bed.

Insomnia and curiosity got me up again when I heard Laura rummaging around in the linen closet off our common bathroom. I got up from my too-soft bed and went to the bathroom door, and found her stuffing something behind the towels. Her first glance up at me was angry and guilty. Her second was all solicitousness.

"Did I wake you? I'm sorry. I should have made sure your door was closed. Forgive me."

I was going to ask what she was doing. Then I reminded myself that I was no one's judge but my own, and I already had enough tallying to do on that scorecard. "I couldn't sleep."

She was so relieved to get away with whatever crime she was committing she actually became sisterly, offering me tea and sympathy and medication. I didn't trust it for a moment, but there was a treacherous weakness in me that longed for . . . I don't know, comfort, perhaps, connection, maybe even just acknowledgment from this woman who had always taken pains to ignore me. We actually might have a conversation for the first time since . . . oh, I suppose since that long-ago phone call she made from Tennessee.

I had to admire her, in a perverse way, as she bustled around, innocent as could be, getting me water for a melatonin pill and something she called a "slumber oil", something that smelled like lavender. She seized my hand, and I steeled myself not to react as she massaged the oil into my wrist.

It was all to divert me, of course. She never even glanced back at that linen closet where she'd hidden her drugs or her dirty videos or whatever it was she didn't want Mother to find. Laura had always been a great sinner—unapologetic, uncaring, and unpunished. Not for her the long struggles with conscience, the self-imposed penances. She, like Augustine, sinned boldly.

I was actually starting to feel drowsy, staring at her special aromatherapy candle as it flickered in reflection on the windowpane. Laura was lingering by the bathroom door, unwilling, I realized, to leave me while I was still awake and able to search for her contraband. As soon as my eyes closed, I knew, she'd be back in the linen closet, moving her goodies to some safer place.

Then she asked me about the convent, her dark eyes bright with interest. I recognized that interest. She'd watched *The Sound of Music* avidly when we were children, and afterwards I came into the bathroom to find her kneeling on the floor, a towel like a veil on her head. She was pretending to pray just like Sister Maria. Now she was at it again, trying on the role of a nun.

But then, wasn't that what I'd been doing for much of the last decade? Auditioning for the role of a nun?

"I might not go back," I said aloud when she asked me what Mother and Ellen were too polite to ask.

For once, Laura was speechless. She wasn't used to candor from me, or, indeed, communication of any kind. Awkwardly, she stammered, "I didn't mean—I shouldn't have asked. It's not any of my business."

"No. It's not." That sounded too abrupt. I was too used to silence—I didn't know how to converse any more. "I'm thinking of leaving the cloister. I think I'm not dedicated enough." It sounded less pathetic than the truth— that they might not take me back. "I don't want to have to ask permission to visit my own mother."

There was, for just a moment, a flicker of question in her eyes, and I read it as if the words were printed on her forehead—*Your own mother? But*— and then the confusion cleared, and she smiled, and all was well, and she pretended she didn't have a moment of complete puzzlement, wondering what mother I was talking about. Not *her* mother . . . oh, yes. I was adopted. I was Margaret Wakefield's daughter too. I was even, though this was stretching things, Laura's sister Ellen's sort-of sister.

Not Laura's own sister, of course.

It was so automatic for her that I could hardly resent her for it. She honestly didn't think of me that way, as her mother's daughter. I couldn't say what I was thinking, that I loved her mother, and she didn't. But that was one of the paradoxical things about real families—they didn't have to love each other, and they could still be each other's family. If Mother and I didn't love each other . . . I'd be no one's at all.

Not that Laura, secure in her blood-tie, cared about that.

"I know that doesn't make any sense to you. You only came back for the money—to make sure Mother doesn't disinherit you." I yanked the unfamiliar pillow out from under me and pushed it onto the floor, refusing to look at her. "I know you don't care about her, but I do. And she needs me."

Laura didn't answer for a moment, and I was forced to look up to see her reaction. She stood there by the foot of the bed, her pretty face serene under the expensive tousled hair-do. I didn't matter even when I insulted her.

"I do understand." Laura went to the bureau and picked up the candle, touching the flame with a bold finger. "You have been so much better a daughter than I ever have. I know adopting you did wonders to distract her from my father's death." Then, in a theatrical good night, she licked her thumb and index finger and squeezed the flame, and the candle sizzled out, in small-town record-keeping.

Mrs. Latham looked up from the file cabinet and shook her head. "Sorry. I've looked through the April 15, 1991, certificates. None with the name of Brian."

"Maybe some of the others? Can I see?"

"No, you can only see your own. But—" her old face softened. "There were three boys born that day in the county. And I know them all. I worked at the grade school when they were there. So—sorry."

He must be used to failure, for it took him only a moment to recover. "Go ahead," he whispered.

"What?"

"Get yours." His eyes were alight now. "That way at least I can see a West Virginia certificate, see?"

I'd been drawn in this far. And I'd never been drawn in before. Never. But for just a moment, I felt sinful again. And besides, I at least knew my birthname. I gave Mrs. Latham my birthdate. "Can you check Terri Price?"

She regarded me levelly. "That's not your name."

I raised my chin and stared directly at her. "It was. When I was born. Please check it."

Brian was standing behind me, and for just a second, I felt his fist punching lightly against my shoulder. Approval. It was almost enough to make me stop worrying that she'd call my mother. Not that I was afraid of Mother's anger—but it would upset her, to know I'd been here.

But it was done. And for an instant there, when I saw Mrs. Latham pull a page out of the folder, I thought maybe it would be worth it.

She handed it over, with a sharp comment. "Nothing under Price. Just the one for Theresa Wakefield."

I hardly glanced at it. But Brian took it from me, studying the form with an air of professional interest.

"That'll be $5," Mrs. Latham said.

I paid the fee and followed Brian out the door, wondering how long it would take for Mrs. Latham to get up her courage to call Mother. They weren't of the same social status, and Mother was inclined to freeze out, in her polite way, anyone she considered to be encroaching.

Brian was going on ahead down the sidewalk, still studying my birth certificate. I said, "Hey! That's mine!" and followed him.

He looked back. "Oh, sorry. But can we sit down for a minute so I can look at this?"

I shouldn't have gone with him. It was folly, to start looking back so far in my life, remembering those early days, that other family. Not now, after two decades of forgetting. I had to think of the future, not the past, of what I was going to do about the convent and my vows. The prioress, in her indirect way, had been saying she didn't really believe in my vocation . . . and wouldn't she know? And didn't I know?

"Your mother," Brian was saying. We found our way to the little strip of park over the river, and without looking up from the birth certificate, he dropped down onto a bench. The park was secluded from the downtown business district by a stand of oak trees, and I relaxed a little beside him. Not that it ought to matter if people saw. But they'd come to the wrong conclusion. Every conclusion, in fact, was likely to be the wrong one.

It was just nice to be with someone who called me Miss and not Sister. Who didn't regard me with that earnest surface-level piety and ask me to pray for him.

Maybe I didn't have a vocation, if it bothered me that others asked me to pray for them.

"See," Brian went on, "it's got your adoptive mother's name here as mother. And the date of issue is years after the date of birth. That's how you know it's an adoption."

"I always knew that."

"Yeah, but if you didn't. That's one way of telling. I read that. It might take six months for an adoption to be approved, so the new birth certificate is always going to show a discrepancy."

I gave in to curiosity and gazed over his shoulder at the piece of paper that retroactively made me Theresa Wakefield. "It doesn't say much, huh?"

"Weird how there's just a line where the father's name should go. I mean, only the original birth certificate, if the father is unknown, it says unknown. That what it says—" He stopped and rustled the paper, and then finished, "That's what it says if, you know, the mother didn't know who the father was."

"There was no adoptive father. Mr. Wakefield died the year before Mother adopted me."

He looked up from the certificate, a frown making a line between his eyes. "That's different. She waited until after he died to adopt? And the court didn't object?"

I took it wrong. I meant to take it wrong. I don't know why. "What? You think a single woman can't raise a child? My mother is very competent. And she had plenty of money for another child. And it was a private adoption anyway."

Brian nodded. "Well, private adoptions are different. But the judge still has to approve it." He glanced back towards downtown. "But I guess in a town named after your family, the judge will probably approve, right?"

Something in the way he said it annoyed me. It was too insinuating. "Look, there was nothing weird about it. My—my birthfather wasn't well. And they were going to have to move, I guess, for his health. And they already had two boys, and not much money. And my birthmother was the housekeeper, so she knew the family, and—"

I realized, as I outlined it, that he was listening politely, but every fiber in him was protesting. "What?" I said abruptly. "What do you think is wrong

"Sort of," Laura said. "A little."

"Why do you ask?" Ellen looked worried. We'd never spoken of this, of my earlier life. I had my reasons—maybe Ellen did too. It can't have been easy to explain to her friends why she was suddenly sisters with the housekeeper's daughter.

"I don't know. Just this talk about adoption. And birth parents. Not too many kids knew their birthparents personally. But I did. For six years."

This was, perhaps, the longest speech I'd given to them since I arrived. I wasn't used to talking anymore; all those long days of silence in the cloister had stolen what little fluency I once had. But maybe the wine had loosened my tongue enough to embolden me—or maybe I thought my sisters would remember what I couldn't.

Laura said suddenly, "When your mother worked here, you'd come over sometime, because you were too little to be in school. You liked Barbies."

I drew in a breath and then let it go slowly. "Yes. You had a dozen or so, didn't you?"

"I did have a lot, and a lot of clothes for them too. Remember, Ellen, we used to sew them up on the sewing machine."

Ellen nodded, her gaze still on me. "The stitches were always set too large. Theresa probably remembers how clumsy the dresses looked." She added, tentatively, "Your mother. Mrs. Price. She once crocheted a tiny little bed jacket for Sports Barbie. Do you remember?"

I felt Laura's glance flick over me, and knew she was remembering too. Cathy had broken her leg skiing that winter, and so Sports Barbie had to be injured too. Laura always liked to draw on real life for her Barbie psychodramas. And my mother—Mrs. Price—spent part of an evening after work making that jacket. I could see her hands, veiny and chapped, with the crochet hook and the yellow and pink yarn. I could remember that now, but I couldn't remember her ever making me doll clothes, or noticing my toys. But Laura was her employer's daughter, a Wakefield, and—

Probably she would have treated me with the same deference, if she'd stayed around after I became a Wakefield myself.

I must have gotten drunk— so weird! I don't think I'd ever been drunk before. And I don't think I handled it well, because the next morning, all I could remember was Mother coming home late that night and Laura looking like she'd been caught having illicit relations with the handyman on the porch swing. I didn't know if this was evidence of an overactive conscience, or a long list of sins.

The next morning Ellen drove me and Mother to the Buckhannon hospital for more tests. As we passed through town, I saw Brian walking along Main Street, looking lost, his hands in his pockets. My heart went out to him. He was so young to confront the questions he was confronting. And from what he told me, his adoptive parents were resistant, and that made it even harder to look for answers. I wondered if he'd found any more information. I raised my hand to wave at him, and he looked up, as if I'd summoned him. He broke into a grin, and I found myself smiling back.

I wanted to tell Ellen to stop the car. I wanted to get out and go over to him and talk some more about our common connection—both of us adopted, both feeling alienated. I was so much older than he was, but he was so much further along in understanding. He dared to ask those questions, at least, the ones I never asked—who are those people who created me? And why did they give me up? And where are they now? And why does everyone think it's so dangerous to want to know?

But I couldn't just do what I wanted. So the day was spent ferrying Mother around to the CAT lab and then to each of the three computer stores along the highway. My concentration wasn't really necessary, so I spent the time thinking about the past, that lost six years before I came to live with Mother.

At the last store, I told Ellen that I'd wait in the car. Once the door closed behind them, I reached into my pocket and drew out the copy of my birth certificate. My original birth certificate. I'd found it in the attic, in the photo album of my first year with the Wakefields. I studied it once again, puzzling over my parents' names, wondering if that would be enough to find them. Wondering if I had reason to search. Wondering what they'd say if I showed up at their door.

The birthdate was the one I still used— that was a relief. I touched it with my finger— September 3. Right around Labor Day, my mother would have borne me, and a few days later brought me home from the hospital, to that little house on the other side of the river.

There was another date in the corner, the "issue date." That one was November 13. Brian would probably frown at that, try to find some evidence there. But he'd grown up in a high-tech time, when you'd never wait such a long time to get an official paper filed. Now it was all probably done by computer, hospital to county clerk in one simple step. But thirty years ago, they probably held the forms for weeks, until there was enough to justify a trip to the clerk's office.

I heard Mother's voice through the open car window and guiltily shoved the page back into my pocket. She and Ellen were approaching, trailed by a teenage boy carrying a big cardboard box. As she got in the car, Mother exclaimed, "We found the perfect laptop! It has a built-in modem! So I can surf the web, just as Ellen does."

Ellen gave me a glance of incomprehension. Mother and computers. But at least it had taken her mind off all those tests they'd run at the hospital this morning.

Sunday I walked down the hill and across to the old church I secretly attended in childhood. Ellen and Mother offered me a ride—the Catholic

Church was only a few blocks from First Presbyterian—but I preferred to walk, just as I used to as a child. And I sat in the shadows behind a pillar, just as I used to as a child. And I found myself watching for my first mother, just as I used to.

On the way home, I stopped at the pay phone outside of Millard's Pharmacy and called Brian. Before I could change my mind, I promised to meet him later that afternoon.

Information is power. That's what Brian said as we sat in the old country diner out on the highway. Not that he had information himself, just techniques for acquiring them.

He waited until the waitress had brought my coffee and his soda, and then, conspiratorially, he dug into the cargo pocket of his pants and brought out a little binder. The sun coming through the diner window glanced off the shiny vinyl cover. "I downloaded this form from the adoption-search website for adoptees whose families aren't being helpful. It's a list of questions that give you more of an overview of the past, what was happening around the time of the adoption, who in the adoptive family might know more than they're telling."

I watched with some anxiety as he opened the little notebook. "Really, I don't want to ask my family. My mother isn't well, and I don't want to worry her with questions. And I've sort of talked to my sisters, and they didn't remember much more than I did."

"That's okay," Brian said, pulling a pen out of another pocket. "It's just an overview, you know?" He consulted the list and asked the first question. "Okay, what was your adoption date, and what was your birthdate as far as you know?"

I didn't know why I answered. I didn't know why I was even sitting here, glancing around nervously whenever the door opened, sure I'd see a neighbor or classmate. But there I was, dutifully reciting the answers to Brian's questions. I suppose I just couldn't ignore it any longer. My birth-family had given me up when I was six years old and then disappeared. My adoptive mother had taken me in and treated me as her own daughter. My adoptive sisters— well, maybe it was the age difference with Ellen and Cathy, and just downright resentment from Laura. But I couldn't say I'd ever felt like I was one of them. So why was I there in that family? Was it really only that Mother wanted me that badly?

Silently I retrieved my real birth certificate, the one I'd found in the attic trunk, and handed it to him. He studied it thoroughly, for longer than it merited. And then he said, "Took them long enough to register the birth, huh?"

I grabbed it back. "They aren't educated people. They probably didn't think to do it until they took me to the doctor or needed to apply for food stamps."

"Okay. And you were adopted when? And how old were each of your sisters then?"

I resented the questions, but I answered. He was only trying to help. I was the one who needed to know, and he just wanted to help me find the truth.

"Cathy, deceased what year?" Brian noted down *1992*, and added, "And how did she die?"

"She was a mountain climber, and she died in a climbing accident. On a cliff outside of town."

He duly took that down, and went on to Ellen— birthdate, college attended, marriage. "Tom O'Connor? Isn't that the guy on CNN?"

In the cloister, no one watched TV. So no one ever asked me about my famous journalist brother-in-law or my famous actress sister. "He used to be. Now he's teaching journalism."

"Do they live here?"

"They live in Virginia. But Ellen's here now, staying at the house. And Tom—well, he's here too."

Brian looked up. "At the house too?"

"No." I remembered Laura's teasing during that pizza party. "He's staying out at the motel on 21, I think."

Brian looked up from his notebook. "I've been kind of sleeping in my car near there. Probably ought to spring for a night's room myself, just so I can get a shower. Which motel is it?"

"The Super-8, probably. The others are kind of sleazy. Anyway."

"Right. Onto the last sister. Laura?"

I managed to keep most of my Laura thoughts to myself, and just told him when she was born and when she left town and when she got her Emmy nomination. I was kind of surprised to realize that's really all I knew about her life out in California. She was on a weekly TV show that got good ratings. She had lots of money and a couple houses. She wanted to get married and have a baby, and I only knew that because she'd gotten drunk and confessed that the other night.

When he was done with Laura's information, he jotted down a list of resources, commenting, "The state doesn't want to tell you much. But you can find out certain things that can lead to other things. That's how I ended up here in West Virginia. No one wants me to know much, but I just keep finding a trail." He capped his pen and put it back in his pocket. Then he ripped out the sheet of paper and handed it to me. "At least it's a start."

"But—" I'd been expecting him to interview me about my birth family, but he was moving restlessly, pushing away his glass, putting down a few dollars, ready to stand up. "I guess you have to go?"

"Yeah, I wanted to check the baptism records of this church in Buckhannon. They'll be open for an hour before their Sunday evening service

he added, "But Ronnie wasn't bad. Well, he was bad, sure. But he wasn't mean."

"Do you remember anything else about him?"

"Nothing you want to hear."

"I do want to hear it. I need to hear it."

He shook his head, but he finally replied, "Like I said, he was angry. He got stuck in solitary a lot. He wasn't one to fight, but he didn't take orders well."

"Did he ever talk about . . . about the family? About me?"

Chief McCain looked out the window at the courtyard square, his eyes distant and unfocused. "He said something once. About hating his parents. Said they gave you away, and threw him away." Then he looked back at me. "But we were all like that. Blaming someone else, you know? Parents were easy targets. I think because we were homesick, and we couldn't stand it that they couldn't take us back."

I found I was gripping the leather chair arm and forced myself to relax. "But it doesn't mean—I mean, you turned around."

"Yeah. Your sister—" He broke that off.

I wasn't supposed to know about his romance with my sister. So I said nothing, and eventually he resumed his narration.

"Your other brother Mitch, he was tougher, I think. A survivor. I remember that much. My dad ran a gym there for awhile. Had a boxing ring set up, and he'd coach me and the other kids sometimes. Sometimes he'd even have illegal matches there at night. Mitch, he used to box there. He was pretty good. Dad said he could end up boxing light-heavyweight if he kept growing like he was."

I remembered none of this. I remembered so little of my oldest brother, just the odd moments, a hulking presence in the kitchen, a hard voice. But I suspect my parents had long since lost control of the boys, and were trying to shelter me from them.

Maybe that was why they gave me up.

It wasn't enough. "Do you recall anything else?"

He thought about this for a minute. "I remember Mitch and some uncle or cousin came to visit Ronnie at Pruntytown. Smuggled him in some cigarettes. Mitch was living with the cousin then. So Ronnie might have gone there after he was released. The cousin was a nice guy, you could tell he felt bad for Ronnie. But he was, well, the holler type." He said this with the usual delicacy of those of us who grew up in town and didn't have much in common with the secretive, suspicious people who lived in the mountain hollows. "I think he was from Rankin. Rankin's down beyond the end of the valley—Canaan, I mean. Way down in Webster County. Pretty far backwoods."

He meant the other West Virginia, the primitive part, away from the ski resorts and whitewater-rafting facilities and our prim little college town. The poorest parts of the poorest state. From my bag, I pulled out the birth certificate I'd found in the trunk. There, in the space for "mother's place of birth," was written Webster County, WV. "You think they might have gone there? My parents?"

"I don't know. I just have it in my mind that might be where Ronnie went, because Mitch must have been there." His gaze was sympathetic. "You really don't know where they went?"

I shook my head.

"You should ask your mother."

This time I didn't even bother to shake my head.

He said, "Look, that's all I know. You could call the county clerk down in Webster."

"Thank you." I rose and left. Out on the street, I hesitated, then walked down to the Chevy dealer, the only place in town that rented out cars.

CHAPTER TWENTY-FOUR

As the convent nurse, I had to keep my driver's license current in case I needed to take a sister to the hospital. I didn't have a credit card, of course, but I was a Wakefield, so the rental agency gave me a car without a demur. The clerk insisted I also rent a cell phone, in case I got lost. "Just call back here, Sister, and we'll tell you how to get wherever you want to go."

That reassurance didn't help me much. I didn't know where I wanted to go, and anyway, I doubted the cell phone would work deep into the mountains anyway. But I followed the map the clerk had given me, and in a couple hours I was crossing into Webster County.

I stopped the car in the parking lot of an abandoned store, and looked up at the broken plastic *Jenkins' Food* sign. Above it was the rounded ridge of the mountains, cutting off the afternoon sun. Rankin was halfway up the road that wound along the slope, and there I hoped I'd find more information about the Prices. Brian might use the Internet, but I'd grown up in West Virginia, and I figured that most people in the mountains would never show up on any Internet search. Better to ask those who knew.

First, while I could still get a signal, I called home. I hoped I'd just get the answering machine, but Laura answered. She had me on the defensive immediately with her news that Brian had been using me to get at our family, and to get at Ellen's husband Tom. I sat there in my rental car, feeling sick, as she accused me of helping him. If I had, it was inadvertent, but she didn't care. And I supposed I couldn't blame her. He'd gotten under my defenses. I was, after all, the most private of people, yet I'd told him things about me and the family that I'd never have told anyone else. He'd played me.

But I almost understood. He wanted so badly to know who he was, where he came from. And Tom had rejected him, refused to tell Brian what he needed to know. Not that Tom deserved what Brian did to him. But it was dangerous to deal with such primal questions.

After I hung up, I sat in the barren parking lot with the cell phone;. I should leave here. Go home. Forget the quest that Brian started me on. Help Ellen—

But even as I thought that, I knew I was lying to myself. I couldn't help Ellen. I was just trying to avoid finishing what I'd started. The looming mountains were spooking me as much as Brian's deception.

So I put the car into gear and started up the mountain.

They were all strange up here on the mountain, strange like the people in the forests of Romania, where I'd served for two years. Insulated and isolated, suspicious and superstitious. The man at the Rankin store said he wasn't sure if there were any Prices still around. All he would do was point up at the dirt road, and tell me about the lumber trails branching off, and the cabins hidden away in the hollows. Used to be Prices up there, he said.

There was a logging trail, or a mining road, every mile or so, up the mountain. I was starting to worry that I'd done real damage to the rental car, so I finally turned off onto one relatively unrutted lane and headed for the cabin at the end. It sat in a clearing, the forest behind it, an old cabin, but with new windows that glinted in the sun. Scattered about in the long grass were neat piles of wood— felled tree trunk and thick branches, still barked.

I stopped the car a hundred yards from the house and sat there for a minute, hearing the birds call in the woods. I'd just ask for directions, I told myself. I'd press the horn and wait for someone to come out.

No. That was rude. People in the mountains took exception to such things. I'd go up to the door and knock and then back off a few feet, ready to run if I had to.

I took a deep breath, got out of the car, and walked towards the quiet cabin.

But I'd gotten only halfway when I heard something behind me— a growl. I turned and saw something silvery-gray, with eyes that glowed yellow. A wolf, only I thought it must have been bred with a big dog, because it had patches of dark on its coat and ears that flopped. And it wasn't scared of humans, the way a wolf should be.

It growled again, deep in its throat. If I ran—

Then I heard a man say, "Stay still." He was right behind me, then right up against me, and I could feel his breath on my neck, his calloused hands on my arms, as he pressed up against my back. It was the closest I'd ever been to a man. Ever. I didn't know that was the way men felt— hard and big and threatening and protective. I didn't want to know it either. I started to pull away, but then the wolf-dog's growl started low again, and the man tightened his grip around me. "Just wait."

He shoved me in the direction of my car and we walked in a way that must have looked, and certainly felt, peculiar— pressed together like a pair of sack-racers at the county fair. When we got to the car, he pulled open the door and pushed me inside.

He slammed the door and walked purposefully away, back to the cabin on the edge of the woods. I could see him better now. He was a big man, like one of those bodybuilders on TV, with a dark stubble of beard and unruly hair, and biceps bulging out under the sleeves of his faded blue t-shirt. I sat there in the car with the window rolled up, sweating and scared, staring at the wolf-dog a dozen yards away. He was staring back at me. Neither of us gave in and left.

A minute later the man emerged with a shotgun. Before I had time to cry out he discharged it, not at the wolf but in front, scattering shot and dirt. The wolf hesitated for just a moment, looking at me, then ran back into the woods.

Setting the gun against a tree, the man came back and opened my car door.

I couldn't breathe. I remembered, back in nursing school, some psychology study on the effects of adrenaline on the emotions—people coming off a roller coaster at a theme park were asked for directions by "an attractive member of the opposite sex", as the researcher put it coyly. A high proportion of the roller coaster riders, it was reported, felt heightened attraction and sexual interest, due to the adrenaline rush of the dangerous ride.

Adrenaline. That would account for the trembling in my limbs, the inability to breathe, the sudden wonderment— this is what Ellen and Laura meant. This was . . . desire.

Danger. Adrenaline. A man. That was all it was, a combustible combination of chemical factors. And I looked in his dark eyes and knew he felt it too, and for the first time in my life I knew that real unity was possible, right there in the tangled grass next to my car.

But even as his hand closed on my wrist and pulled me from my car seat, I remembered it all—my past and my plan and myself. This wasn't what I was seeking, this hot bright claim. And just as his mouth closed on mine, I got my hands up between us and shoved at his broad chest.

I had just a second's taste of him—it was so alien, so sweet and dangerous, that taste.

With a rough laugh, he released me. His hands dropped from my arms, his body pulled away. My blouse felt damp there, where we'd been joined, but I didn't know if it was his sweat or mine.

"It's not safe here for you," he said. His voice was rough too, but it was a town voice— educated, at least a bit, not the sullen half-words of the mountain folk. "You better get on back to town." He walked away, back towards his cabin.

"Wait!"

He turned, and I saw the light in his eye, his arrogant stance. He thought— he thought I was going to let him. Let him take me, there on the unmown grass. I had to speak quickly, before — before I felt that again, or felt it enough.

"I'm looking for a house. It's supposed to be off the dirt road, but I haven't seen the name on any mailbox."

"Who you looking for?"

"The Prices."

And then the heat in his eyes gave way to wariness. "What do you want with them?"

"Someone down in Rankin told me they live up here. I—I used to know them."

He studied me now. After a moment, he shook his head. "Don't know you."

"I know." I was impatient now, angry at him, angry at myself, for that moment when we might have—"I said, I'm looking for the Prices."

"I'm the only one around here. And I don't know you. Now goddamnit, get back to town. I got to get hold of that wolf and take him back up the mountain a ways."

I felt behind me for the car. The metal under my hand was hot from the sun, but I leaned back anyway. He was the only one around here . . . "What is your name?"

He gave me an annoyed glance as he picked up his gun. "Price. Mitch Price."

And then he walked away, back to his cabin, without a glance back at me.

It took me a minute to get going, and by that time he'd disappeared indoors. But slowly I crossed the yard to the front porch. To the left of the house was a lean-to, and even from here I could recognize the carved wooden statues underneath, a half-dozen of them covered in clear plastic, all of them variations of the Blessed Virgin.

Surely there were no Catholics back here. Snake-handlers, yes. Maybe the Mitch I remembered, the one who quit going to church right after his confirmation, had found his faith again.

I knocked on the door and waited, and eventually he opened it and stood there, his face closed and grim. He didn't want to let me in, but he could hardly send me away. Mountain hospitality was a complicated matter, but he'd introduced himself, and so I was due a minute or two.

So with ill grace, he stepped back from the door and let me pass into the clean-swept, almost barren front room. "What do you want?"

It was hard, after—after what happened, to say the words. "My name is Theresa Wakefield."

He barely responded, and for a second I thought I would have to explain. But then his eyes narrowed enough that I knew the name had struck a chord with him. But still he did not speak.

Finally I said, "I was adopted when I was six. Before that, my name was—"

"I know what your name was." He stared at me for a moment, then abruptly turned away, heading into the next room.

Slowly I followed and stood in the doorway. It had once been a bedroom— there was still a cot pushed against the wall, neatly made— but now it was a workroom, flooded with light filtering through the motes of sawdust. Along the wall were four more Virgins, each in a different pose, all in rich burnished hardwood. They were beautiful, austere, traditional. They did not look as if human hands had crafted them. But as I thought that, he took hold of the unfinished work on the table, just grabbed her by the shoulder, and picked up a carving knife. It was no more than a shape at this point, but he must have had a picture of her in his head, because he applied the knife to the mantle area with gentle, ruthless assurance. It was going to be a Madonna, only there was no place on her lap for a child. Mary after the crucifixion.

He wasn't even looking at me. So I had to speak, and it was not easy, after a year of cloistered life, to start a conversation. "I wanted to find my family."

"Why?"

The question came sharply, but he never looked over at me. "Because—" It shouldn't be so hard to explain. I'd rehearsed this with Brian, but the script seemed inadequate, and the truth was —I didn't know. Twenty years I'd waited. Why now? I'd met this boy who was looking for his family, and I decided to keep him company?

No. Because I needed to know. Because the prioress was right. I was running from something and I couldn't choose my future until I faced my past.

Because the family I had didn't feel like a family. Because Mother was sick and she would die someday and I would be alone.

"Because it's time," I finally said.

Now he looked at me. He regarded me for a long time, and I thought he must be remembering the moment near my car. But he must have concluded, as I did, that it was best to put such an awkward moment away. This was all new, and required renewed focus. "Terri," he said. He wasn't addressing me, really, just repeating the name as if he had to remind himself. "What do you want?"

I couldn't remember any of the little speech about reconnecting. So I said, "I just wanted to see my family."

He glanced around the workroom, as if someone might be hiding among the wooden statues. "I'm the only one here."

"I can see that." I took a deep breath to smooth out my tone. "I thought you could give me their phone numbers."

"Everyone's dead."

I stared at him. But he'd gone back to carving his Madonna, his knife scraping gently at her shoulder. The scratch of his knife was rhythmic and low. He looked medieval there, a big man, bent over his craft, the sun dusting his shoulders with light. I had come such a long way— oh, not in distance, but in spirit, and there was nothing here but a man who wouldn't even look at me. "Your—our parents?"

"Dad died a few years after you left. Mom—she had cancer. Lingered for awhile. Died, after a couple years."

"But Ronnie?"

He looked up, just for a second, before he went back to his work. "Yeah."

"They're all—" I could finish, so he finished for me, hard, quick. "Dead. Yeah. Bad time."

I whispered, "Bad time . . . after I left?"

"Sure. I suppose. When we moved away, anyway. Same year you left. It all went to shit." He wiped the knife on a leather strap hung off his belt, and finally gave me another glance. "Dad just got worse and died. And Mom. She was always depressed. Ronnie went to reform school. He wasn't a bad kid. But he just wasn't interested in much of anything. Drugs. That's all."

"Why didn't you contact me? Didn't you know where I was?"

He shrugged. "Sure. More or less. We knew Mom's rich boss had taken you. Bought you. That's what Ronnie always said."

"That's not true. Mother didn't—"

"Yeah, I know. I kept trying to tell Ronnie that if you'd been paid for, we wouldn't have been poor anymore."

He sounded cold and cynical and dismissive. I struggled to save whatever connection we'd established. "But you could have contacted me. Why didn't you?"

"Mom wouldn't let us. She told us to leave you alone. Let you live your good life. She'd given you up so you'd have a good life. She kept saying that. A good life with your new family." He palmed the knife and used his finger to brush away some sawdust on the curve of the statue's arm. "She always said that." Matter-of-factly, he added, "We'd have ruined it, you see. Your good life. So we had to stay away."

I sat there at his oak table, staring hard at his abandoned Madonna. There was so much lost—so many years. "But when—" I couldn't call her Mother. "When she was dying. You didn't call me."

"She wouldn't let us. She was happy in the end, thinking of you in your good life." He turned back to his statue, his knife in hand. "And afterwards— well, what was the point?"

"But you and Ronnie—"

"Look. We honored her wishes. She didn't want us disrupting things for you." He paused and then added, "And we would have. White trash, you know."

"You aren't—"

"Give it up. It's not like the words matter."

He was implacable, standing next to that half-formed statue, refusing to look at me. It seemed almost impossible, that this family had an entire existence and I didn't know. That he had been hating me like this and I didn't know. I didn't know. There was the emptiness that had frightened me, that had sent me searching. And now I found only more emptiness to fill it.

"Tell me," I whispered. "Where was she when she died?"

He glanced back towards me. Not at me. "Charleston. South

Charleston."

"When?"

"Ten, eleven years ago."

Eleven years ago. My hope that I'd been away doing mission work in Romania then faded. That was several years before I'd entered the convent. I'd started nursing school in Morgantown that year. If there had been an obituary, I had missed it.

"What about Ronnie?"

Now Mitch turned and looked at a closed door, across the little living room. "Last year. He died here."

"How?"

He didn't answer for a moment. Then he said, quietly, "He was clean. That's why I brought him here, to get him away from all that. But he'd wrecked his health. One morning his heart gave out. He didn't wake up." He shook his head. "They're all buried together. Mom's family plot, down in Paulsen."

It seemed impossible that all this happened and I didn't know. But I'd spent most of twenty years trying not to remember. "You weren't alone, were you?"

"Nah. My uncles and two cousins came to the burial. It was okay."

"Will you show me?"

He glanced again at the closed door, and then, finally, he looked square at me. "No. I'm not going down there. But I'll give you directions."

I didn't want to go alone. Not this time. I was always alone, somehow. So was he, I thought, now. But he didn't have to be. "Why can't you come with me?"

He shrugged and looked away. "I don't go down the mountain much anymore. Just as far as Rankin to ship the carvings, and get supplies. No real need to go down the rest of the way."

"But—"

"No. I've seen enough family graves to last me a lifetime. They can cremate me. Just let me blow away."

I tried once more to convince him to come with me, but something flickered on his face—panic. And I stopped. He didn't want to leave here. He had his reasons.

I rose and picked up my bag. It couldn't end here, could it? But what could I say to this silent man, up here with his wooden saints and his memories? "Your carvings are lovely. Where do you sell them?"

"Churches. Rich Catholic people. The Wheeling archdiocese commissioned this one, for a grotto outside the bishop's office. I don't know what it's going to look like after a couple winters outdoors."

I looked out the window at the little lean to, where other virgins stood shrouded in clear plastic. "Do you have a special devotion to Mary? There are so many of her."

He gave a short laugh. "I don't believe any of that. I just carve what they want to buy. Virgins and Madonnas sell best. Always have. Even back when Michelangelo was carving his marble."

I couldn't bear it any more—all the loss, his cynicism, his lack of care, his pain. But I had to ask. "Do you remember Wakefield? When we lived there?"

He shrugged. "I guess. We were in a lot of places, after we left there. All the towns kind of blend together. Wakefield's just another place we lived."

It was as clear a dismissal as I was going to get. But I reminded myself that I had come here without his invitation, came and interrupted his day, his work, his life. I hesitated, and then reached into my bag and pulled out a card I'd picked up from the rental car office. I jotted down my new cell phone number. Somehow I knew he would never call the Wakefield house. "Call me if—well, if there's anything you think I should know."

Leaving the card on the table, I went to the door. "Thanks," I said. It was inadequate. It was all I had.

"Let me go out with you," he said. "That wolf might still be hanging around." When we were out in the sunlight, walking across the grass towards my car, he said suddenly, "So. Do you have it? A good life, like Mom wanted?"

I considered this, considered the years that separated me from her decision, her wish. "I have tried. To be good. I—did you know? No. Of course you didn't." I stopped near my car, a few feet from him, and he stopped too, and looked at me. "I joined the convent. Would—would she have wanted that?"

He regarded me, my civilian clothes, his face flushing a little behind the several-day stubble. He was remembering that moment when he'd held me—so wrong on so many levels. "The convent. Well. I don't know. She was always praying for you. So maybe she would have been happy to hear you're a nun."

"I'm not. I was for awhile, but I'm with a different order now, and I haven't taken my vows."

"Okay," he replied. "She'd be okay with that too. She just wanted you to be happy."

"What did you want?" I whispered.

He tilted his head to the side, as if he'd never considered this. Then he said, slowly, "I just wanted to forget. Not to care. Me and Dad. That's what we worked on. Forgetting. But Ronnie and Mom. They wouldn't give up remembering. They just kept remembering. And now they're dead, and you're here. And it doesn't make any fucking sense."

He opened my door and I got in, and he closed it firmly, and walked away.

I'd done that so many times—walked away. I should have let him go back to his bare cabin and his wooden Madonnas. But I couldn't. I rolled down the window and called to him. "Mitch. Wait."

He stopped but didn't turn. I spoke quickly. "Do you remember when they gave me up? Do you remember what they said? What you thought?"

Finally he turned and came back, and his face was bleak. "I was fourteen. Sure I remember."

"What?"

"Mom took you with her. To work, she said. Dad stayed away all day. Drinking, I guess. We didn't see him at all. And then Mom came back alone, and she said you were going to stay with the Wakefields, and they were going to give you a good life."

"What—what did you think?"

"I thought . . . I don't know. I thought—" He shook his head. "I don't remember. Ronnie thought they'd sold you, like I said. But I didn't think they'd do that."

I just couldn't leave without asking. "Was it something I'd done? Something I was? Was that why they gave me away?"

"You mean, were you bad? Christ, no. If they were giving away bad kids, they'd've given me and Ronnie away, not you." He smoothed a hand down the hood of the car, his fingers light on the hot metal. "I figure it was triage, you know. I guess I thought she wanted you away from the trap we were in. She thought she could still save you. Not us. Just you."

"Did you talk about it?"

"Just with Ronnie. For awhile. Couldn't say your name to Dad—he'd go off on a bender. And Mom would go off to church and pray more. So we didn't talk about you. Only sometimes Ronnie would get high and talk about finding you and bringing you home. But I'd tell him he was stupid. There wasn't any home anymore."

And then he turned and left me.

CHAPTER TWENTY-FIVE

The cemetery in Paulsen, like everything else in that town, was shabby. I walked past leaning gravestones, hardly able to read their faded lettering, until I found what Mitch had termed the family plot—a dozen old stones by a corner of the rusting iron fence. A maple tree shaded the oldest graves, but the newer ones were out in the sunshine, and I could read the epitaphs plainly. Peter Price, beloved husband. Joan Price, beloved mother and wife. Ronald Price, beloved brother. Just the names, the pro forma messages, the birth and death dates.

I sank down beside Ronnie's grave. I remembered him as a boy—sharp-featured and clever, adept at card play and magic tricks. And then he stopped—or rather, my memory of him stopped, and I sat there, my hands gripping the long grass, and it was as if I was staring at the grave of a young boy. A life cut tragically short. But I stared at the recent death date carved into the stone, and reminded myself that he had lived into adulthood, had time to grow up and make choices and explore the world.

I pushed at the soft earth and rose to my knees. Grooming graves was a woman's job. Mother made us girls help her take care of the Wakefield family graves, though she hired college boys to weed the more distant relatives' plots. I knelt in the dirt and yanked the dandelions, tossing them over the old fence. But there wasn't much I could do about the overgrown grass and the bare patches on Peter's grave. I sat back on my heels and let the breeze push my hair back from my face. I couldn't do anything here. I couldn't make it right or make it meaningful. It was time to leave.

In the car I used my water bottle to wash the dandelion spores from my hands, then started the engine. The sun was already sliding behind the mountains, even in the middle of June, and that meant shadows on the twisted mountain roads. It was at least a two-hour drive home, and I didn't feel confident enough of my driving skills to drive in the long mountain dusk. And the despair was creeping over me. I never cried, but I was afraid that I might start crying, alone in my car, driving home.

So I stopped just outside Paulsen at the only motel and took a room down from the office. It was hard to get the key to fit, and the door squeaked loudly as I opened it. But at least it closed tight, and the dark room smelled of cleaning supplies instead of smoke. Setting my bag on the bed, I went into the bathroom to wash up, and almost didn't hear the tinny ring of the cell phone. I dug it out of my bag and, after a few seconds, realized I had to flip it open.

My first incoming call. No one had the number except Mitch.

He spoke so low I couldn't understand him, and I had to ask him to speak up. I could hear his deep breath on the other end of the line, and then he said, "Look. I didn't tell you this, because I don't like what it means. What it means about my parents, and my dad. But it's been so long, and they're dead, and you say you want to know."

"What?" I whispered.

"I remember when Mom came home with you."

That was all, and I had to prompt him. "Home from the hospital?"

"No. That's just it. I don't remember her being pregnant. I was eight, and I wasn't stupid. I knew about women getting pregnant. My aunt had just had a baby a year before."

Cousin Phil. Suddenly I remembered. A nasty tale-telling boy, a year older than I. "I don't understand what you're saying."

"I'm saying that I'd remember Mom being pregnant. I was old enough. And I'd remember her going to the hospital. But I don't. She never got big, and she wasn't ever sick, and she didn't go away for days like she would if she'd gone to the hospital. She and Dad just went somewhere and came back the next day, and they came back with you."

I shook my head. It made no sense. "But— but what does that mean?"

Another deep breath. "Ronnie and me, we never asked. We knew we weren't supposed to ask. But I figured—well, I figured Dad had gotten some girl in trouble, and Mom had agreed to raise the baby as her own. It was, you know, one of those family secrets. No one said anything, not the aunts or Dad or Mom. You just weren't there one day, and you were there the next."

I had to repeat it, and it still made no sense. "You think I wasn't your mother's child?"

"Not like Ronnie and I were." Roughly he added, "Look, she loved you. You were her favorite, not that I blamed her, stuck with two boys like me and Ronnie. You were her little princess. So it's not like—"

The muscles in my hand clenched on the small phone. "But then she gave me away."

"Well, she must have had her reasons." He was silent for a moment, then he added, "You said you wanted to know. So that's all I know." And then he hung up, and I sat there with the phone pressed painfully to my ear until it went numb.

I kept the cell phone the next day. The car rental agent showed me a couple tricks, like how to see the details of the last incoming call. I jotted Mitch's phone number in my little notebook, promised to return the phone in a few days, and walked home. After years in Romania, where every medicine order and patient admission meant three pages of forms to fill out, it was oddly good to be back here, where all I had to do was say my name to

The Year She Fell

get special favors. They knew my mother would make good even if I stole the phone.

Not that I would. Mother never had to clean up after my messes. Cathy, Laura, even Ellen— Mother had to deal with their big and little scrapes. But I didn't cause her much trouble.

Not until now, that is.

I'd gone to Mitch looking for answers and instead got only more questions. And I couldn't escape the truth any longer. The answers were here, at home, with my mother.

But Mother wasn't there. Her car was still missing from that long driveway up to the house.

I felt like I'd traveled for weeks, but it had been less than two days since I'd been home.

It all hit me as I entered the door. I'd only been seeking some information, but that innocent inquiry—maybe it wasn't so innocent. This might be what I was secretly hoping for, to bring down this house somehow. I was like that boy Brian, wasn't I? Willing to wreck what I had for what I couldn't have. I just didn't have his recklessness.

Brian was waiting there on the porch in the late afternoon sun. Just sitting on the steps, waiting. He looked young and abashed and tried to speak. But I pushed past him and went inside the house. I heard Laura in the kitchen, and without much volition I found my way back there through the dark hall. The light was pouring in the wide windows, outlining Laura at the sink as she washed coffee cups. I didn't know her. I never had. She didn't know me.

But she turned when she heard me. For an instant, I thought she might hug me, but she stopped a couple feet away, drying her hands on a towel. "Theresa! We were a little worried."

"I'm all right. I just didn't want to drive home in the dark."

She gave me a tired smile. "I'm impressed you drove at all in the mountains."

"I drove very slowly. It took me four hours to get back here."

"Well, sit down. I just made some raspberry iced tea."

I took a seat on one of the scarred oak chairs. "Tell me what happened."

And so, as she busied herself, putting ice in tall glasses and finding long spoons, she said, "Tom's at his hotel. No—no harm done."

And then, succinctly, she summed it all up. Brian had come looking for the identity of his birthmother, and she and Ellen had figured out that it was Cathy. "And Mother knew," Laura said bitterly. "All along. Or at least she had a letter from Brian, and hid it. She'd written down a bunch of dates, see, working out the timing. So she knew."

For once, I was in accord with Laura. We were just discovering how

232

closely Mother kept her secrets. "How is Ellen?"

"Okay. She went to find Tom. I don't know. I guess he's pretty mad that she—and I— didn't tell the police about Brian." She took a sip of her tea. "But Ellen didn't think he'd hurt Tom. And she didn't want him to go to jail."

"I saw him sitting outside. So I guess he's not going to jail."

"Well," she said ambiguously, "it helps to know the police chief." She shook her head. "He's still out there, huh? He's waiting for us to welcome him into the family, I guess. But— he's like Cathy, that way. Headstrong. And he never thinks of consequences."

She was trying to be conciliatory, I realized. Otherwise she would be demanding why I'd been helping him. But now, I supposed, she felt herself equally culpable. Sisters united in sin.

"So he's our . . . nephew?" I asked. The term sounded so strange. I thought of him as "Brian", and yet, he was my sister's child.

Laura took a quick glance back through the door to the hallway. "Our nephew. And Ellen's—I guess stepson. Since Tom is his father."

Then it hit me finally—that Tom must have slept with Cathy. Laura saw my shock and immediately began explaining. Tom didn't know it was Cathy. He and Ellen were broken up at the time. Cathy had sought him out for some unknown reason, vengeance maybe. "No one understands why. She just did it. And never told anyone about the baby." She busied herself at the sink, washing up a stray cup. "I knew she was pregnant. I just happened to stop there on my way to New York. But she said she was going to get an abortion." She glanced back at me, belatedly remembering how my church felt about abortion. "I guess she didn't. And she put Ellen's name on the birth certificate. And then she's dead in a year."

"What do you mean?" I said slowly.

With an abrupt gesture, she shut off the faucet. "I don't know. Why would she put Ellen's name down? Unless she wanted to lead the boy to us some day? But she wouldn't have needed to do that unless she knew she wasn't going to be here for him." She turned, leaning back against the kitchen counter. "I thought she was wonderful. So beautiful and brave. I always admired her so much. But to do that to Ellen—"

I had been living the last week in a roil of emotion, my own fears and desires and regrets. But now, I felt overwhelmed. Ellen's pain and Laura's anger and Brian's need, they were like a dark cloud surrounding me. I didn't want to think of Cathy taking some vengeance on her little sister, or planning for her own death. And I didn't want to think about those graves in Paulsen, that other family I'd lost, or Mitch, alone and embittered on that mountain, carving his statues and shutting out the world.

And Laura didn't help. She didn't say anything more at all about Cathy. She just put the pitcher of tea into the refrigerator and glanced around the kitchen. "Clean enough to pass Mother's inspection when she gets home. I'm going to hit the parlor next."

I didn't offer to help. It only reminded me that Mother would be home soon, and that only she could answer the questions I'd suppressed for so long.

Finally I took my bag up to my room and got unpacked, and stood there by the window, looking down at the boy sitting on the steps. The truth was, I didn't want to face Brian, knowing now that he had used me. It shamed me that I had trusted him so readily. I had never been the trusting sort, but he seemed so . . . plausible. Of course he did. He had researched the family. He knew I was adopted. And he knew how to reach me—asking my help, and then offering his own. And all along, he was planning.

Finally I forced myself to walk out onto the porch. Brian was still sitting there, his hands on his knees. He looked up, and then quickly down again. "Sorry," he mumbled.

I was still too much the nun to sit down on the steps beside him, or to forgive him too quickly. Instead I crossed the driveway to the bench by the rose bushes and sat down there, breathing in the scent. "You lied to everyone."

"Just you," he said. "I told everyone else the truth." After a second, he added, "Except about the gun, I guess."

"The gun?" I echoed.

"I don't have it anymore. The police chief took it."

I sighed. "You're lucky this is a small town. You'd be in jail otherwise. What were you thinking?"

He reached down to pull up a blade of grass that was growing up between the stone steps. "I guess I was thinking that I needed to know. That knowing is better than not knowing. And—" He glanced behind him to make sure the front door was closed. "And he wouldn't tell me the truth. He's supposed to be a journalist. They're supposed to get the truth out there."

"No matter who it hurts?"

He split the blade of grass lengthwise, then again. "Isn't it better to know and be hurt than not know and be hurt?"

"I don't know—" I didn't know. Was I better off knowing that my family had fragmented, broken, died? Was I better off knowing that Mitch lived silent and alone and bitter? Was I better off knowing that I still didn't know how I came to be, and how I came to the Wakefields? "But I do know that violence is wrong."

It sounded patronizing even to my own ears. But it had an effect. Brian ducked his head again and dropped the grass blade onto the step.

"Yeah. I screwed it up. I know it. I knew it when I was doing it. But I did it anyway." He glanced over at me, and then away. "At least now I know the truth."

"At least now you know the truth," I echoed. Then I added, "But you don't know much else. You don't know why. Why Cathy did this. Why Tom wouldn't tell. Why she gave you up."

"Yeah. Just the facts. They're not enough, are they?"

"I've always known who my birthparents were," I said. "But it turns out to be so much more complicated than that."

"I guess." He glanced quickly at me, then away. "I figured that when I saw your original birth certificate, how long it took to register the birth. I thought, well, maybe they'd tried to give you away then, but not gone through with it."

Mitch hadn't said anything like that, but maybe he wouldn't remember. Maybe they wouldn't have told him. Or maybe— maybe he was right, and there'd been another mother, another birth certificate, that his parents hadn't made me either.

Brian was regarding me sympathetically now. "It's hard, huh? I thought—I guess I thought finding out the answer was what I wanted." He looked bleakly down at the town. Everyone was driving home from work now, and Main Street had what passed for a traffic jam in Wakefield. "But I wanted more than that really. I wanted . . . I don't know. Birthparents who welcomed me."

"And you found that your birthmother was dead."

"Yeah." He raised his head, and I saw in his eyes a hurt that I understood. "When did she die?"

I had to count back, through all the intervening years. "Sixteen years ago? No. Seventeen."

"I was just a baby."

"Yes."

"How?" he whispered, and I remembered asking these questions of Mitch just yesterday. When. How. Why didn't I know.

"It was a climbing accident. Cathy was a mountain-climber. She was rappelling one afternoon off a rock face just east of here, and her harness malfunctioned. Or she had it buckled wrong. She liked to rappel the rocks around here. And jump off bridges."

He frowned, puzzling over this. "She sounds crazy."

I almost smiled. "Well, she was, a little. She liked to take risks." With men too, apparently. I didn't understand it.

"What about him?"

"Tom?" I thought of my brother-in-law. I hardly knew him, even after so many years. "I guess he liked to take risks too. He's always going off to war zones."

"Yeah. I know. I read about him on the web." He stopped, as if he suddenly remembered he'd used me, too, to get information about Tom. "He probably hates me now."

"You should have thought of that before."

"I should apologize, huh?" He scuffed his ugly army boot against the bottom step. "Not that it'll matter. It won't get me anywhere."

I said grimly, "You don't apologize because it'll get you somewhere. You apologize because you're sorry for what you did."

"I totally screwed it up, didn't I?" And then he rubbed his face with a fist, and I realized he was crying.

I sighed. We were supposed to be peacemakers, those of us who had dedicated our lives to the Church. We were supposed to help heal rifts. But I'd always been better at healing bodies. Finally I stood up. At least he was taking my mind off those graves back in Paulsen. "Look. Go get some sleep. Tomorrow morning, I'll take you to see Tom."

The next morning, Brian apologized, and Tom accepted it, or at least didn't reject it. He was cool and annoyed, but controlled. It could have been worse. Ellen, at least, went out of her way to be nice to Brian, taking him home from the motel in her car and getting out the photo albums and spreading them over the coffee table. She was very polite but distracted as she turned the pages and pointed out yet another photo of Cathy on horseback, Cathy in climbing gear, Cathy graduating from Loudon.

Brian looked up at me just once, his face stricken. Quietly I bent and from the table took the envelope containing Cathy's medical records. Out in the hall, I went over the charts one more time, puzzling.

It was easier to translate the medical jargon than to remember how complicated my life had become.

I wasn't used to this, not since I'd left all the anguish of the clinic in Romania. I wanted to retreat to the quiet sanctuary of the cloister— but Mother Prioress would just tell me I was escaping, and she would be right.

I heard the front door open, and, glad to get away from the tension, I dropped the file on the chair beside me and rose. Mother was at the front door, halfway into the house, staring at her overnight bag. "Mother?" I said, and slowly she looked up at me.

"I forgot my laptop," she said in a wondering tone. "I can't believe it."

"It's all right, Mother." I almost told her it wasn't the worst thing that was going to happen today. But I couldn't bring myself to reach out to her. She'd withheld so much knowledge from me, and now it turned out that she'd kept Brian's letter from Ellen. So many secrets . . . and some of them were mine.

Ellen heard us and came out into the hall. In a tight voice, she said, "Mother, perhaps you can join us. There's someone we'd like you to meet." She took Mother firmly by the arm and drew her into the parlor.

I stood by the door, longing for escape, feeling sorry for Brian. Whatever he had done, he didn't deserve to be trapped in there with my mother when she was feeling defensive. His . . . grandmother.

Ellen was at the desk, rummaging through the lower drawer. I could see the bitterness on her face as she pulled out a folder. "I found this. It's got

Brian's letter to me in it. Opened. You knew about him. And you didn't tell me."

Mother wasn't ready for this. She had the expression of someone who had just awakened— blank and startled. My sympathy was stirred, and I had to grip the doorframe to keep from going to her.

Ellen, usually so calm, was shaking as she tried to hand the folder to Mother. "Tell me why you thought I shouldn't know."

Mother took the folder but didn't open it. She held it to her chest and murmured, "I was just trying to protect you."

"It didn't work." Ellen gestured to Brian, who was sitting abashed on the window seat. "He felt ignored. And so he decided to go to extremes. He abducted Tom. Do you understand? Mother?"

Mother slowly turned her gaze on Brian. He looked down, and I couldn't see much trace of the confident boy who instructed me in the investigation of adoption. I wondered how long he had been without a good night's sleep.

Laura slipped past me into the parlor, hardly sparing me a glance. This was her moment, I knew. She'd always hated our mother, always distrusted her, and now she finally had reason. And so she joined with Ellen, the two of them talking in low, angry voices, accusing Mother of lies and deception and secrets. Always secrets, more secrets.

Brian was sitting there, his back stiff against the window. Tears were running down his face. Through the glass, I saw Tom getting out of his black Jeep. He took one glance over at the window, and then away from Brian.

I felt disconnected and disoriented. Brian had lied to me, of course, but I should be his friend—he needed one now. He came here expecting to find a family. Maybe that was foolish, but I understood. And what he found was anger and dismissal. And the one he'd come for, his mother, had been dead most of his life.

I should reach out to him. But Mother was talking, justifying herself. She would have contacted Brian eventually, told him the truth. She just had to get a few things straight before then.

Ellen left then. She must have seen Tom's car. Automatically I stood aside to let her by. Mother turned too, as if she was going to follow. But I didn't let her even start across the room towards me. "Mother. Wait. I want to know too. Why am I here? Why did you adopt me?"

She looked at me finally, her brow furrowed. "You know why, dear. I've told you. Your father was ill. Your mother needed help."

"But she's not my mother," I said, and the truth of this shivered through me. "She didn't give birth to me. I know that now. So she gave me up. Now tell me why. Why did you take me?"

Mother reached out a hand to me, but I didn't take it. "Come, dear, this isn't the time to worry about something so deep in the past."

"You can stop lying, Mother," Laura broke in. "I know why you hid that letter from Brian. And I know why you waited until Daddy died to adopt Theresa."

I hardly had time to realize what Laura was saying—that she knew where I came from, why I was here. She'd never said anything to me, but now—

Mother was shaking her head in that placating way. "Laura, you're just trying to stir things up. Theresa is with us because we love her."

"It's because you're hers, Theresa." Laura was looking directly at me now. "She went away one spring and had you. She couldn't keep you because Daddy would know she'd been cheating on him. But once he died, she took you back. She gave you up and then she took you back."

"No," I whispered. And yet—

Mother's eyes were blazing as she stared at Laura. "You—you're wrong. You—" She swallowed, once, twice, convulsively, putting her hand back and finding the arm of a chair. She balanced against it and took a deep breath. "Don't say anymore, Laura."

Her face went very pale, and before I could react, Brian jumped up from his seat and took a few long strides to her side, and he was there to catch her when she fell.

CHAPTER TWENTY-SIX

Later, at the hospital, I found my way to a quiet place down the corridor from Mother's room—an inner staircase, smelling of metal and cigarettes—and dialed the number I'd already memorized. And Mitch answered, his voice distracted but strong, and some part of me marveled at the thought of him standing over his medieval art, talking on a cell phone.

All in a rush, I presented him with the supposition. Perhaps I'd been the product of an affair between his father and my mother—Mother, I meant—and his mother agreed to raise me. And then, when Mr. Wakefield was dead, Mother took me back.

I heard something drop to the floor. His knife, perhaps.

"Mrs. Wakefield?" Mitch's astonishment was answer enough. "Uh, no." After a pause, he said, "Do you remember my dad? He was, you know, rough. He was a coal miner. His fingernails were always black. And when he shook his head, coal dust came out of his hair. She'd never have—" he stopped again, then resumed. "Anyway, he was all union. He wouldn't mingle with management."

"I believe you," I said. I couldn't imagine it either. It was an answer, but it couldn't be the right answer. "I am just trying to make sense of it, and—"

"Why don't you ask her?"

Simple. Direct. Impossible. "She's in the hospital. Her condition is a little precarious now. I can't upset her, just because I want to know."

He was silent for a moment. A man accustomed to silence, up there in his solitary world. His own cloister. Finally he said, "Look, I'd like to help you. But I can't come down there. I — I'm tired of that world down there, and all the troubles. I just—"

"Want to be left alone," I finished. "Yes. I know. I understand." I did, actually. It was another escape, his mountain refuge, but who was I to begrudge him an escape? "Thanks," I said, and hung up. I dropped down on the cold ridged metal step and thought of Mother in that room, hooked up to the telemetry, her condition too fragile to risk. I'd have to find out the truth myself.

When I finally tracked Laura down in the hospital cafeteria, it was late enough that it was almost full dark. Laura was sitting in a booth under a dark window, drinking coffee and staring at some baseball game on the television monitor. As I watched, the cashier came over with an order pad and a pen, and Laura smiled and signed her autograph. Even so late, she looked good. She was never as beautiful as I remembered Cathy being, but she was casually elegant, her hair tousled just so, her skin aglow in the harsh light.

I got a coke and sat down across from her. She raised her cup in some kind of welcome. "How's Mother doing?"

Laura had been banished early on, because her presence made Mother more agitated.

"She's asleep. They've decided it wasn't a full-fledged stroke, but she's got to be kept quiet."

"So no more questions, huh?"

I fiddled with my straw and didn't look at her. "What you said really upset her."

"Yes. I'm sorry. It must have upset you too."

"I want to know why you said it. Where you got that idea."

Laura rose. "Can we walk somewhere? Hospitals make me nervous."

So silently we walked out the emergency room door, past the little courtyard where patients snuck off to smoke, and through the floodlit parking lot. The river was two blocks away, and we headed for that. It wasn't till we were on the sidewalk overlooking the 10th Street bridge that Laura answered me.

"I always suspected it. It was so weird, the way she always showed such interest in you." She started down the block away the bridge, and I had to walk fast to catch up. "Maybe you don't remember, but when you were little and your mother would bring you to the house, Mother would walk you down to the Dairy Queen for an ice cream."

"I don't remember," I said softly.

"Well, I do, because it annoyed me that she did that for you, and never for me. She didn't like me, I know—it's not like she wanted to spend time with me—but she was hardly the warm generous type."

I had to protest. "She's always been generous and warm to me."

"Exactly," Laura said. She put her hand gingerly on the metal railing that bordered the riverbank. The sidewalk was rutted here, strewn with gravel, and she was picking her way carefully in her expensive high-heeled sandals. "She isn't that way by nature. And yet, with you, even when you were with the Prices, she would get all . . . fluffy."

"You noticed," I said, trying to sound skeptical.

"Well, of course. She was *my* mother, and if she was going to buy anyone ice cream, it should have been me. So I noticed. And I also noticed that when Daddy came home, she'd send you back to your mother, whatever room she was cleaning. Mother didn't want him to see you, or see you with her."

I took a breath of the cool evening air. It hurt in my throat, and hurt in my chest. "But there was more. You said she went away the year when I was born. But how could you remember that? You were just a little girl."

"I remember because Ellen and I got to be alone with Daddy for months, and that was wonderful. We had so much fun." She glanced apologetically at me. "I'm sorry. This can't be easy to hear."

"No. It's all right. I want to know." I considered what she had said. "You said she was away for months. What did she say she was doing?"

"Oh, it was when she and Cathy were doing the equestrienne thing. She was going to horse shows, supposedly, driving from one city to another, being a judge. But she dropped Cathy at a horse school in Virginia, to polish her skills."

"But if it was only few months—"

"They left here before school ended. Cathy missed a whole grading period. But she made it up at the Virginia school."

"You think Cathy knew."

"No. I don't know. I can't believe she did. But Mom was using her as an alibi, I think. They weren't even together that spring."

"Was my—Mrs. Price cleaning the house all that time?"

Laura frowned. "Yes, I think so. The house was cleaned, anyway, and I think I'd remember if we had a new housekeeper while Mother was gone. And," she added, "I would have noticed if the housekeeper were pregnant."

I'd already accepted Mitch's assertion that his mother had not borne me. But the rest was hard to accept. "You think Mother concealed her pregnancy for months, and then went away and had me and—and what? Gave me to the housekeeper?"

Letting go of the railing, Laura stopped under a streetlamp and reached into her purse. She brought out a little foil square and ripped it open, and pulled out a wet-wipe and fastidiously washed her hands. "I don't know. I think they must have worked it out ahead of time, and she delivered the baby— I mean you— and met your parents somewhere and handed you over."

"But—" I took another deep breath. "But why would they take me?" Before she could answer, I said, "Mitch—my . . . their elder son—told me he always thought they were paid to give me up. But maybe they were paid to take me."

Laura dropped the foil and the wet-wipe into the litter can hanging on the railing. She didn't reject what I had suggested. She didn't even react. That probably meant she agreed. Finally she said, "I didn't figure this out till a lot later—till Daddy died and the first thing she did was adopt you. I mean, it couldn't have been two months after his funeral that you came to live with us. And all she would say was that your parents needed help, and so she adopted you to help them."

"You hated me. I remember that."

She shrugged. "I lost my father and my position in the family, all at the same time. It wasn't your fault, but I guess I took it out on you." She gazed over at the bulk of the hospital, gray in the twilight. "We should probably get back. Ellen's going to worry if she can't find us. And maybe she'll remember more for you. She's four years older." Her mouth twisted in an ironic smile. "And she's a lot more objective about Mother than I am. Maybe she'll have a different perspective."

The street was deserted except for a couple of parked cars. We crossed it and walked back to the hospital. Ellen was sitting in the waiting area outside of Intensive Care, making notes in a journal. She closed it as we came in. "I'm trying to write a sermon for when I get back to work. But my thoughts keep scattering." She gestured towards the closed door to the unit. "They said we should go home for the night. She's sleeping."

We were just entering the main lobby when a man rose from one of the waiting room chairs and came towards us. It was the college president, Dr. Urich, in casual clothes as if he'd come off the golf course. "I just heard," he said. "How is your mother?"

It was a small town, and bad news about an important citizen traveled fast. Ellen said politely, "She's sleeping. But she's doing better."

Laura said, "Don't worry. She's not in real danger."

And I heard myself chiming in, "Yes, don't worry. She'll live long enough to sign that new will for you."

As he opened his mouth to protest, Laura grabbed my arm and dragged me out the hospital door, Ellen close behind. They collapsed into laughter against the railing.

"You are so *bad*." Laura looked back through the glass door into the lighted lobby and started laughing again.

"Well, it's true," I said. "That's what he's worried about. That she'll die without signing the new will."

Ellen, shaking her head, led the way back to her car. "You know you stole Laura's line. That's what she was dying to say."

"But I was way too polite," Laura said, opening the door. "Unlike Sister Marie John here."

She was grinning at me as if she approved. As if we were kindred.

And then, serious again, she said, "So go ahead. Ask Ellen."

So as we started home, I explained to Ellen what Laura and I had been supposing— that Mother was my mother in truth. Ellen was silent until she pulled to a stop in our driveway. "That's pretty wild."

"I know," Laura said. "But so is Mother grabbing up Theresa like that, just after Daddy died. She wanted her badly. And she had to have some way to make the Prices give up the child they were raising. Like Theresa was hers by right."

I wanted to believe it. It would mean I was wanted—wanted by Mother, and wanted by the Prices. This way they wouldn't have given me up for money or because I was too much trouble, but because they had no choice.

It was too tempting. It played too close to my fantasy.

And it meant Mother had strayed from her marriage. And given up her own child. But maybe it was enough that she'd taken me back—

Ellen turned off the engine and we went into the house. It was silent enough that we could hear the crickets calling in the garden through the open parlor windows. Laura led the way to the kitchen, flipping on the lights as she went. Ellen and I sat down at the table while she opened the refrigerator and studied the contents.

"But wouldn't we have noticed?" Ellen said. "Wouldn't Daddy have noticed?"

Laura looked back from the refrigerator. "We were just kids. And anyway, the reason I always suspected was that was the spring and summer you and I spent alone here with Daddy. Remember? Mother was doing her show-horse judging tour while Cathy was in equestrienne school. Or so she said."

"And she's always been a big woman." Ellen shook her head. "But Daddy would notice, wouldn't he? I mean, he wasn't the suspicious type, but really."

"Maybe he did notice. Maybe—" Laura glanced over at me. "Maybe he knew about the affair, and let her stay with him as long as she gave Theresa up."

I said, "Mitch thought that I was Mr. Price's child by some other woman. I just called him and asked if Mother could have been the other woman. But he thought that was unlikely. Impossible."

Laura took out a pitcher of lemonade and closed the refrigerator door. "No, I don't think it could be him. Jackson said something odd this morning. He said Mother had come to his office and forgot her laptop." She got glasses out of the cupboard and filled them carefully. "And she'd also forgotten a DNA report. She'd wanted the DNA of someone— and it had to be related to this. I mean, it had to be. And hasn't Mr. Price been dead for years? So she couldn't have gotten a DNA sample. It had to be of someone alive now."

I nodded slowly. "The real father, I guess."

Laura took a seat and cupped her hands around her glass. "You know what she told Jackson. He said she had some crazy story about tracking a sexual predator in some chat room. I mean, can you imagine?"

I said slowly, "Maybe, well, you know, it's part of her condition. Maybe she'd had some mini-stroke already, as we suspected, and she was being paranoid."

Ellen put her head down on her hands. "I just don't know. All this— concealing Brian's letter, and suddenly wanting a laptop so she could investigate some weird issue, and she suddenly takes off for Charleston, only she wasn't headed for Charleston."

"Maybe she's in worse shape than we thought," Laura said. "Guilt eating away at her? Keeping this secret for so long? And getting the letter from Cathy's son—"

Ellen raised her head. "Of course, the letter said he was my son. But she must have figured out pretty quickly that it was too close to Sarah's birth."

Laura frowned. "I wonder if she knew. Suspected. Because the only reason I realized Brian was Cathy's and not the child of someone else was that I'd known Cathy was pregnant. And I only knew because I dropped in on her that fall. Maybe Mother knew, or found out later." Her mouth tightened grimly. "And maybe it all came back when she got Brian's letter. Maybe she blamed herself because she'd given up a child too—"

I didn't want to think about Brian, off somewhere sleeping in his car, I supposed, miserable and lonely and mourning a mother he never knew. "I wish Cathy were here for him."

"I wish she were here," Laura said, "just to tell us what she remembers. She was the eldest, and knew Mother best. But—" she sighed and rose from the table. "It's been a long day. Let's get to bed."

We spent the next day at the hospital, taking turns in the waiting room. Around noon, Brian snuck in with snacks and drinks for us, and hung around until Ellen took pity and offered him a tour of town sites, like where Cathy had gone to grade school and won the softball tournament— and her grave. I wondered if she would drive him out of town to the cliff where Cathy fell.

I got to sit with Mother for an hour or so, watching her face as she slept. I thought I knew her, but now I wasn't so sure. Did my birth shame her so much that she had to hide it?

Finally I went home to change and make some dinner. Then I just sat in the kitchen with my rosary, feeling the old rosewood beads bump through my fingers as I said each Hail Mary. There was always peace in this ancient exercise, but seldom any illumination. I'd never been the sort of nun who needed only to pray to learn. I always had to think and hurt to gain any wisdom.

The doorbell pealed in the hallway. I stuffed the rosary into my skirt pocket and rose, wondering what new catastrophe was going to befall us.

But there, outlined by the porch light, was Mitch. He'd shaved and put on a shirt that buttoned and jeans with intact knees. "I thought maybe we'd go find the old place," he said.

I stared at him for a moment, then looked back at the empty house. "Why not?" I closed the door, then followed him down the steps and past his pickup truck. "We're walking?"

"Don't know if I'd be able to find it any other way. Never had a car till we left here."

I was feeling breathless, overwhelmed. He said nothing more as we walked down the street that fronted the river. He didn't ask about my mother in the hospital, or about what I'd learned, or what I feared. There would be no small talk with him, I thought. No easy converse, no easy comfort from him. We just walked, side by side, to the bridge.

Mitch stopped there and looked out across the river. "I haven't been back here in, I don't know. Twenty years."

"Now do you remember how to get there?"

"Sure." He gestured across the bridge to Gemtown, on the other bank of the river. "Couple streets over. It's coming back to me."

And then, without waiting for my agreement, he strode across the bridge, and I had to run to keep up. But the air was cool there above the river, and I didn't have to think of Mother in the hospital as long as we walked along in silence. When we reached the other side, I pointed across to a high white steeple silhouetted against the dark mountain. "That's St. Edward's."

"Yeah. Well. Didn't spend much time there." He glanced over at me with something like a smile. "Should see if they need a Madonna, huh?"

"Schools always need Madonnas."

"Convents are more into the virgins, in my experience."

He said this pragmatically, and I guess to him it was the sort of marketing information he needed in his business. But for some reason, it made me want to laugh nervously. I covered it up with a cough.

"So where's your convent?" he asked.

"Outside of Pittsburgh."

He glanced over at me. "You decided whether you're going back?"

I looked back at St. Edward's, where I'd first decided to be a nun. "No. I can't, now. I realize I went in for the wrong reason— to find my place in the world. I thought I'd gotten lost, and that was the only place to find me."

"You wouldn't be the first to turn to the church for a refuge."

"It didn't work. I kept switching. Mission work. Hospital work. Cloister. I didn't fit into any of it."

He gave me a half-smile. "Know the feeling." And then he was silent again, but it was an easier silence now.

"Ronnie used to walk me to school this way," I finally said. "First grade." That was the only grade I'd attended before I was adopted and started going to the public school. Ronnie was in 5th grade then—he must have been held back at some point.

Mitch nodded. "He was a good kid. I mean, a bad kid. But good in the ways that counted. Took care of you. I couldn't be bothered." After a moment, he added, "Sorry."

"That's okay," I said awkwardly. It wasn't like there was anything to forgive at this point.

The street was potholed, spotted with rough black clods of broken asphalt. Across the river, I could see my own house, the Wakefield house, big and imposing, a seldom-used but still solid summerhouse jutting out over the water.

Mitch was studying it too—the big house. "So Mom cleaned that whole place. Until you went to live there."

There were a couple of generations of class resentment behind that comment. And I didn't know how to respond, except defensively. "She was well-paid, for these parts."

"What, for the work, or for giving you up?"

That silenced me. And we quit trying to talk on the rest of the walk. We passed the old Union 76 station where I used to spend my quarter allowance on candy. It had been replaced by a new Shell with pumps that took credit cards.

Then Mitch turned the corner. It was as if his feet and legs remembered how to get home. He walked with long strides to the next block, and then stopped, waiting for me to catch up. "Down there," he said, pointing down the street. On either side it was lined with little frame tract houses. The lawns, side by side, were closely mown and edged with shrubbery.

But the small green house to the west was surrounded by knee-high weeds and a rusted fence. On this long summer evening, the neighbors were out, sitting on their old porch furniture. They stared at us as we walked by. We were strangers now, although I thought I remembered the young man leaning against the porch rail as a boy in my first-grade class. He said nothing, and Mitch said nothing, walking with his hands in his pockets and his expression closed.

He stopped on the walk in front of the little green house. It was shabby, sided with faded asbestos shingles, the screen door hanging off one hinge. The windows had that emptiness that signified that no one lived there anymore.

"It wasn't so bad when we had it," Mitch said, as if in apology.

"I remember it as so much bigger."

"You were a lot smaller then."

I followed him around the side of the house, and got to the back and remembered that it used to be fenced in, because we had a dog. I couldn't believe I'd forgotten the dog. "What— whatever happened to Pepper?"

"Pepper." The quizzical tone of his voice indicated that he too had forgotten about our fox terrier. "Yeah. Near the end, Dad got to be allergic to animal fur. So we had to take Pepper to the pound."

"Oh."

"She was really Ronnie's dog. He loved her most."

For just a second, I wanted to protest that I loved her too. It came back to me now— sitting on that old back porch with Pepper, watching the cars creep up the alley in the evening. I'd packed away her memory the way Mother packed away my parochial school uniform.

Ronnie wouldn't have done that, I supposed.

The alley was still there, but rutted and overgrown now. I crossed to where the gate used to be. Mitch joined me, a dark form in the twilight, and I led the way down the alley to the pool of light cast by a lone streetlamp behind the neighbor's garage. "It hurts to remember. Hurts to forget too."

"Yeah. I know. Listen." He surprised me by taking my hand. He didn't look at me, however. "That last year, before Ronnie died. He wanted to come find you. He'd gotten straight, and I guess he wanted you to see him that way." His grip tightened. "He was all excited about it. But—but I didn't want him to leave the mountain. I figured, you know, he'd either find you or not find you, and either way, he'd get hurt. And he'd be out there, in the world, and he'd start using again."

My hand was trembling in his, and my voice trembled too. "That's okay."

"No, it isn't. You don't understand. I could have come with him, kept him straight. But—" He shook his head, half-smiling. "I was living with a lady, there in the cabin. And she was . . . you know. High-maintenance. I didn't want to leave her alone there, because she might, well, leave me. She left anyway, a couple months later. And by that time, Ronnie decided I was right. Said that Mom didn't want us to bother you. So he never brought it up again. And then he died, and I know he felt . . . unfinished. And it was my fault."

I felt oddly like laughing, imagining this tough, big man worried about his high-maintenance lady. But it was sad, too, that he blamed himself. I wiped my wet cheek with my free hand and said, "No, it wasn't your fault. You were just trying to protect him. And I don't know what would have happened, if he'd tried to find me. My mother—she might have . . . " I swallowed and tugged my hand free. "I don't know what she would have said if he'd come to the house looking for me. She probably would have lied. Said I was still in Romania. Or that the cloister didn't allow me any visitors. She had— has— so many secrets. We're just figuring that out. And so Ronnie probably wouldn't have found me anyway. And that might have hurt him more."

"Okay." He looked around us, at the trash heaped up against the neighbor's brick retaining wall, and added, "Let's get out of here."

We retraced our steps back to the bridge, and when we got there, I said awkwardly, "Thanks for coming."

He shrugged. "Just don't like coming down here. Up mountain's . . . easier."

"Well, you're here now." I looked away, over the river at my house. One or both of my sisters must be home, because the kitchen window was a square of yellow light. "I'm sorry about the phone call earlier. You must have thought I was crazy."

"Yeah, well. You really think Mrs. Wakefield was your mother?"

"It—it seems plausible. Laura—my sister—I guess has always suspected that, that Mother waited until her husband died to adopt me because I was the, uh, the product of an affair. And I guess she left town that spring and

247

summer before I was born, supposedly judging at horse shows."

Slowly he replied, "The one thing that was hardest was Mom giving her child away. It never made sense to me that she could do that. And Ronnie— he couldn't get past it, kept thinking it meant something. Don't know, like she was trying to protect you from us. But if you were really a Wakefield— what could Mom do? Even if she didn't want to, she'd have to let you go."

I took a deep breath and let it out. "I suppose it is better. I don't have to feel so . . . so abandoned. Or rejected. But it worries me too. You know, that it's what I want. To feel wanted."

"Yeah. So automatically you're suspicious you're making it up." He regarded me with a half-grin. "Maybe you should spin it positively. Two families wanted you. Only one could have you. Lucky for you it was the rich one."

I had to smile back. "That's not really the way I look at things. Positively, I mean."

We started across the bridge, and he said, "Course if you're right, that means . . . weird. That we're not related."

This silenced me. This made him feel better, that somehow it was better for his family if I wasn't really theirs. And maybe he was right. But still—

Finally he prompted, "You're not still thinking that my dad—"

"No! No." I sighed, letting go of the memories of that first family of mine. "I was just trying to make it make sense. But my sister told me something—she said that my mother had been trying to get some DNA tested, and we figured out it must be the father's. And your father died a long time ago. So it can't be his DNA."

He regarded me quizzically. "But why wouldn't she know?"

"What?"

"Why would she need to check DNA? I mean, unless she was really getting around, she'd know who the father of her own child was, wouldn't she?"

I opened my mouth, then closed it. He was right. Mother wouldn't need a DNA test to identify the father. "But why then? Unless I was hers, why would she go to so much trouble to keep me close and get me back?"

Mitch considered this for a moment. He didn't seem shocked at all of these scandalous doings. I guessed where he came from, he learned to be tolerant. "Maybe you're still family. Like her sister's kid. Or her husband's kid by another woman. Or—"

I thought of what Laura said about that time I was born. She and Ellen were left home with their father all spring and most of the summer, a halcyon period, from Laura's perspective. But Cathy—

I took off at a run towards home, hardly hearing his startled yell. When I got back, breathless, to the porch, he was right behind me. And he was with me when I went in to tell my sisters who I was.

CHAPTER TWENTY-SEVEN

JACKSON

Small-town policing is all about discrimination. I don't mean racial discrimination. I mean the discrimination that lets a cop decide not to arrest the kid smoking dope behind the stadium, or the old guy shoplifting lipstick from the Walgreens. You learn quick what will deter and what will aggravate. So while I'm for sure hauling a drunk driver down to the city lockup and charging him, that town drunk staggering down the street, I'll just take him to his house and shove him through his doorway. First do no harm—the cop's motto.

It's all about outcome. And that takes guesswork. Clairvoyance even. Got to predict if reform school will destroy this kid, or actually reform him. Tougher than it sounds. I was one saved by reform school, or at least by the cop who sent me there. So I'm mindful of the possibility that what hurts most now might help most in the future.

The truth is, for most small-town criminals, getting caught is deterrence enough. It's humiliating to get caught drunk and disorderly by your former geometry student. And it's scary for a married banker doing a late-night audit with a teller to look out his windshield and hear a cop, hand on a gun, say, "Heard someone yelling. That you, Mr. Peterson? You all right?"

So when I was cruising one night over by the college, I didn't arrest the town matriarch when I caught her rummaging through the trash bags just inside the college gates.

It was a moonless night in late May. The streets were deserted—our town is full of working-class people who have to be up for the seven a.m. whistle—and the air was damp with mist. We're in a valley, but still twenty-two hundred feet above sea level, so the nights are usually chilly well into spring. I wasn't enough of a wuss to turn the car heater on, but I admit I considered the idea long enough to dismiss it.

When I got to River Road, I rolled down my window, and it was all so quiet I could hear the water rushing by thirty feet below the guardrail. Tug Lewis was reporting in on the radio that Gemtown was secure, and he was stopping at the minimart for some coffee. The dispatcher told him to bring some Oreos back.

I noticed the trash bags and barrels dotting the sidewalks and driveways, and remembered it was Tuesday, and tomorrow, way too early, the Roemer

Refuse truck would be coming around to do the weekly pickup. I was just thinking I had to stop by my house and get the garbage out when I came around the corner onto College Ave and saw something moving behind a heap of three trash bags.

Too big for a raccoon. Dog probably. I was a cop, not a dog-catcher, and besides, this was along the maple-lined row of brick faculty houses. I was still annoyed at the president's refusal to compensate the department for the nine man-hours of traffic direction during graduation last week. If a dog ripped up and scattered professorial trash all over College Ave, served him right.

But then someone stood up. Wasn't a dog then. I cruised down the road, thinking it might be some fraternity prankster. But the college was out of session.

I flipped on the beacon lamp mounted over the side view and angled it to illuminate the trash bags. There was the perp, spotlighted a couple dozen feet away.

Okay, even for me, trained as I am to expect the unexpected, this was . . . unexpected.

And I decided this was the time for discrimination, not to mention discretion.

Couple reasons. First, well, if I remember my criminal justice class lectures, it's not actually a crime to steal someone's trash, as long as it's out on public property. And these trash bags were sitting out there on the city sidewalk. Second, the trash thief was none other than Mrs. Margaret Wakefield, town matriarch, city councilwoman, and, for a few minutes twenty years ago, my mother-in-law.

Now I didn't know what the hell she was doing, but I knew I wasn't dealing with an unregenerate criminal here. And so I pulled up at the curb right beside her and said in a casual tone, "You lose something there, Mrs. Wakefield?"

She'd been so intent on her task, whatever it was, she hadn't noticed me before that. Now she looked up, and I was struck by her complete lack of panic. I mean, she should have been panicked. She was caught. But she just said, "Chief McCain," in that lofty tone of hers, like I was standing at the podium in the City Council room, requesting more money for Kevlar vests.

"Mrs. Wakefield." I got out of the car and stood there, arm on the frame of the door, waiting to see if she had some good explanation for her actions.

She didn't even bother. She opened the last trash bag and started rummaging through it.

I closed my door and came round the front. "Mrs. Wakefield," I said again, this time shining my flashlight on her.

She looked up at me, frowning. I've never figured out if she actually forgot I was once briefly married to her daughter, or if she was just too proud to acknowledge it. Rich people really are different, as some author said. Or after so long, there was no way an investigation could end well. It's hard enough to get an indictment and conviction on a date-rape case, even with physical evidence. But a year later? No way.

But that didn't mean I could let it go. If he was still out there, still walking around, still dating, that probably meant he was still raping. Silence might save Laura's career, but it might doom other women.

There had to be a way . . .

I'd half-formulated a plan—needing only the identity and location of the rapist—when the entire Wakefield family followed the matriarch down that path to madness.

It was a weird coincidence that Tom O'Connor, the journalist, was kidnapped while I was in bed with his sister-in-law. For a day or so, I thought maybe it wasn't a coincidence—I don't know, like they wanted a potential witness out of the way, or wanted me distracted. But pretty soon I acquitted Laura of conspiracy, at least pre-crime.

Still from the first, there was something off about this kidnapping. First thing—no one gets kidnapped in Wakefield. A non-custodial parent might keep a kid a couple extra days, requiring a visit by an officer, and, if things are slow at the courthouse, the assistant prosecutor, just to subtly remind the offender that this is a crime. But a real kidnapping? Of an out-of-towner? I have to say, of all the crimes I'd anticipated when training my officers, this didn't even register.

As I drove to the crime scene, I ran through the possibilities. Means, motive, opportunity. A foreign correspondent might have made a few enemies, but why wait till he comes to this remote mountain town to strike? You practically have to be a native to find your way here through the hills, and getting out in a hurry—well, the nearest major highway is forty-five miles away along sharply graded twisting roads. And strangers, especially foreign strangers, get noticed in Wakefield. The arrival of an Arab or even a European would occasion a few calls to the police station, and we'd gotten none of those.

It didn't take me long to conclude that it was an inside job.

I stood in Tom O'Connor's motel room, trying not to choke on the chloroform fumes, surveying the scene. CNN was on the TV; the laptop was powered up and connected wirelessly to the Web. I used a pen to punch a key on the laptop, and saw that the victim had been answering his email and broken off mid-sentence—something about a student's spring semester grade, nothing interesting. Next to the keyboard was a glass, half-full of whiskey. I bent to smell it. Good whiskey. Strong enough to momentarily overwhelm the sweet-sick smell of chloroform. But there was no liquor bottle on the desk or dresser, or in the wastebasket.

The door was clean. No sign of a break-in. Looked like he let the assailant in.

Now granted, this was Wakefield, and even an out-of-towner would know that the crime rate was pretty low. Still, this O'Connor guy, by all accounts, had worked in the most dangerous places in the world, and already lived through one kidnapping. So would he have opened the door to a stranger? I didn't think so.

We had a good little crime-scene team, a regional group fresh off training at the FBI. I stepped back to let them do their work, and continued my line of thought. What was he doing in a motel anyway? He was married to a Wakefield, and the Wakefield mansion had plenty of room for guests. Like his wife's room, to start with. There was no sign of a woman's presence here in the motel room, and anyway, I'd seen Ellen in the grocery store a few days ago, buying perishables. No refrigerator here, just a bucket of melting ice. And Laura had sure made it seem like she and both her sisters were staying with their mom in the big house.

So why wouldn't the husband be there too, sharing Ellen's room?

In my experience, spouses were usually considered part of the family. I couldn't imagine Michelle's family relegating one of the spouses to a hotel room. Even since the divorce, her brother kept a guestroom for me when I came down to visit Carrie. (No hard feelings—Michelle and I were so different, no one expected the marriage to last a year, much less thirteen.)

Of course, Michelle's family was way into togetherness—that was one of the problems we had; we had to live within a block of her parents and across the street from her sister, and I couldn't miss the family dinner of a Sunday unless I was on duty. But even in my family—the felony-trash type of family, full of backstabbing and betrayal and turning state's evidence—you were expected to crash at the parents' house with the spouse, significant other, or current one-night stand.

That was really the sticker. Married couples in the same vicinity don't usually sleep in separate places. Unless, of course, they're on the outs.

From the first moment I talked to Ellen O'Connor, there in her mother's parlor, I knew something was wrong. She was worried, but not distraught. She seemed more like a woman whose husband had gone missing than one who was pretty clearly abducted.

Then again, maybe she was just a woman not all that much in love with her husband, caring enough to worry, but not enough to fall apart. Even then, she'd likely be anxious about a possible ransom. It just didn't . . . feel right. One of those cop-intuition things that aren't worth squat in front of a judge. *No, your honor, I don't have any evidence, but it just felt like she was lying.*

I didn't come outright and accuse her of it. That would just shut her down, and she'd end up more cagey. But I sure thought Laura would be more honest with me. Looking back, I don't know why. Because I was the law, and didn't trust me with those secrets.

"So we're okay?" Laura's voice was hopeful. Her face was luminescent in the golden late afternoon light.

"Sure. Case closed."

"Can I stay tonight?"

I got up off the swing, and went to my front door. "I don't think so, Laura. You go be with your family. That's what's important. Everything locked up tight. No tabloid's going to be investigating the TV star's family secrets, don't need to worry about that. No headlines about your man-trading sisters. No research into your past, turning up that teenaged marriage, right?"

She was regarding me warily, but reached out her hand as if to draw me back. "Jack, let's——"

"No need. You got what you wanted from me the other night, and you got what you wanted today. I think our case is closed too."

I walked into the house, closed the door behind me, went to the kitchen and poured myself a shot of JB. Listened hard. The window was open, and I could hear the porch swing creak, and then a car door slam. She'd given up. Good.

CHAPTER TWENTY-EIGHT

When I got to the station the next morning, my secretary Sheri rolled her eyes and mouthed, *Trouble*. In a normal tone, she said, "Mrs. Wakefield is waiting for you." She inclined her head to the little waiting room off the lobby, outfitted with cable TV and Kleenex boxes, as it was used mostly by those waiting for their husbands or sons to be released from the drunk tank.

Ho-kay. I didn't waste any time speculating about what information she would demand I reveal or conceal in regard to her son-in-law's abduction. I just called her into my office.

She was weighted down not just with the usual old-lady big handbag, but also a laptop case. I reined in my speculations again as she sat down, and just waited for her to speak.

Finally, once she'd gotten the laptop case arranged on her lap, she did. "Chief McCain. I was hoping you had the result of that DNA test."

Hmm. Not what I expected. "Sure," I said, getting up and locating the file in the cabinet. I didn't bother with the caveat about how I shouldn't be doing this for a private citizen, and all that. This was the town, after all, that let the previous police chief smuggle heroin for ten years. I figured I was okay spending $50 on a city-councilwoman's vanity DNA research. "Not sure what you're going to make of it, without another sample to match it to," I said as I handed the VNTR sheet over.

"Thank you," was all she said. She read through the text as if it made sense to her. Maybe it did. Even when she finished scanning it, though, she didn't stand up.

She didn't ask about her son-in-law. She'd been out of town, I recalled. "Have you been home yet, Mrs. Wakefield?"

She slid the report into the pocket of her laptop case. "No, not yet. I've just come back from a visit. Now can I show you something?"

"Sure," I said, hoping it wasn't more dental floss.

She pulled out her laptop, set it on the case, and booted it up. "I saw you on the news, that interview, when you spoke of Internet predators. I did some of my own research . . ." She rose and with an unexpected awkwardness, shuffled with the open laptop to my desk. She set it down on the edge then turned it around so I could see.

What I saw was an Instant Messenger dialogue box, the type I used to keep in touch with my daughter during the week, you know, *so how was school today; did you finish your math project; oh, dad, come on, that's not due for a week.* I found myself unwillingly impressed that Mrs. Wakefield, of all people, would know about this technology.

The cursor was blinking beside the user name: justinfan222.

Mrs. Wakefield had resumed her seat, and was regarding me expectantly.

"Okay," I said. "You did some research on Internet predators. And?"

"And I learned that they approach teenagers in chat rooms. And then they approach them using this Instant Message program."

I told myself to be patient. She had a point. She must have a point. And even if she didn't have a point, she would soon be out of my office and I could get back to my own Internet research— cheap last-minute flights to New York. "Yes, that's one way they approach the kids."

"So I got an account. Those technical support people are really quite helpful."

I didn't know what was going on, but I felt dread. "So what did you do with this account?"

"I went to some of those chat rooms. I pretended to be a teenage girl. Successfully. It is," she added, "more a matter of poor punctuation than anything else."

Dread spread. "So what happened?"

"As I expected. I was approached by a predator. He thought I was a fourteen-year-old girl. And he suggested that I meet him."

I found myself struggling to keep up. "The problem is, Mrs. Wakefield, you're not a fourteen-year-old girl."

"He didn't know that."

"But—" But it's not your job. But this is nuts. But—"What do you need from me?"

"Well, I need you to arrest him, of course."

Right. "There might be jurisdiction problems." I pulled my thoughts back together. "It might be a federal offense. More FBI than Wakefield PD."

That's what we always used to do, back at the Bristol PD, when the local schizophrenics would call and whisper that the mayor was trying to break into their bathroom or that space aliens were sliding probes through their dryer vent and stealing their underwear. *The mayor? Well, sir, that's official corruption, and the state police handle that. Space aliens? Hey, Joe, aren't space aliens counter-terrorism? Yeah? Okay, ma'am, that kind of complaint goes to the FBI. Here's the number of the field office in Knoxville.* The fibbies just loved that.

"What if it's a local man?"

So much for passing the buck. I wondered if she'd really snared a local guy, or if it was all feverish imagining. Why she'd be imagining Internet predators, I couldn't say. "Is it?"

She just gazed back at me, like a suspect who knew her rights because she watched *Law and Order*.

I sighed. "I don't know if it's a crime if there's no actual child involved. I'd have to check with the prosecutor about that."

"The policewomen who pose as prostitutes aren't really prostitutes either, and yet you can arrest the men that approach them."

She was crazy, but she was sharp. I said, "Soliciting for prostitution is itself a crime. Maybe soliciting this way is a crime too—the prosecutor will know. Why don't you email me the logs of your messages, and—"

"The logs?"

"You did keep a log of the messages back and forth?"

She pursed her lips. I took it that the answer was no. Maybe she didn't get that far with the helpful technical support people.

"Okay. No log. Well, why don't you give me his name, and I'll see what—"

She rose and closed up the laptop. "I will provide you with logs."

"Mrs. Wakefield, you know, the FBI has special agents who—"

"As I said, Chief McCain, I will get you those logs. Within the week." She slid the laptop into the case and set it down on the chair. "What else do you need to start an investigation?"

I resisted the impulse to rub my aching forehead. "The name of your suspect, if you know it. His Instant Messenger ID. The chatroom you found him in—"

"Very well." She gathered up her purse and left my office.

I thought of calling her back and explaining about the whole son-in-law abduction thing. But then I decided Laura and Ellen could do it themselves. Introduce her to her new grandson, all that.

I went back to work. That is, I called my first lieutenant and switched a few shifts with him, and went online to reserve a flight to La Guardia. Then I unbuckled my holster and locked it away in the safe in the wall. I was legally allowed to carry a gun on a flight, as long as I registered, but that would mean an hour or more of delay at each airport. Best leave it behind. Not like I meant to shoot anyone.

A quick trip to the training supply locker, and I was ready to go.

But as I was closing my office door, I noticed Mrs. Wakefield's laptop case, still there in the armchair, the folder sticking out of the front pocket. I sighed and went to the phone.

Laura answered. It took me a moment to remember why I called. I did remember it wasn't to beg for another chance. "Yeah. Look, Laura, your mother was just here. Tell her she left her laptop here."

"She was there? At your house?"

"Office."

"Why?"

I thought about disclaiming any understanding of it. But if Mrs. Wakefield was going senile, her daughters probably ought to know. "Look, she's not really making any sense. She came in with some story about some Internet predator she's trying to attract by pretending to be fourteen."

Laura's silence had that stunned quality. Finally she said, "You're— no. You're not kidding. Okay."

"There's something else weird. Few weeks ago, she wanted a DNA sample analyzed. She picked up the report today. Only she left it here with the laptop."

In a whisper, Laura said, "Whose DNA?"

I had a sudden attack of discretion. "It's just a report. No names." I glanced at my watch. I had a long drive to the airport. "Look, I got to go. Just tell her my secretary will have the laptop."

"Okay. Thanks. Jack, listen—"

"I'm on my way out. Talk to you later."

I hung up, and headed out the door.

I'd done my research at peoplemagazine.com and other star-chasing websites, and so I showed up at the Poison Club in Soho around midnight. The suspect was known to hang out there every evening after taping of his lousy inauthentic NYPD cop show. (Among other things, he keeps a machine gun and grenades in the trunk of his squad car. Right.)

A quick search of the block and I located his vehicle—a steel-gray Hummer sitting squarely and illegally in the dark alley behind the club. I walked along the driver's side, using the floodlight over the club's back door to see inside. The lock was the kind easily jimmied by someone who knew what he was doing. And I knew what I was doing. I pulled on a pair of light cotton gloves and popped open the driver's door lock in about 20 seconds. When I retired from the police force, I'd have all the skills needed for another job.

The muted music from the club suddenly grew loud and the light yellowed as the door opened. I ducked down behind the car, one hand on the damp brick of the ground, the other around the flexible plastic jimmy strip. I could smell garbage from the overflowing dumpster at the end of the alley, and that gave me an idea. When the footsteps receded and the music went soft again, I stood up and paced off the distance between the front of the Hummer and the front of the dumpster. Twenty feet. Enough to cause some damage? Probably.

I checked my watch. Haldrick supposedly had to be in makeup (yeah, real macho) at seven a.m.. It was now almost twelve-thirty. I sat down on the Hummer's broad front bumper to wait.

It didn't take long. I heard a man's voice, rough and low, in the front of the alley, and hunched down. When I heard a woman pleading, however, I slid to the side of the Hummer and glanced over. Two figures were silhouetted in the light from the street. They were struggling in that ambiguous way people struggle when they don't want to make a scene—the man pulling at her arms, the woman drawing away and murmuring, "No, it's okay, let me go." No screams, no blows.

But then he pulled her into the alley. "Come on, come on. Let's go."

The woman's voice was slurred. "I don't feel good. I want to go home."

"I'll drive you home. Just come with me."

"I don't want—"

He slammed her against the tailgate of the truck. I felt the vibrations go through my back and as I charged, instinctively reached for my missing gun. But all I had for a weapon was my fists—and the element of surprise.

I got a hold of his leather jacket with one hand and his jaw with the other, yanking his face away from her and hurting him enough to make him let her go. I had just a glimpse of her terrified face as I pulled him away from the car—she thought I might be another attacker. "Run," I yelled at her. But her reactions were slowed. She stumbled away from the car on her high heels, and fell to her knees before scrabbling up, holding onto the alley wall.

He was protesting, loudly and obscenely, and I considered a chokehold, just to shut him up before he got the attention of a bouncer. But I didn't bother. He was all buffed gym-muscle, without any real strength, and his attempted blow barely rattled my arm. I jammed him up against the car door, grabbing his leather lapel and tugging it so that his face bulged red and he stopped yelling to gasp for breath. "This is for her, and the other one you raped too," I said, staring right into his eyes.

He was trying to speak, so I eased up fractionally on the pressure at his throat.

"Which one told—"

I didn't want to hear more. Didn't need to hear more. I slammed my fist into his face, right where the nose met the forehead. Not hard enough to fracture the skull, but hard enough to break his nose and knock him out— and bruise my knuckles pretty good, even through my gloves. It had been a long time since I got to hit someone like that (it's sort of discouraged by police forces these days), and it felt good to hear the crack, to feel the give. Triumph. Vengeance. My turn.

He slumped against the car, and I hauled him up, and settled him against the side of the building. I found his car keys in his jacket pocket, and leaving him there, I climbed into his idiotic Hollywood-militaristic mobile. It took me a minute to get the damned thing going, then I buckled the seatbelt—it looked like a seatbelt on the space shuttle, ready for five Gs— and shoved down the accelerator. It lumbered forward, hitting the dumpster with just enough force to buckle it slightly without initiating the airbag.

I left the car running in second gear and went back to haul him up. He muttered something, but never woke up as I put him in the driver's seat and pressed his face against the steering wheel, leaving a nice imprint of blood and snot. Then I gently shut the door and, stripping off my gloves, left the alleyway.

The woman was sitting slumped on the curb. There was music pouring out of the club's front door, but no one had noticed her. Or they figured she was just another drunk. I sat down beside her and said, "I got to call the police." Best to go with the cover story. "He got in the car and tried to drive, but hit the wall. Might be hurt."

She lifted up her head and stared at me. Her eyes were glassy and unfocused. I'd seen enough drunks to know this wasn't from alcohol.

"He drugged you. That's why you're feeling so weak."

"He was going to rape me."

"Yeah. Like I said, I got to call the police."

I watched her eyes, and I could see it happening. She was making the same decision that Laura did, to conceal the crime. She was going to refuse to report it. She looked ashamed as she tried to explain. "He's famous. It'll get into the tabloids. There'll be photos of me, and I—I just can't. And he'll probably get off."

I took a deep breath and let it go. It wasn't my decision. And I didn't have any right to judge her. "Okay. But I'm going to get you a cab and send you to the emergency room. You might have a concussion."

I got her into a taxi, gave the cabbie $10 and told him to take her to nearest hospital. All the while I had my hand in my pocket, fingering the pills I'd gotten from the training supply locker at the stationhouse back home. I walked back to the actor's car and opened the driver's side door. He was still slumped there, unconscious. He looked like just another drunk-driving accident.

But that wasn't all he was. I withdrew the tablets and gazed at them in the dim light. Planting the goods. The first step down the slope of corruption for a cop. I'd never done it before, not in fifteen years.

But sometimes getting justice requires creativity. I used the hem of my t-shirt to wipe the tablets clean, then let them drop on the seat right between his legs. And then I crossed the street to the pay phone and dialed 911 to report a drunk driver crashing a fancy Hummer in an alley behind that trendy club Poison.

I waited down the block till the squad cars arrived, followed seconds later by a video truck from the local news. Watched as the beat cop hauled him out of the Hummer and the video cameraman zoomed in. He'd still be shooting when they found the pills.

In a few days, the police might (or might not) announce that the tablets with the rohypnol markings weren't actually rohypnol. (After the last police chief's activities, I thought it best to use fake drugs in training sessions.) But by that time, the word would be out. The macho Hollywood star wasn't just drunk; he was in possession of date-rape drugs.

It wasn't really planting evidence to put a couple of aspirin with false markings. Anyway, that's what I told myself as I caught a cab back to the airport.

The next day was my court day. That is, I sat in traffic court and stood up every time my name was called and read from my notes about what I'd witnessed on my one monthly traffic shift about this speeder or that red-light-runner over there contesting his ticket. It didn't take much effort or attention, which was good, because I'd managed only a couple hours sleep after the flight and the long drive back from the airport. I put in another couple hours on paperwork, and went home too tired to do more than kick off my shoes and flip on CNN and drop onto the couch to wait for the entertainment news.

Laura arrived just in time to watch with me. I could tell from the look on her face that this same segment had been repeating all day, and that she had some suspicion, don't ask me how— anyway, she sat down next to me, bumping her bare ankle against my shin, and took my hand as we viewed the cop show star get hauled away by the cops.

She watched with professional interest as the publicist faced the camera and said that the actor didn't know where those date-rape pills had come from, that he knew he'd had too much to drink as soon as he started the car, and started to get out, but must have knocked the shift into gear accidentally, and rumors that he'd left the club with an incoherent woman were just that, rumors . . .

I'd gotten away with it. It felt good. I'd reformed, sure, but there was still the felon-within that got a charge out of committing a crime and getting away with it. (The cop-within started to argue that what I did wasn't really a crime—using force in defense of another was legal . . . but faking an accident wasn't, for sure.) I knew they'd have no chance of tracking me down—not like anyone would guess some small-town cop would be wreaking revenge.

Laura didn't say anything, just did that thing women do because they're sure it's got to turn guys on, rubbing at my knuckles with her thumb. Harder and harder rubbing. I kept my jaw clenched tight to keep from yanking my hand back.

"Gee," she said. "Your knuckles are kind of bruised. Maybe I should massage them even more."

I kept quiet. But then the segment ended, and she let go of my hand, and rose. And then, before I could react, she climbed into my lap, and I realized that little blue sundress must have cost so much, Laura didn't have any money left over for underwear.

When I could breathe again, I said, "I guess this means you've gotten over that intimacy phobia, huh?"

Her answer was to slide her hands around my back. I pulled her close to kiss her, but felt the shoulder holster hard between us, and moved to unbuckle it. "No," she whispered. "I want you to leave your gun on."

From phobia to serious kink. I must be better at this sexual healing stuff than I ever realized. But fifteen years of training jammed in between me and my lust-fogged brain. "Wait," I said, and pushed her a few inches away, damning my own responsibility. I managed to get the automatic out and removed the clip and the round in the chamber, tossing them on the coffee table. Then I replaced the gun in the holster and looked up to see her mouth droop sulkily.

"I'm sure you had the safety on."

"Yeah, but now I won't be distracted, worrying that something you're doing to me is flipping it off. Think about the headlines then."

I prevented any further protest by kissing that sulky lip of hers, and she sighed and whispered against my throat, "You forgive me?"

"You do something wrong?"

"Yeah. You've just forgotten."

I did remember, but I didn't care, not anymore. Laura had more secrets than anyone else I knew, at least on the outside of a jail cell, but I didn't care anymore, and not just because she was undressing as much of me as she could without disturbing the shoulder holster. I didn't care because she was so complicated that she couldn't help but hide things, and it made her mysterious to me, and it always had.

Laura broke free of the kiss and pushed at my chest. "Jack, listen. I—I know you didn't like my decision. You know, not to report him. And I know this—this thing you did was to fix that. And I know you must have risked a lot to do it."

"Did it for you." I bent to whisper this into her throat. "Because you're mine, and no one gets to hurt you."

And she drew in her breath, and I felt the pulse pounding in her throat, and she never told me I was wrong.

An hour or so later, she got up and disappeared into the bathroom. The quickest of showers, and then she came out and started to dress. "I have to go back to the hospital."

I was fogged from an excess of sex on a minimum of sleep. "The hospital?"

"Oh. I guess you didn't hear. Mother had another episode last night. A mini-stroke, they're saying." She sat back down on the bed and I took her in my arms. Her hair was still damp from the steam. "And it's my fault," she added, burrowing her head into my shoulder. "You wouldn't believe what I said to her."

"What?"

"That Theresa was her child. I mean, her illegitimate child that she adopted back after Daddy died."

Okay. That was another one for the Jerry Springer show. Now I vaguely recalled Laura's dark mutterings back when we were kids, of her mother's strange decision to adopt a half-grown child the first year she was widowed. Even then, I guess, Laura had her suspicions.

I tried to process this, put it together with the DNA and the Internet predator investigation and—and I couldn't. Probably Mrs. Wakefield's irrationality was a symptom of her physical decline, some neurological misfire. Paranoia, delusions of grandeur—

But still. "She didn't pick up her laptop."

Laura pulled away. "I forgot to tell her. We got started arguing, and then she felt ill—"

"No matter. I'll keep it for her." And maybe check through it, just in case she actually had made some kind of Internet contact . . .

"They won't let me go into her room. I upset her too much. But I still ought to be there."

"Come back later, okay? Doesn't matter how late. I don't have to be at work till noon."

And she pushed me back onto the bed and kissed me quick and promised to come back.

The next morning, Laura slipped in the backdoor, coming up against me with a sigh. "Making breakfast?" she asked, looking longingly at the omelet I was frying up. "I don't suppose that's an egg-white omelet."

"Nah, babe, here in the boondocks, we go ahead and cook the whole egg. I'll share with you."

So we sat down out on the porch, watching the sun break over the mountains. We had one omelet, one plate, two forks, and she ate a third and I ate two-thirds of the cholesterol. "How's your mom?"

"Better. Her vital signs are good, and she's awake. But we can only go in there for ten minutes, and we can't say anything to upset her."

"I guess you got a lot you can't say, huh?"

Laura sighed and put her head back against the porch railing. "More and more every day. Last night Theresa—" She broke off.

"What?"

"You don't want to hear all this family junk."

"My town, remember? And my secretary has better sources than the CIA. Trust me, I'll hear it eventually."

She groaned. "If there's gossip, Mother will—" Then she sat up straight. "To hell with it. It looks like Mother has been lying for thirty years."

"So did she admit she was Theresa's birthmother?"

Laura suddenly got occupied gathering up the dishes and the crumpled napkins. "Uh. Well. I might have been wrong about that."

"How?"

"I had the right idea," she said, a little defensively. "Mother hid a pregnancy almost thirty years ago. But we think maybe it wasn't hers." She set the dirty dishes on her lap, the forks arranged just so. "Cathy was with her when she went away that year."

I shook my head. "Your sister Cathy? But she would have been just a girl."

"She was fifteen."

That stopped me. I had a daughter not much younger than that. Slowly I said, "And your mother arranged it all. The adoption."

"That's what we think. That Cathy told her, and to hide the pregnancy, they made up this story about how they were going on the horse show circuit."

"I thought the story was supposed to be that the girl was visiting an aunt."

Laura made a face. "Oh, I'd forgotten that. That's what Mother told everyone when you and I ran off together. Probably they all thought I was pregnant."

I thought about this. Neither of us returned to the high school to hear the gossip after our elopement. "Says something, doesn't it, that she'd rather have people speculating that you had a baby, than that we got married."

"My mother does have her values. Illegitimate children can be dealt with. Unfortunate marriages, however—" She reached over and touched my leg, just to make it clear she was being ironic. Then she rose, holding the dishes in both hands. "Back then, that's what they did, you know. Went away, had the baby, gave it up, never mentioned it."

I followed her into the kitchen and we started washing up. "You know, it almost beggars belief that your sister would manage to have two babies no one knew about."

"Mother knew about the first. And I knew about the second. At least I knew she was pregnant." Laura scrubbed at the omelet pan, her face tight, her gaze focused on the scrub brush. "And she wouldn't be the first to, oh, re-create an event. Try to get it right this time."

"Yeah, you know, going after your sister's boyfriend is the way to ensure you get it right."

She looked up, mad, and threw the scrub brush at my chest. I caught it, but it still sprayed soapy water on my t-shirt. "Come on, Laura. Maybe she did it to get her revenge on the male gender."

Laura sighed and took the brush out of my hand. "Or get back at Mother for making her give the first baby away. Not that I blame Mother, really, if it's true. Cathy wasn't old enough to raise a child. And I think she was trying to protect Daddy too. He was never in very good health, and to learn that Cathy had been in such trouble—"

I was a father myself, and this bothered me. Just seemed like their father had a right to know if his daughter had gotten into that sort of trouble. So he could . . . take action. Break the guy's leg or an arm, maybe. Okay, that was the father in me speaking. The cop said, "If she was only fifteen, and the father was older than eighteen, it's a crime."

"I don't think that's an issue," Laura said, "The father was probably a boy in her class. Just the usual teenaged romance gone wrong."

I thought of what I remembered of Cathy Wakefield. She was still dominating the high school when I was starting junior high, and everyone knew her. She was tall and lithe and reckless, and every boy I knew felt a combination of lust and terror. Maybe more terror than lust, because we figured she could snap our puny little spines if we looked at her the wrong way. Somehow I doubted a boy her own age would have had the courage to knock her up.

And besides—

Laura was continuing. "But Mother—this is the part that gets to me. She didn't want Theresa to be far away. So she got the housekeeper to adopt her. It's all so weird. Theresa's . . . well, the one she thought was her birth brother, Mitch. He said that his mother raised Theresa as her own, never even said she was adopted. And then Daddy dies, and Mother snatches the child back." She dried her hands on the dishtowel and looked over at me. "I got the idea it kind of messed up his family, to lose a child that way."

"Yeah. I knew Mitch. I used to hang with the other brother Ronnie. And, not that I remember his little sister much, but no one ever thought of her as anything but his sister. We all thought it was pretty strange when she was suddenly given to your family. Well, not so strange. You were rich. They were poor. We figured it had something to do with that. Like your mother bought her. Only the Prices didn't seem like they had any more money afterwards."

"But Mother—" She sighed. "She wanted what she wanted. Her grandchild, raised as a Wakefield. And that's what she got, I guess. I wonder what Cathy thought. Whether she agreed to Mother's action."

"How much later did she go after Ellen's boyfriend?"

"He wasn't Ellen's boyfriend then," Laura said, as if that made all the difference. "But it was several years after Theresa came to us. I mean, it wasn't a reaction to what Mother had done. I don't think." She folded up the dishtowel and put it on the counter. Then she came to me, putting her head right against the soap blotch she'd made on my t-shirt. "I wish Cathy were here. I wish she could explain it. But it had to be so painful, treating her daughter like a sister. And for part of that time, when Theresa was first adopted, Cathy was there at the college, a half-mile away. She couldn't ever get away from remembering the mistake she'd made." After a second she added, "Not that Theresa is a mistake."

"I know what you mean." She was warm and slender in my arms, and I wanted to take her back to bed. But even as I formed the thought, she sighed and pulled away.

"I saw her, you know. Cathy. When she was pregnant with Brian. I wish she would have said something then. I was so aghast, you know. I probably wasn't as open a listener as I should have been. Maybe she would have explained why she'd done it again. Why she'd done it in a way that was sure to hurt Ellen."

"But she told Tom, right? He knew about the child all along."

"Well, not from the first. She told him just a few months before she died. And I'm not sure he believed her." Laura brooded for a moment, and then said, "She must have felt like it was a bad recurring dream—having a baby and then giving it up. And she had so little time left."

"So how's Theresa dealing with it?"

Laura shrugged. "She's pretty disoriented, I guess. But she said it kind of fits. Ironic. She's lost a brother—Mitch—but gained another one. Brian. Her half-brother."

"This is so . . . West Virginia."

She didn't have the brush to throw at me this time, so she balled up her fist and punched my arm lightly. Then she sobered. "It's really hard for them both, I think. Theresa has to face that she's been lied to all these years—and in the name of love. It wasn't just Mother who deceived her, but the Prices too. And Brian—well, here he's been searching for his birthmother, and he finds out that she died when he was a baby."

"Yeah," I said over my shoulder, as I went into the bedroom to dress for work, "what a shame. There's a parent he can't kidnap and hold hostage."

She followed me in, angry now for real. She stood in the doorway, hands on her hips. "That's not fair. He's just a boy."

"He's old enough to go to prison for kidnapping. Now that would make him maybe think being an over-privileged adopted kid wasn't so bad after all." Couldn't help it. I didn't like the kid and his whiny quest for his identity, or whatever he called it.

"Don't be mean," Laura said. "He's not the first teenager to go to extremes."

This might have been a reference to our elopement twenty years ago. Or it might just be a general observation. But it wasn't the same at all. I did my time in jail. This kid got off scot-free, which, in my experience, was usually what happened to boys with family connections.

Class resentment was an ugly thing. I let it go. "Can't be pleasant, to find out all this about Cathy."

She settled against me, her shoulder nudging at my chest. "I'll be okay. It's worse for Theresa. Her whole life turns out to be a series of lies." She sighed. "I guess I have to stop thinking of her as my sister, and start thinking of her as a niece. Remembering to send her a check on her birthday."

"And taking her up to Charleston to go Christmas shopping at Kauffman's."

"And go with her to see Beauty and the Beast." She pulled back and looked up. She was smiling, and beautiful, and it made me think we had a chance—Too early to worry about that now, I told myself. Just . . . enjoy what we had while we had it.

CHAPTER TWENTY-NINE

It was a slow afternoon, which was always good. But the FBI APB reports didn't grab me, and after awhile I got up from my desk and addressed something that was nagging at me. Best not to ask my secretary for help. I found my way to the storage room and quickly located the right file drawer— the last chief had his faults, but at least he insisted on regularly scheduled filing.

The folder was a little dusty, but thick with photographs. I took it back to my office and closed the door. I had been in Bristol when Cathy Wakefield died, and didn't hear about it till years later. So my knowledge was limited to "climbing accident," which wasn't all that unusual around here, where climbing schools were almost as common as ski schools, and greenhorns fell off mountains with some regularity. What was unusual was a local dying in a climbing accident. Not that locals were such great climbers— only that very few were dumb enough or reckless enough to take up that hobby. Mountains were for mining, logging, and skiing, not climbing.

But Cathy Wakefield wasn't the normal local. She was reckless and athletic, and probably no one was surprised when she took one risk too many and it killed her.

What nagged at me was Laura's suggestion that the accident wasn't an accident.

There were some cops who believed, just like Freud, that there were no such things as accidents. They assumed every single-car accident was really a suicide, that every accidental overdose was really planned. These cops tended to be cynics and pretty grim about life, but they also tended to be right. Suicide is always suspected when the accident victim is young and single, or old and sick. Not that we share our suspicions with the family— what good would it do? It makes them guilty as well as grief-stricken, and sometimes it screws up the insurance settlement too. Better to say, "He fell asleep at the wheel," and leave it at that.

So I leafed through Cathy Wakefield's file, looking for evidence that the investigating officers were thinking suicide. The signs were there, if you knew how to read the reports. The observation about oddity of her rappelling alone in the late afternoon, when the mountains cast deep shadows across the hollows. A tinge of skepticism that an experienced climbing instructor would buckle her harness so wrong that she fell out of it. The mention of her recent return to her mother's house after two years away.

I went to the storage locker and removed a climbing harness— we had the equipment because sometimes we'd have to help locate a stranded hiker. Then I took the harness and the folder out to my squad car and drove across the river, past the gas station public phone where someone had called in to say a pickup truck was abandoned on the old bridge, up the other side of Croak Mountain. From there, the road wound down, switchback upon switchback, three miles in driving distance, but nine hundred vertical feet from the pine ridge to the river. The river bottom was a place known to every teenager in town because of the little sandy beach, just past the rapids. We used to have parties there, taking the path down beside the bridge, dangerous, yeah, when you were carrying a 24-pack, but seldom lethal.

I parked the car on the gravel shoulder just this side of the bridge, and walked up along the road to the spot where Cathy had hooked her rope. The guardrail was old and dented by collisions, but when I put my hand on it, I could feel scrapes in the warm metal. The gouges were recent and sharp. Climbers either didn't know that one of their number had died here, or, more likely, took the stories of Cathy's death as a challenge.

I gripped the guardrail and leaned out over the cliff. I'd done a bit of rappelling myself, for the department here and in Bristol. Plus it was part of the curriculum at reform school, you know, all that Outward Bound shit, sending us out in the wilderness so we'd learn survival skills. Mostly what we learned was how to hide our stash of weed from the counselors. But those of us who grew up in the mountains had a healthy respect for heights. I took a deep breath of the cool air, gazing down through the two hundred-foot drop to the rocky river below.

The canyon face would have been an easy rappel for an experienced climber, and an easy climb back up. It was the sort of climb Cathy probably did just to pass an hour or two, as another woman might shop in a department store even if she didn't have much to buy.

But no one died during a shopping trip.

She'd fallen while rappelling down, or while climbing back up, and landed down there on the sand, just beside the river.

I got the folder from the car and sat down on the guardrail, looking through the accident-scene photos. They were sharp and well-framed, probably taken by the photographer at the newspaper. I pulled out a magnifying glass and studied them one by one.

Cops get used to seeing people they know lying dead. In Bristol, it was usually our homeless pals, the ones who got themselves arrested every week so they could get a shower and a few decent meals. Then one or the other would be found lying dead in an alley, from heart attacks, mostly, or pneumonia, but sometimes a beating that went on too long. It wasn't particularly weird seeing them dead. They looked half-dead when they were alive.

It was different, seeing the pictures of Cathy Wakefield's body. Even splayed out on the little sandy shore, she looked young and fresh and ready in her nylon climbing shorts and tank top. Her eyes were open and her face unmarked. There was no sign of injury, though the autopsy report had listed a fractured skull and a crushed ribcage as causes of death.

Tragic. Waste. Lost.

I spent some time studying the picture of her harness. The leather was unbroken, the buckles intact. But the strap was dangling loosely. A stupid mistake. An amateur mistake.

Or not a mistake.

I pulled my own harness on, fixing the line between my legs and buckling the straps. Hmm. To fall out of the harness- as she must have done, to end up down on the beach without it— she would have had to be dangling almost upside down. Even without the strap tightly buckled, the leg lines would ordinarily keep her solidly in the harness. Unless she was upside down and fell out.

Okay, I'd been known to end up dangling headfirst when I was learning to rappel. But she wasn't a beginner. She was a professional climber. She wouldn't make the mistake of neglecting to tighten her strap and then finish up by turning upside down. Unless that's what she planned.

She was the purposeful sort. Made a goal (like getting her sister's boyfriend) and went after it. If she wanted to kill herself but spare her family, she'd do it right. She'd make it deniable enough that the small-town cops and the coroner would ignore the evidence and call it an accident.

And that's what she'd done. Didn't matter now. Not like I was going to say anything to the family, after so many years. I just needed to know for myself. For Laura.

I squared the photos and started to put them back. But I hesitated, looking once more at the photo on top, of the body laid out in the sand. There was an indentation a yard away from her outstretched hand, just inside the yellow police tape.

When I got back to the office, I took one copy of each photo of the sandy bank and cut out the half with the body. Then I took them down the street to the camera store. Judy was intrigued by my request— usually she just got requests for extra prints of wedding photos, she said— and took an hour off her other work to blow up the images, then scan them and put them on a CD.

When I got back to the office, I spread the blowups on my desk and stuck the CD in my computer. I went through the four pictures, zooming in on that dent in the sand.

It was a shoeprint. And in the middle was a rectangle— a logo.

No one in this town knew more about shoes than Laura. She'd know what that logo was, I'd take a bet on it. I was looking back and forth from the big photo to its counterpart on my computer screen, when Laura came in response to my call.

She looked sweet and pretty, refusing to meet my gaze. I didn't know if this was an act, playing shy now that we weren't in bed. Whoever knows with an actress. But I called her over. "Come here. Look at something for me."

As she approached my desk, I reminded myself this was her sister's death scene. The photo was cropped, but she might recognize the muddy shore there, that particular bend of the creek. I zoomed in so that all that showed was the shoeprint.

I got up from my chair, and gestured for her to sit down. "There. Look at the footprint." The rectangle in the middle showed up well, but the logo was blurry. "I figure you know more about shoes than anyone in town—"

"Bass," she said right away. She hardly had to glance at the image. "A man's shoe. Probably one of the less-expensive ones, a moccasin, I bet."

I leaned over her shoulder and studied the image. "How can you tell?"

"Oh, we all used to wear them in high school, no socks. Remember?"

"No. I think I wore the same pair of Adidas running shoes for most of high school."

She shook her head. "And I still dated you?"

"At least I wore socks."

Laura frowned at the screen again. "Anyway, it's definitely Bass. And a moccasin. Probably with a leather thong tie." She actually looked a bit nostalgic. "They were kind of cute, in a clunky way."

Our class graduated just a year or so before this photo was taken. "So only teenagers would wear them?" A teenager didn't fit my preliminary profile.

"Oh, no. They were classics. Still are. Well-made and not very expensive. Sort of, oh, preppy athletic ecological. Easy to walk in."

Hmm. "Could you hike the mountains in them?"

"I doubt it. They weren't that rugged, and you can see that the tread isn't that grippy. No ankle support either. They were more for taking walks around town."

"So who would wear them? Around here?"

The urgency in my voice must have alerted her, because she stared hard at the image, and when she spoke, her voice trembled a bit. "Someone, I don't know. Not rich, but not poor. Concerned with image but not, oh, ostentatious. A lawyer on the weekends. A banker. A teacher up at the college. I mean, this isn't the most trendy town. They go with the traditional."

Why anyone bothered with psychologists, I couldn't say. Laura and her shoe analysis trumped any profiler I'd ever known. "Were they sold here in town, back when we were in high school?"

"Sure I bought mine at Mabley's."

Mabley's was an old family-owned shop, still run by the old man who was old back in those days. I wondered how long he kept records. Not this long, I'd bet.

"So why am I looking at this?" Laura asked. "Is it a crime scene?"

Belatedly, I decided to be upfront. Maybe, you know, start a new trend in our relationship. So, gently as I could, I said, "With all these new revelations, I started wondering about your sister's death. And these are photos of the accident scene."

She pushed back the chair and started to rise, but fell back. She didn't seem angry, at least. Anguished, maybe. "Why? What were you wondering about?"

"The police force then wasn't really well-trained. And there weren't any accident scene teams nearby, and there's no sign they called in the state police team. So I thought they might have missed something."

"Jack—" Laura put her hand on the screen, her fingers touching the photo of the sandy shore. "Look. I know what you mean. And it's nothing we haven't all suspected all along. But—"

She suspected, and didn't report it? Or maybe I wasn't understanding her. "You suspected all along . . . what?"

"You know." Laura's face now was wet with tears, but her voice was even. "We always suspected that maybe Cathy—well, brought the accident on herself. At least Ellen and I did, and Mother maybe too."

I relaxed a little. They'd only been concealing the suspicion of suicide. And yeah, probably it would have helped if they'd shared it, but they wouldn't be the Wakefields if they could be open and direct. I looked over at the folder which contained all the reports on Cathy's death. "Yeah. Well, that's probably what the detective thought too. But there's no use worrying a family that's already grieving. So the official verdict was accidental death."

She was silent for a moment, staring out the window. "It did make it easier. To believe that, or at least to pretend to believe that. But when we learned about—about Brian, we couldn't help but think that she'd been depressed afterwards. Now we find out that he was the *second* baby she gave away—"

"And this one, Mom didn't manage to retrieve."

Laura whispered, "I have thought such a terrible thing about Mother for so long. That she betrayed my father, and Theresa was the result, and she hardly waited for him to be buried before she took Theresa back again. And the truth was . . . more complicated. Maybe worse. Cathy was so young—she couldn't raise a baby, I know. But Mother taking Theresa back later—it might have seemed like a rebuke. And so Cathy had another child. And if she told Mother about that—Mother could have been so disappointed . . . Cathy was supposed to be the golden girl, you know. The one who always triumphed." Laura took a deep breath. "Mother might have said something angry. And she could be looking back and feeling guilty—afraid that she drove Cathy to this."

She looked tired and strained, and I wanted to take her to bed—just to hold her until she fell asleep. For so long, she'd tried to get away from this family of hers, all the sorrow of her father's death and her sister's, her mother's coldness. And yet she couldn't let go. Now she was back again, suffering with her sisters. I knew her, knew the apartness of her—but she couldn't stay apart now. And I might just be making it worse.

I went ahead and said it. "Maybe your mother has figured something out. Maybe she's learned something new, and that makes her think that she was wrong about what happened."

Laura's eyes cleared and focused on me. "What do you mean? That it was an accident after all?"

"No. Not an accident. Not suicide."

"You don't mean—" She stopped. "What do you mean?"

"Your mother has been looking into something. Ever since the kid wrote that letter and she intercepted it." I watched as the realization dawned in her eyes, as the horror started.

"No. You're wrong. You must be wrong."

"She's been keeping it from you—like she's kept everything else. But she's suspected someone."

"Maybe she's just crazy," Laura said desperately. She knew better—her mother was a lot of things, but not crazy. "She's been acting crazy—changing her will, and suddenly leaving town when we're all here. It's not like she's been really rational lately."

"But what if she has a reason for all this? And she's not telling you?"

"But Jack—" After a moment, she finished, "You can't really be thinking that someone else was involved."

"I don't know. And after so many years, I probably won't ever know. But—" I gestured to the computer screen. "I thought I'd look at the photos. And found that."

"The shoeprint."

"Yeah."

"The police were walking there."

"You wouldn't catch a cop or a deputy in a shoe like that, even off-duty."

"Then it was the photographer. Or whoever found the body. Or it was there before she fell—" Laura pushed her chair back from the desk and rose. "It doesn't mean anything."

"Maybe not. But your mother was looking for something. Someone. All this DNA stuff and Internet predator business—she was looking for something."

"But Jack—"Laura took a deep breath. "Look. She's probably looking for any reason to believe it wasn't suicide. Because she has to wonder if she'd done something differently, Cathy would have made another decision. But that doesn't mean she's right. She's just not reliable."

"Maybe she is, about this. Maybe she's on to something. And if she's right—then someone's walking around thinking he's gotten away with it." It felt simple to me. You didn't let criminals get away with crime. But then, I was a cop.

Laura wasn't. She came to me and put her hand on my arm. Softly, she said, "Jack, please."

"I'm just going to look into it."

"Please don't. My family has been through so much this last couple weeks. I don't know if we can take another blow."

"I'll do it quietly. Won't hurt to look into it."

Her hand dropped from my arm and she moved back a step. "Won't hurt? Of course it will hurt." The entreaty was gone. Now she was angry. "It will bring it all back. And there's been enough pain already, don't you think? Mother in the hospital. Ellen finding out about Brian, and about Cathy betraying her. Brian learning his mother is dead, and his father doesn't want him."

"Could be that little abduction thing getting in the way of paternal love," I suggested, but she wasn't listening.

"And Theresa discovering that everything she thought about her life was a lie."

"What about you?"

She walked to the door. "I'm okay."

"Just worried that all this is going to get into the tabloids, huh?" It wasn't a nice thing to say—it might not have even been a true thing to say. But I was pretty fed up with it all. She was using me, using my protectiveness, to manipulate me. I'd proved already that I'd bend the law for her, and she meant for me to do it again.

"It's not about the tabloids. It's about protecting my family."

"Right. Because thirty years of hiding the truth has worked so well."

"Thirty—" She fell into a stubborn silence.

"Yeah. You don't think your father might have liked to know he had a granddaughter? Might have liked to know that his daughter—his teenage daughter—had a baby. Might have liked to help out." Thinking of my own daughter, not that much younger, I added, "And he might have liked to have a talk with the guy who got her into that situation. But your mother kept the secret, and so did Cathy. And what did you get from all that secrecy? Cathy ended up angry and desperate, didn't she? And she had another child she never intended to raise."

Laura was silent, and I had to add, "And maybe it got her killed."

"By whom?" Laura shot back. "Did it ever occur to you that Tom would have the best motive to kill her right then, just after she'd told him about the child?"

That stopped me. It was hard to think of Tom O'Connor as a murderer—if he'd been that, he would have killed the kidnapping little jerk off. "Yeah, well, if he did it, then he shouldn't get away with it."

"And if he didn't—and he didn't. The idea is absurd. If he didn't, and you drag him and Ellen and their daughter through an investigation and a trial, what good will that do?"

"If he didn't do it, then he doesn't need to worry."

Laura's eyes narrowed. "And in the meantime, what are you going to be doing? My mother is sick. Her condition is precarious. Stirring up the past for no good reason—that won't help her."

"If it was murder, then there's a killer out there walking around."

"And you know that because there's a shoeprint."

I didn't bother to tell her about cop's instincts. She'd only point out that none of the cops involved seventeen years ago had the same instincts. I just said, "I'm going to look into it."

"No."

"It's not your call."

She stood at the door, her face angry and anguished. "I don't want you to do this. It's just going to hurt us more."

I regarded her, and I actually considered what she was saying. The cop in me was insisting that justice had to be done. But the lover in me just wanted to soothe her.

The cop won. Or at least persuaded the lover that it did no good for Laura to keep on denying the truth. They'd done that long enough. "I'm just going to make some inquiries."

"You mean, talk to my mother." She opened the door and stood there, half in, half out. "You don't care that she's sick, that she's not in her right mind. And you don't care about me or my sisters. You just care about your case."

"I'm doing it for you."

"I don't believe you." She took a deep breath. "I mean it, Jackson. You keep on with this, hurt my family, and we're through."

It pierced me, that flat remark of hers. And I shot back. "I don't take well to ultimatums."

"It's not an ultimatum. It's just a warning." She pulled the door shut behind her.

I wanted to call her back, remind her that it was her family that kept us apart in the first place. That she and I were one of those family secrets her mother kept hidden away. That truth was good no matter how it hurt.

But I just let her go. I'd win her back not with pleading, but with results. If I solved this mystery, she'd come back to me. I knew it.

Or hoped it, anyway.

CHAPTER THIRTY

After Laura left, I spent an hour online, using Nexis to track down Tom O'Connor. He was filing stories from Europe during the week of Cathy's death. I had to admit to a certain relief. My instincts told me the man wasn't a killer. And clearing him meant clearing away one of Laura's objections to my investigation.

Then I packed up the forgotten laptop and headed over to the hospital to visit Margaret Wakefield.

Her room was in the new wing, through a shiny, fluorescent-lighted corridor and past a silver and pink nurses' station. The orderly was just leaving with the dinner tray as I entered her room. She sat there, propped against the pillows, reading away at some thick hardback book. Not for her the easy diversion of a TV show, I guessed. There was an IV in her left arm, but the telemetry machine stood in the corner, turned off.

"Mrs. Wakefield," I said, and she looked up.

She was pale, and her hand trembled as she set the book down on the coverlet. But her voice was strong enough. "Chief McCain. How . . . kind of you to visit me."

It was barbed just enough to remind me that she was no one's fool. "I brought your laptop. And I have a few questions."

"I'm very tired," she said, her gaze sliding away.

"I won't take very long." I set the computer on the side table and took a seat in the chair near the window. I didn't take out my notepad. This was a conversation, not an interrogation. At least that's what I wanted Laura to think if she happened to come in. "Tell me what you're looking for. What the DNA was about. Why you're worried about Internet predators."

She looked over my shoulder, out the window, at the fading evening light. "I have a granddaughter. Your mention of predators worried me. That's all."

"And the DNA?"

She sighed. "A silly notion."

"You're not a silly woman."

She smiled. In another woman, it might have been coquettish. On her, it looked grim. "I can be. I have been."

"I have something to show you." I took my time plugging in the laptop and loading up the CD of photos. Then I set it on the bed beside her and waited till the first photo appeared on the screen. "That's an accident scene from 17 years ago. Do you recognize it?"

"The beach. Under the Kaskco bridge," she whispered. She couldn't take her eyes off the picture, and I was glad I'd cropped out the body.

I hit the mouse key and zoomed in. "There—see that? A shoeprint. And it doesn't belong to any cop. Someone else was down there on the beach, before the police arrived."

She just kept looking at the screen. Finally I said, "No one noticed it at the time. But I've gone through the file, and I've been out to the bridge." When she didn't respond, I added, "Here's what I learned from the report. At about seven that evening, someone stopped at the Shell station on Croak Mountain Road and called the police from the pay phone there. It was a man. He said that a Ford pickup was abandoned along the bridge and someone should come tow it away before dark. The chief sent a wrecker there, and the driver saw the rope dangling from the guardrail. And then the body. One of the officers recognized your daughter, and—"

"And I was called to identify the body." She said this with a strange sort of determination. "My nephew said he would do it. But it was my duty."

"The report says that she buckled the harness wrong. Did you believe that?"

She sighed and finally looked straight at me. "No. Cathy didn't make stupid mistakes like that."

"So you thought—"

"I thought she'd done that to disguise her suicide." Well, Mrs. Wakefield wasn't one to mince words. She'd kept quiet about this for almost two decades, but when she admitted it finally, she said it straight out.

"Why did you think that she'd commit suicide?"

This time she wasn't so quick to respond. Finally she replied, "She had been . . . behaving erratically, those months before."

"Did you know she'd had another child?"

"No." This she said firmly. "I didn't. She told me the first time. But the second time, she hid it. She stayed away from home for months, and arranged the adoption herself."

I didn't ask what Mrs. Wakefield would have done, if she'd been in charge. Instead I said, "Then a few months later, she went to Europe to visit Ellen and Ellen's new baby."

She didn't reply, so I continued, "And then she came home. And a few weeks later, she was dead. What happened to make you conclude she'd killed herself?"

She didn't flinch from the blunt language. But she wasn't ready to be candid yet either. "The circumstances of the accident. And the timing. She wouldn't ordinarily have been climbing that late in the day, when the light is fading."

"But no note. No warning."

"No."

I waited. Finally she added, "She was in a . . . cheerless mood. I remember that. She usually liked coming home, liked seeing old friends. She was . . . something of a star, you know."

There was the ghost of pride in her voice, and I thought unwillingly of Laura, another star come home—but not to a proud mother. "But she didn't meet with friends this time?"

"I don't think so."

"So she stayed home with you most of the time."

Reluctantly she nodded.

"You must have talked."

Another nod.

"She told you something. Something that later made you think that she was in—" I had to search for the words. "In despair."

"Yes." This was just a whisper.

"And it wasn't about the second child."

"No. I didn't know about him—until he wrote here to Ellen."

"It must have been about the first. Theresa."

She didn't answer, so I pushed on. "This was just a few years after you took Theresa back from the Prices. Adopted her. And you didn't know it, but it was on Cathy's mind because she had to give up another child."

"She accepted what I'd done. For Theresa. But it . . . bothered her. She took it as a rebuke. That she couldn't forget now, no matter how she tried. But it was too late. It wasn't as if I could give Theresa back." She pushed back slightly, into the pillows, and said, "But Cathy would rather have forgotten having her. Forgotten conceiving her."

"And she told you that before she died."

"Yes."

"And she told you something else. Something about the father. Something you didn't know before." I was guessing. But I was right.

"Back when she was just a girl, and she came to me and told me she was pregnant . . . she said that a boy in her class was the father."

"But that wasn't true, was it? And she corrected that, before she died."

"She told me she had to speak the truth. She said it was an older man. A teacher."

Very softly, I said, "Why did she tell you at that point, after so many years of silence?"

Mrs. Wakefield was silent for a moment, gazing out the window at the fading evening light. Finally she said, "Now I understand. She realized that she had . . . gone off track. That she was—what do they call it? Acting out. Being self-destructive. She didn't say that, but now I understand. Seducing her sister's boyfriend . . . giving up another child. Taking greater risks in her climbing. And she realized that it was because of what happened to her years earlier."

"It is rape, you know. Even if it seemed consensual. She was under sixteen."

"I know. Now. But then, I thought it was a boy her own age, just two children who got carried away. That the best thing to do was handle it discreetly. And I did." Her manicured hand moved slowly on the coverlet, stroking the wrinkles smooth. "But then, finally, she told me the truth. And she said that she wanted to——"

When she didn't finish, I finished for her. "She wanted to prosecute. To expose him. To put him in jail."

"Yes."

"What did you say?"

Another moment, and a sigh. "I said she couldn't. It had been too long. And Theresa would learn the truth. And we would never recover from that."

Theresa would know the truth now. The wall of secrecy was cracking. "What did Cathy say?" "She . . . agreed. Finally. She understood that it would hurt Theresa most of all."

"And she died——"

"Two days later."

She laid her head back against the pillows, and I let her rest for a moment. Then I said, "Something happened this spring to make you think it wasn't suicide after all. That she was killed."

She sighed again. "First was that letter, from that boy. Brian. He addressed it to Ellen, because that was the name on his birth certificate. But I knew right away it couldn't be Ellen who delivered him. And I thought perhaps it was Cathy."

"What else?"

She hesitated, then said, "There was a sketch. Her father had made one for each of the girls. Just a study of a landmark on the Loudon campus. He so hoped they'd all go there—but only Cathy ended up enrolling." She looked away again, out the window, as if she could see across town to the campus. "What with everything, I never noticed. But Cathy's sketch disappeared at some point. I didn't know it, but she'd given it away."

"To the teacher."

"Yes. Even when she was just a girl, she attended the summer camps and classes at the college. And so, I suppose, she thought that would be a lovely gift to a teacher there."

"And so, this spring, you saw the sketch."

"Yes. It was on the wall of an office there on campus. I'm sure he never realized the significance of it. Perhaps he didn't even recall where he got it."

"And that's when you started your investigation."

"Yes."

"When you gave me that DNA sample—you were trying to prove that this man was Theresa's father."

"Yes. I was going to get a hair from Theresa's hairbrush for comparison. But . . ."

"You realized that if he was the father, he might have killed Cathy."

"I thought she might have gone to him. I had discouraged her from going to the authorities. I was thinking of . . . us. She was thinking of other girls he might hurt. So she might have called him, asked him to meet her. Confronted him. Threatened to expose him."

"Who is it?" I knew, but I asked anyway.

She turned her face away. Gently I said, "It's the college president, isn't it? He was a teacher there at Loudon when Cathy was a teenager. He went away, and then came back recently as president. And he hung that sketch she gave him in his office."

"He wanted to cultivate me. As a donor. So he invited me to his office when he first came in as president. It is hard to imagine—how he could invite Cathy's mother. Hard to imagine such . . . ruthlessness"

"You've been trying to trap him. Pretending to want to donate money to the college. Trying to find him on the Internet."

"There is a Loudon College recruitment chatroom, you see. I thought I might pretend to be a teenage girl."

It was hard to imagine, this proper matron searching for clues, conducting her own investigation. "What else?"

"Recently he spoke to my garden club. He mentioned an ex-wife. I went to see her. I didn't tell her why I was there, and she gave me little help. But she was obviously antipathetic to him. She was quite adamant that she had sole custody of their son, and that the child seldom visited his father."

"Why didn't you come to me?"

She shrugged. "You wouldn't have believed me. You were not interested in pursuing the Internet angle."

I didn't bother to point out that Mrs. Wakefield hadn't given me much to work with. I just said, "And if I did investigate, it would become a criminal matter. And it would all come out— about Cathy being molested. About Theresa."

"Yes. I thought . . . I thought perhaps I would just ruin him. Destroy him professionally somehow. I thought I'd promise the college a big gift, and then withdraw it, and tell the trustees that he was rude to me. Or trap him in a compromising position on the Internet. I don't know. I thought I could ruin him."

I could hardly argue with this. It was exactly what I'd done to that rapist in New York, now all over the airwaves protesting that he didn't know where those date-rape drugs came from. It was some sort of justice. But murder, if that's what this is, required more than just ruination.

"But now I know. And I can't bury it. You know that."

"You are a police officer. You investigate. Arrest. Prosecute."

"Yes."

She whispered, "Are you certain?"

It was like the transfer of a terrible duty. And for the first time, I felt a connection to her. I said, quietly, "I'll make certain."

She gripped my hand. Her touch was hot and dry and papery. "It could . . . destroy everything."

"You have lost it all anyway. Everything the lies created. Your daughters didn't stay with you. They didn't do what you wanted. They didn't love you more."

After this harsh assessment, her hand fell away from mine. And then, in only a whisper, she said, "My husband never had to know. He died thinking that Cathy was still safe with us."

"But she wasn't. You couldn't keep her safe. Not by keeping this all secret. And she finally realized that, didn't she?" It was cruel, sure. But that was because it was true. "She finally realized that she was wrecking her own life, trying to get back at men. Trying to get back at you."

"She wanted something I couldn't give then. Approval. To bring it all down."

"But now—"

She started to cry. It was a frightening thing, to watch a woman like that cry. She cried silently, her face hard and her eyes fierce.

That's when Laura came in, her shoes tapping lightly on the tiles and then halting. I looked around and saw her standing there, framed in the doorway. She took one look at her mother and said icily, "Jack, that's enough. I asked you not to—"

"It's all right," Mrs. Wakefield said. "It's all right."

I rose and Laura took my place on the bed. She sat there, just a foot away, both of them rigid. Then Laura awkwardly reached out and patted her mother's hand. "We know, Mother," she murmured. "Don't worry. We know. Theresa knows. We'll be okay."

Mrs. Wakefield gazed down at their joined hands. Then slowly she withdrew hers. Laura made a little noise, something between a gasp and a sigh, and started to rise. But then her mother leaned forward and put her arms out, and Laura hesitated. Then, careful of the IV lines, she came into her mother's embrace.

CHAPTER THIRTY-ONE

It was dark, or as dark as a June evening gets, and Laura and her sisters were shadows against the greater darkness of the old house. I found them in the backyard, Laura and Ellen at the picnic table on either side of a flickering citronella candle, and Theresa on the Adirondack chair. The kid—Brian—was hunched up on the stairs of the deck. I guessed he had more success with his birthmother's sisters than with his birth father—who had gone back to Virginia without making whatever acknowledgment the kid had been wanting.

"Come over here," I told him, and sullenly he moved towards me. In a second I had him against the railing of the deck and gave him a quick pat down, with maybe a little bit more neck-grab than was recommended back at the training academy. He squirmed, his breath coming fast and scared. I let him go, though I kept his pocketknife.

"Is that really necessary?" Theresa said.

"Sure is. Get one chance in this town, and he's already used it up." I watched him walk back to the steps, sulky and disarmed, and turned to see Laura's smile. She hid it quickly, but I saw her mouth curve in the candlelight. I guessed she didn't like him all that much either.

Or maybe it was just that macho displays made her hot.

No reaction from Ellen. Maybe she'd run through her patience with the boy. Or maybe she was wondering about her husband.

Anyway, I asked Laura, "You filled them in yet?"

"As much as I know. But Mother said you'd explain."

And so I did. I told them about their mother's suspicions, and about her conversation with Cathy just before the accident out on the bridge. At first, they didn't ask any questions. Stunned, I guess. Then Theresa made a noise—very quiet, almost too quiet to hear over the calls of the crickets in the grass. And finally she said, "You're trying to say that I'm the product of statutory rape?"

"That's what we suspect."

"And that he m—"

She couldn't go on. I couldn't blame her.

"Look, nothing's certain. But it's not just your mother's suspicions. The police had questions at the time, and I do now. Someone left a footprint—a Bass moccasin shoeprint—there at the scene. And it never made any sense that she'd be climbing that time of day, and make an amateur's mistake."

Laura said slowly, "You think she met him there. By the bridge. To confront him." After a pause, she added, "She always kept her climbing equipment in her truck. Just in case she got a chance to climb."

"Yeah." I leaned against the railing, chose my words carefully. "She wasn't climbing that day, I don't think. I think she probably just wanted to talk to him. And —"

"He knew how to climb." Ellen spoke for the first time. "That first summer camp, he took us all to search for lichen on the cliffs. He showed off, rappelling down and climbing back up." She added, "But Cathy was better even then. He called her his best student."

Theresa had her hands in her lap, and stared down at them. "I always knew . . . that I was the child of sin."

Ellen was there in an instant, kneeling at her side. "That's not true. You know that God doesn't visit the sins of the father on the child. You were innocent. Nothing about this means anything about you."

Laura came closer, put her hand on Theresa's arm. "Besides, you're good. You've done nothing but good things in your life. No sins to speak of."

"You don't know," Theresa whispered.

"I do know," Laura said firmly. "The only reason you think you're a sinner is that you have such high standards for yourself. You're way better than average."

Brian finally spoke up. "You are good. You helped me, even though I was lying to you."

He huddled into himself, and I could imagine what he was thinking, that he'd brought this all down on the family . . . well, maybe he wasn't thinking anything like that. I wasn't sure the kid had that sort of self-awareness. And anyway, I was the one who kept saying the truth should come out, so if his lies led to this revelation, I should be thanking him.

He probably shouldn't hold his breath waiting.

Theresa accepted her sisters' embrace, and she put her head down on Ellen's shoulder. After a moment, Laura rose and came to stand by me. "Do you have to?"

"You know I do."

Theresa looked up. Even if the flickering candlelight, I could see the anguish on her face. "I was—was *sired* by a child molester, you're saying. And when she went to him to make him face what he'd done, he pushed my birthmother into a ravine."

That was a pretty concise summary, so I just nodded.

Theresa pushed Ellen's arms away and stood up. Her face was hard now. "Then get him. Get him for her sake. And mine."

A quarter-hour later, Laura was still arguing temperance and caution and all that good Wakefield stuff. "Can't you just . . . ruin him? Like you—"

She broke off, but I knew she was thinking about the number I'd done on the man in New York. That wasn't murder, however. "If I got enough evidence for murder, I'd have to take it to the prosecutor. But—" I shrugged. "After seventeen years, I don't know whether we can find much evidence. The shoeprint is intriguing, sure. But those shoes are long gone."

"What do you need?" Ellen asked.

"A confession would be good. On tape. But I don't think I'm going to get that." I thought with some longing about my former force—a half-dozen detectives and cutting-edge wiretap equipment. "My best chance is trying to trap him. Your mother was trying to do that, pretending she was a teenage girl, trying to entice him in a chatroom."

Ellen and Laura exchanged glances. "So that was what all that laptop interest was about," Ellen said. "And she wanted help in figuring chat software out. And finding Loudon College chatrooms. And all that time I just thought she was trying to keep up with the times."

"Well, she cottoned on pretty quick." I tried to think through the angles. "I'll have a tech look at her laptop, but I don't think we're going to find anything. She didn't keep logs, and somehow I doubt he did either."

"He doesn't know that she didn't keep logs."

It was the boy—his first contribution. I looked down at him, sitting hunched on the porch step. "What are you suggesting?"

"I don't know. I mean—" he floundered for a moment. But he was in the generation that grew up with Instant Messenger, and it didn't take him long to figure something out. "If he thinks that the police are investigating his chats with girls, well, maybe he'll do something stupid."

"I can't just forge logs." Unfortunately.

"Yeah, well, maybe just implying you got them? And implying you can track down the other PC used in the chats? I mean, you know. Every computer's got a unique IP number, right?"

"Right," I said slowly. "So you're saying, if he thinks we can trace it to his computer . . ."

"Maybe he'll confess to something," Ellen said. "Something not so bad. Like he might try to say that he did have a chat, but he didn't know she was underage. And once you get him in an interrogation room, well, he'll be looking at the end of his career."

"He might say something incriminating," Theresa said. She was still shaken, but she sat ramrod straight in her low chair. I wondered what it was like, to want vengeance on the man who sired you. She was tougher than I'd be, after so many revelations coming so fast, and none of them good.

I pushed away from the railing. "Well, let me see what I can come up with tomorrow. I'll keep you informed."

Laura followed me around the house to my car. I held out my arms, but she kept her distance. "Jack, if you can get him on some Internet predator count, then maybe that'll be all you need."

"I can't get him on that," I told her wearily. It had been a long day, and it looked like it was going to be a long, lonely night. "He probably didn't break any laws with your mother. It's not like she's actually a teenager. So we just have to hope he screws up somehow. And he's a college president. He should be smart enough not to screw up much."

Laura's eyes narrowed, and she said coolly, "Well, he decided to mess with my sister, and I think he screwed up then."

Decades ago—but I didn't say it out loud. I had to believe there was a chance to catch him, even though this was about as cold as a case got. I might have to settle, as Mrs. Wakefield thought, and Laura wanted, for just ruining him. Could ruin myself in the process, of course.

I thought briefly that I should take this to the prosecutor, get a go-ahead on what amounted to a sting operation. But this wasn't the bold, risk-taking sort of prosecutor you got in big cities. This was a good old boy with a thirty-five-year-old law degree and a big mortgage, who spent a lot of time worrying that actually prosecuting anyone might cut into the private practice he had on the side.

The college president was an important man in town, and he would have some powerful allies. If I started going after him, and couldn't finish, well, I wouldn't be Wakefield police chief much longer.

As I got in my squad car, Laura was still regarding me warily. In some ways, she had the most to lose from a trial. Outside of this little town, no one cared about me or Mrs. Wakefield or even the college president. But Laura was out there in the public eye every day. And for a semi-famous person, she kept a fierce hold of her privacy. If this investigation developed into a trial, she'd be a featured player in tabloid stories. The spotlight would be on her, but for all the wrong reasons.

I couldn't let that stop me. But maybe I'd find a way.

She was still standing there, silhouetted in the driveway, as I drove off.

It took the morning and half of the afternoon to set everything up— calling in the off-duty cops, assigning them to quadrants, recruiting my fake computer techs. Getting an appointment with the big man on campus.

The college spread out on the north side of town, a small tidy campus grouped around a central red-brick quadrangle. It was all quiet and lush in the afternoon sun, the lawns almost empty now with most of the students gone.

I'd actually gone to college back when, gotten a degree in criminal justice. But my college was a barren stretch of concrete low-rises on the edge of downtown Bristol. Tuition was cheap enough that the department paid for it, and classes were held at night and on weekends, because most of the students worked. There weren't any dances or football games or marching bands. Just the grind of adults and their cheerless career-driven studies.

Loudon, on the other hand, was a real college, with dormitories and bearded professors and sororities. Weird that every time I set foot on this campus, I felt like I was on a movie set. It just seemed a world apart from the real West Virginia, where a lot of kids didn't have textbooks or toothbrushes, and working men didn't have work. But the college was the only thing that kept Wakefield's economy relatively stable. So I made sure my department worked well with the administration and the tiny college security force whenever there was a football game or some fraternity had an extra-wild party.

Ridell, the security chief, a frail man with a bad cough, was waiting for me in the administration antechamber. He tried to get more details as we walked into the office, but I didn't say much until we were sitting there in front of the desk, with President Urich there, his hands clasped on his blotter.

I did my best not to gaze at the framed sketch drawn by Edward Wakefield. But I could see it there, in my peripheral vision, just over the president's shoulder. It was right underneath a photo of him with some governor or senator.

Could he have kept it, if he'd killed the girl who gave it to him?

Well, hell, that was a stupid question for a cop to ask. There were men who didn't worry about such contradictions. That's how they went on, achieving their goals, succeeding at whatever criminality they chose. They didn't look back at the damage they'd caused.

It's just most of them didn't look like this guy. Most of them didn't teach botany and hit up old ladies for endowments. Most of them didn't look calm but concerned when I arrived.

It wasn't that I didn't suspect him. I did. But I had to keep an open mind. And I had to admit that Urich was pretty plausible. He looked shocked, but in that college-president responsible-for-students way, when I explained about the Internet predator who was using a college computer for his predation.

Pretty plausible. If I didn't already suspect him, I probably wouldn't suspect him. He coughed a little and asked if this could be handled quietly, the reputation of the college, all that, just like any college president would do. And I had to take a slightly tougher tone, just like any police chief would. "The more cooperative you are, the quieter we can be."

"What can we do?" he said, his hands out, palms up.

"First, you agree to a search and I won't have to get a search warrant. Search warrants, the newspapers could find out about." I didn't bother to mention that the local editor could probably be prevailed on to keep that quiet. "We'll send in a couple technicians, no big deal. They'll look just like regular computer techs. But they'll be checking every PC owned by the college—in the computer labs, and the library, and the offices."

"That could take weeks," Ridell, the security chief, protested. "Got to get access, maybe permission, passwords . . ."

"Well," I said easily, "takes that long, we can bring in the FBI, I suppose. They have plenty of agents can do this."

Urich's face went a little pale. "No, no, I'm sure that won't be necessary. Maybe you should start with the library. We don't require passwords to use those computers, and townspeople have been known to gain access."

Townspeople. My people, that is. Not college people. "Sure. We'll start there." That meant, if he was actually chatting up teenagers, he wasn't doing it from the library terminals. "How many students you have here for the summer session?"

"About two hundred."

"And about half are male?"

"Yes, I suppose." Urich's eyes narrowed. "You think whoever this was—he's been doing this during the summer session. So he's still around."

I shrugged. Best to let him wonder and worry. "I didn't say that. How many faculty and staffers are still here?"

"We keep some on ten-month contracts. About half will be off now. And most of the faculty takes the summer off for research."

"But they could be doing research here, using their offices and the library," I said. "So what's the breakdown of how many are still on campus this summer?"

Urich glanced at his security chief. "What would you say, Bill? About one hundred fifty?"

Ridell sat up straighter and tried to look knowledgeable. "Uh, a lot of the professors went off to Europe and the beach. But there are twelve teaching summer classes. And maybe another dozen using their offices. I think they're cutting paychecks for about one hundred twenty people on the staff. Got to keep the place running. But some of those are seasonal employees, like gardeners. Don't think they'd be accessing the computers."

"No." I looked at Ridell and said, one regular guy to another, "This fellow seems pretty, what do you call it. Erudite. You know what I mean."

Ridell nodded. "Big words."

Urich picked up on this—that the recipient of the chat must have kept a record somehow. And I didn't even have to out-and-out lie.

"What exactly are you hoping to find?" Urich said. "Logs of conversations?"

I shrugged. "If he was a really stupid erudite guy." Couldn't help myself. I had to add, "Of course, anyone who has to hang out with 14-year-olds to feel like a man probably is pretty stupid."

"Got that right," Ridell growled. "Should be put in jail with some real tough guys, and find out what it's like to be molested, huh?" Then he glanced at his boss, and down again. "Just saying. We don't want jerks like that at Loudon."

"So you'll be looking for logs?" Urich repeated.

He said it in a way that made me think he wasn't actually stupid enough to keep logs. But then, I didn't expect that he would be. I had a fallback plan. "Logs, sign-on names, whatever. And you know—" The kid Brian had written this down for me, and I memorized it, so it came flowingly from my tongue: "See, every computer has a unique IP address. So we just need to look for that IP address, see who was logged onto the college network the right time—easy enough." I added the kicker. "He might try to delete stuff, but you know, nothing is ever really erased on a hard drive. So if there's anything to find, we'll find it."

He was quiet for a moment. Not so plausible now, I thought. Not that the pensive expression on his face was any kind of evidence. Finally he said, "What do you need?"

"I'll need your techs to work with mine, starting immediately. I'll need a record of all the college's computers. And I'll need a pass key to the offices."

We worked out the details, me and the security chief, while Urich sat there quietly. But he rose as I did. "I'm sure this can be . . . handled without undue difficulty," he said.

Without undue publicity, I was supposed to understand. A good college president sentiment. "We'll do our best," I said, and headed out.

I had it all set up. I had five off-duty officers in civilian clothes walking around the campus, watching for straying computers. I had Theo, the recruit who liked to come in on his off-time and install new hard drives and sound cards, waiting at my car. And I had the kid Brian waiting there with him.

"Theo's in charge, you hear?"

"Yeah, okay." Brian looked like a videogame junkie, not like a police officer, but then, Theo didn't look much like a cop either. They were both pretty weedy. But that was fine. They were just supposed to look like they knew computers. So they were both in the uniform—that is, faded t-shirts and olive-drab cargo pants and webbed tool belts, just like any techie.

I gave the boy a hard look. "I'm going out on a limb here, kid. You being a civilian and all that. You just do like we discussed, check out the PCs and Macs, don't talk much. Got it?"

"Got it," he said, gazing down at his Doc Martens. Then he looked up, sincerity sitting odd on that defiant face of his. "Thanks. I just wanted to help. Because it's my . . ." it took him a moment, but he finished, "my mother."

Theo was looking away politely, pretending not to hear. He didn't know much, just that he was supposed to pretend to look for a specific IP address, but if he found anything suspicious at all, he needed to confiscate the computer. And he needed to watch out for anyone trying to sneak out with a computer or hard drive. Or anyone who looked like he was doing some major erasure.

I walked with them into the big granite-faced library. The atrium lobby was brighter than a library should be—the ceiling four floors above was splintered with skylights. Urich was waiting by the terminals—the card catalog terminals. Somehow I doubted anyone would troll for jail bait there, so I said in a low voice, "Don't waste too much time on these—head over to the admin building in a few minutes. Start at the first floor, and make plenty of noise."

It wasn't much of a plan. But if Urich had done anything wrong, maybe he'd panic. If not, well, I'd probably blown the whole Internet predator angle. And I didn't think there was much chance I'd make a charge on a seventeen-year-past murder stick.

Brian fiddled in his tool belt and pulled out something square and blinking, and, with a muttered apology, pushed past Urich to the first terminal. I could see the effort it took the boy to pretend nonchalance, so close to this man who might have killed his mother. Maybe he wasn't such a worthless over-privileged whiner after all.

Or maybe he was a worthless over-privileged whiner who could keep his mouth shut.

Anyway, Urich watched them for a moment, then followed me out to the quadrangle. "I'd really prefer—"

"I know. Discretion. Sure. That's why they're dressed like techs and not cops." I was watching him pretty closely, and I thought he looked spooked. Then again, nervousness wasn't unlikely in a college president who thought his school might soon be featured on CNN Headline News. "I'll let you know if they find anything."

He sighed, and held out his hand. I took it, trying not to flinch.

It was late afternoon, the sun edging down behind Lantry Mountain, so the light was gold and green. The two men students walking on the quadrangle paths glanced curiously at me, but then cast their eyes down, hiding whatever minor transgression made them feel guilty. I walked to my squad car and made a big show of driving off, just in case Urich was watching. Then I went back to the department garage and changed to civilian dress and an unmarked car.

I drove along College Avenue, past the faculty houses, and back onto campus using the service road. In the parking lot, I parked between a couple other cars, hidden in the shadows of the HVAC plant, and waited, leaving the motor running and the air conditioning on.

The radio crackled with the usual traffic messages as what passed for rush hour passed in Wakefield. I sat there, with that as my background music, watching the back of the admin building. The shadows were lengthening as evening came on.

When the cell phone rang, I thought it must be one of my officers, reporting someone exiting, laden with PC. But it was Laura. "Where are you?" She was still reserved, I could tell, but at least she was asking.

"On a stakeout."

"No. I mean, where exactly?"

I debated. Imagined her here, beside me, maybe laying her hand on my thigh. Sue me. I'm a man. "Behind the admin building, in the parking lot. Facing out—back lane."

The Wakefield house was only a half mile away, so it was just a couple minutes before the headlights broke the dusk around me. She parked a few cars down, and I leaned across the front seat to shove open the passenger door.

She slipped in, and I smelled her faint perfume, and she settled back against the seat with a sigh. She turned her head and regarded me in the half-light from a distant streetlamp. "Bored?"

"Lonely."

She turned to the side so she could lean past the computer sticking out of the dashboard, and she nestled her head against my chest. "This isn't a good car for making out."

"I don't know. I've never tried it." I tilted her face up and kissed her, and we forgave each other—for being who we were, for having conflicting values, for expecting too much. Anyway, I thought that was what the kiss meant, and she must have thought so too, because she kissed me again.

But even then, I kept my gaze over her shoulder at the back of the building. We should give up and go home, I thought, but it was only desire talking. Stakeouts often lasted for hours, and it made sense that Urich would wait until it was dark and everyone had gone home before he made his move.

If he was going to make a move at all.

She sighed and settled back into her seat. "What are we waiting for?"

I explained the whole flimsy strategy to Laura—the sting to trap Urich in some evidence of guilt.

"I can't believe you're using Brian."

"Why not?" I knew I sounded defensive. "He's not in any danger."

"Not that. I was just thinking that you kind of held him in contempt."

"Well, sure. Nasty little jerk, he is. But . . . but he's got a right, I suppose. And at least this time he isn't breaking the law."

She stared into the gathering dusk. "Is this the right way to go?"

"Yeah. The truth is always the right way to go."

She gave me a slight smile. "That sort of attitude would put the TV industry out of business."

"Except for reality TV."

"That's just as invented as the show I'm on."

We sat there in the dark, listening to the radio static. Holding hands. And I wanted to ask her like I would have when we were kids—Are we okay? Are we together? Is this for keeps?

But I was grown-up now, and I knew nothing was for keeps. We had what we had, and for as long as it lasted, and that was as long as we appreciated how lucky we were to get another chance. I wasn't going to force the issue, because it still felt so fragile. But we were here together now, and that was more than I'd ever let myself expect.

A slice of yellow light in the second building over. The science building, I thought. Could be just a student leaving the back way—

But it looked like Urich, stuffing something in his jacket pocket, looking around, then stepping carefully down of the loading dock.

"Get down." I urged Laura's head down below the dashboard level and leaned back myself, back against the seat. I kept my gaze on the man walking through the line of cars to a black Mercedes parked in front of a Reserved sign.

I let him get in the car and out of the parking lot before I reached over and opened Laura's door. "Out."

Laura just pulled the door shut again and buckled her seatbelt. "No way."

"I don't have time to argue—"

"Then don't. Get going."

I was three parts annoyed and one part charmed. "Could get scary. High-speed chase, all that."

She shrugged. "Big deal. I had a bit part in *Speed*. I was one of the passengers on that bus. I bet you drive better than Sandra Bullock."

She trusted me too much. Always had. When I was a wild teenager driving too fast on the mountain roads, she trusted me. When she was so sick and I told her I'd take care of her, she trusted me. And she trusted me now. Again.

I put the car in gear and eased out into the road, and then picked up the radio. I instructed my officers to station themselves near the major intersections and the three bridges and wait for my word. No need to spook him— but if he was going to toss his evidence into the river, I wanted someone to witness it.

But Urich was cagier than that. He drove along the river road, just under the speed limit, windows rolled up. I hung back a few cars, staying focused on the distinctive Mercedes taillights. When he turned onto the north bridge, I followed him, keeping one car between us.

"Where do you think he's going?" Laura whispered, as if he might be listening.

"Up Croak, I guess." I peered into the gathering darkness, trying to assess his plans. "He's going to cross the city limits if he gets down the other side—"

"Is that a problem?"

"Nah, I'm deputized for the whole county. Little arrangement between the sheriff and me." As the Mercedes started up Croak Mountain Road, its taillights trailing red in the dark, I reached over to the dash and flipped on the little mini-camcorder. Never knew when that would come in handy.

Just as I cleared the bridge, the car ahead peeled off to the west, leaving me exposed. I let Urich get farther ahead, then followed, up the winding road towards the ridge.

"You don't think he's going to go to—to the scene?"

I mentally scanned the next few miles of road. The gorge where Cathy fell was another two miles up the hill, beyond the final climb to the ridge of the mountain, and a mile down on the road heading down the other side. Just inside the city limits. "That would be too incriminating, I think. He'll probably toss it before that."

Laura's face was anxious in the dim green light from the dash. "But if he knows someone's behind him, a potential witness . . ."

"Don't worry." I slowed until he was around the bend, and then I flipped off my headlights. We used to do this, when we were young and stupid—any boy with a car to drive and a girl to impress. Drive the mountain roads in the dark.

And it was pretty dark, for June. There was no moon, and a high cloud cover, and the lights of town were erased with the last turn of the road. But I'd driven this road enough, as a teenager and as an adult, that I knew every bend and turn.

On the right, there was nothing to worry about—just the jagged rock face the road carved out of the mountain. But on the left, I could see through the feathering of brush the sharp slope, rocky and rugged. Only a couple hundred feet here, but another half mile up, and the drop would be five hundred feet.

I felt Laura's tension as we inched up the darkness. My window was cracked open, and I could smell the mountain laurel in the cool evening air and the musky smell of last year's leaves. We turned a switchback and there were the taillights ahead, also climbing slower now that the danger was greater. "Can he see us, do you think?" Laura whispered.

"I doubt it. We're far enough back, and no lights. He had his windows closed, so he can't hear us either— think we're okay."

And then I saw it, the taillights swerving—into the scenic cutout overlooking French Valley to the east. I slowed, almost to a stop, and Laura leaned forward, peering out the windshield. A hundred yards ahead, there was a sudden flash of light—the dome light coming on as the car door opened. He got out of the car, silhouetted in the yellow light and the darkness beyond. I idled to the side of the road, the one against the cliff, heard to the quiet whir of my camcorder, and gave the viewer a little shove in the right direction. I didn't know how much it would capture, but combined with our eyewitness testimony, it might be enough—

He slammed the door shut and crossed the few feet to the guardrail. He was just a dark form as he stood there looking out over the dark valley, and I thought maybe he was thinking of that other cliff, that other day, on the other side of the mountain. But then his arm rose, and something arched out over the guardrail and into the empty night.

Laura took a sharp breath, and I put a quelling hand on her arm. "Wait," I said, low and quiet, and she settled, waiting.

I watched him get back into the car, and listened to his engine roar in the hush. "Hang on," I said. And then I flipped on the lights, hit the siren and beacon, and jammed on the accelerator.

He was quick, I'd give him that. He had the car in gear and out into the road in seconds. But he couldn't turn back down the mountain, not with me in the way, so he headed up to the ridge. His headlights shot through the darkness, up into the night, deflecting off the trees that lined the gorge. And his red taillights were right ahead of me, swerving to the left at the ridge of the mountain, drawing me on.

I knew this road like I knew the streets of my first beat in Bristol, like I knew the back alleys of Gemtown. And I knew over the ridge, the road stretched out for a hundred yards before heading down the other side, twisting back and forth over the river gorge.

"Do you, uh, have a plan?" Laura asked as we jammed left as the road turned.

"Plan?" I replied, like I'd never heard the word before. The exhilaration filled me and I pushed the accelerator up a notch, closing the distance between us and the car ahead. "Don't need a plan. I know this road. And he doesn't."

She said in a small voice, "Okay."

"Trust me."

And in a slightly stronger voice, she said, "Okay," and she gripped the armrest between us as we veered right, down the other side of the mountain.

"Call in," I said, past a tight throat. "Tell the dispatcher to notify the sheriff— have some cars waiting over by Ellett—set up a stop." The last thing I wanted was to take this chase into the little hamlet at the bottom of the mountain.

Laura complied, taking only a few seconds to figure the radio out, and crisply relayed my instructions to the dispatcher. If Toni was surprised to hear Laura on the radio, she didn't give any indication. She just said, "Tell the chief we're on it," and left the channel open.

So we raced down the mountain, my car taking each turn with a squeal of tires that echoed in the hollow. The wind rushed in through the cracked window, and I could hear the night noises, and Laura's startled laughter as we jammed into a switchback and she was thrown back against the seat.

The taillights slid around a curve. He was trying to outrun me, and he had the advantage of a hundred yards and a German-engineered car—and an empty passenger seat. He could take more risks. He didn't have much choice. But I had the experience of someone who learned to drive right here—a reckless kid taught by a reckless older brother. I gunned the engine and jammed the brakes, sliding around the turn, and headed down into the darkness of the mountainside.

I just needed to keep him in sight.

But he pulled around the next curve, disappearing except for a flash of lights through the trees. I sped up, gripping the gearshift with my right hand. Then I felt Laura's hand, hot and tight, on mine.

I pulled free of her, just to grab the steering wheel with both hands, just as we rounded the turn. My tires squealed as the car swerved into the far lane, but I righted the progress and headed down. Urich was ahead of me, taking the corners tighter and more economically in his European car. He was a good driver—I'd give him that much. And a smart one.

What was I going to do if I caught him? He'd fled from a pursuit—a minor crime, but one he could argue away. The hard drive might have some evidence, if we could recover it, but surely not of a long-ago murder. He could get away with it, more smug than ever, having beaten back the challenge.

"Don't worry," Laura said beside me, her voice low against the singing of the wind. "We'll get him."

All I could focus on then was the hairpin curve ahead. I jammed on the brakes, slewed sideways, and for a second saw the trees ahead and not to the side, and thought we wouldn't make it. But the tires gripped, and we swung around, and we were after him again.

But he'd pulled too far ahead and I almost lost him. His lights disappeared, and for a second, I couldn't place him. Then I remembered the old mining road that cut off to the south a half-mile before the bridge. I sped down the last road section, but I couldn't make the sharp turn he'd made, not without slowing down. Cursing, I came to a stop in the middle of the pavement and backed up, then turned onto the rutted dirt road. I had to be careful here, more careful than he, because I had Laura with me, and she was more important than getting him. I growled as I saw his taillights swerving ahead. The road came out where? The frontage road near Lasted? Or—

"The pit," Laura whispered, and suddenly I remembered. At the end of this road, a slag dump had, over the decades, filled in with snowmelt and river runoff, and generations of kids had gone skinny-dipping there in the cold dark water, miles from the nearest authority figure. We'd done it ourselves, that summer so long ago. There was the boarded-over mineshaft on the left as the road curved right toward Lasted. But straight ahead, there was the pit, just past a flimsy chain barrier we used to drive under, and a wooden fence—

"Hold on," I said as I caught sight ahead of the abandoned mine. I turned the lights off again, slowing down and letting my instinct direct my steering. Then the road dipped up, and I saw his taillights just ahead, bouncing up and down as he negotiated the ruts. I flipped on my brights, surprising him, and he accelerated convulsively. He missed the turn to the right and crashed through the chain, and through the fence, and the

Mercedes sailed out, and flew twenty feet before crashing into the pit, sending a shockwave of water back towards the shore.

I slammed on the brakes and shoved the shift into park. Then I was out the door, the ground solid beneath my feet. The car, caught in the beam of my headlight, was sinking fast into the pit's depths. The light glinted off the crushed frame, the broken windows. In a few seconds, the cabin would fill with water.

"Call it in!" I shouted to Laura. Then instinct took over. I kicked off my shoes and was pulling off my shoulder holster when I felt her hands tight on mine.

I pulled free. "I've got to go after him."

She was beside me then. She took hold of my arm again, a firm, gentle grip. "Stop," she murmured. "Think of your daughter. Think of me. Don't risk your life for someone like him."

I hesitated, and the car slipped under the surface, and Laura set my hands free. I stood there staring at the dark water, and listened to her call this in, asking for the sheriff to send a diving team up to the old mining pit.

She was right. He'd called this fate down on himself, and it wasn't my place to get in the way.

CHAPTER THIRTY-TWO

I had a nightmare that night, about drowning. Occupational hazard. I woke up, wanting to find Laura beside me—I'd gotten too used to her too quick. But I sat up in the darkness, chilled to the bone, and remembered that she was back with her family.

But the sun had hardly crested the mountains to the east when she arrived at my door. She was dressed simply, for her, in a tank top and shorts, and her eyes were tired. We'd been up late at the old mine, watching while the state police divers searched for the body and finally dragged it to shore. Now I faced a day of questions—an important man had died, after all.

We had to get our story straight, I reminded myself, and headed for the coffeemaker.

"Okay," I said a few minutes later, when we were settled out on the porch with our coffee and our view of the ski slope. It was a startling green under the motionless ski lifts. "We were driving out that way, and saw a car turn towards the old mine, and I got concerned and followed it."

"And we got there just in time to see him unwittingly drive into the lake," Laura finished.

"Right." It was . . . wrong. Wrong that I was making up this story, however close it was to the facts. This is what criminals did.

But there was too much at stake, and nothing to gain by being too candid.

Laura looked down into her coffee cup. "So does this mean that the whole Internet and murder issues stay . . . under wraps?"

I shook my head. "Depends on what's on that hard drive. And I'm going out to look for it soon."

Laura insisted on going along, and watched in silence as I gathered up my rappelling equipment from the back closet.

When we got out to the scenic overlook, I took my time hooking up the harness. It was a cool morning, with mist clinging to the edges of the valley. As I looped the rope around the guardrail, Laura came close. "Be careful," she said, bending taking hold of the rope just beyond the knot, like she could by brute force keep me from falling.

"Don't worry. It's not a sheer drop."

No, not a sheer drop—just a steep incline, covered with brambles and wind-stunted trees that caught at my boots and snagged at the rope. But I made my way down slowly, watching all the way for some sign of the hard drive. Once I hit the sloping bottom, I unbuckled myself and let the rope dangle as I prowled around, searching the tall grass.

And then I saw a glint of metal in the sun. Maybe just a soda can, tossed from a car— but I crossed the few yards and my hand closed on the flat cool rectangle.

I stuffed it in my shirt, reminding myself that it was probably damaged and useless. And even if it wasn't corrupted, he would have deleted anything criminal. And yeah, Theo could say all he wanted that nothing could ever be completely deleted, but somehow he wasn't able to recover the March expense reports that I'd managed to send into the ether last month.

But whatever was on the hard drive scared Urich enough that he wanted it lost forever. And that was reason enough to put my hands back on that rope and make the hard climb back up the ridge.

Laura held the hard drive on her lap all the way back to town. "Do you think—" she started, and then said, "It doesn't matter, does it? He's dead." She gave a small smile. "You should have seen my mother's face this morning when I told her. She was so . . . triumphant. It was better than any medicine. They're going to send her home later today."

"That's good." I thought of the tangled skeins of family ties, and said, "What about Theresa? How'd she take it?"

Laura sighed. "She was very quiet. I think all along she'd been hoping— I don't know. That she'd find her old family, the Prices, and it would feel right, and everything would fit again. But there isn't anyone really left in that old family, and it wasn't even her family, as it turns out. And the truth is so terrible."

"But at least it's the truth," I said. I had to make that point. The truth was better than a lie.

Laura said doubtfully, "I suppose. And she's still got us. More than ever, maybe. And she's got Brian. And that Mitch Price. He turns out not to be her brother, but at least he's a connection to the past."

"What about Ronnie?" I asked. "The other Price boy."

Laura's frown of concentration eased as she remembered. "Oh, yeah. Ronnie. I think he's dead. She didn't say specifically, only that all the Prices except Mitch were gone."

I spared a thought for that broken boy I'd known so long ago. I could have gone that way, I knew, graduated from reform school to jail to death. But something along the way diverted me, gave me hope for something better.

As we crossed the bridge back into town, I glanced over at Laura. "So what's next?"

She knew what I meant, but pretended she didn't. She wanted me to speak the words, I realized. All she said was, "I guess it depends on what's on this hard drive."

"Yeah." I took the long way around to the courthouse square, but it wasn't till I was pulling into my reserved slot that I could speak with the appropriate casualness. "So when are you headed out?"

She kept her gaze down on the gray metal of the hard drive. "I don't know. I need to get Mother settled. She'll need a nurse's aide, I'm sure. But—" Her mouth quirked in a wry smile. "I left a hundred thousand dollar remodeling job in the Hamptons, so I probably ought to get back there."

"And renew acquaintances with your architect." I couldn't help myself. I had to say it.

She gave me a quick glance as we got out of the car, but all she said was, "I probably ought to make sure that he didn't run off with all my money. Or put a fountain in my living room."

She was waiting for me to say something. I was waiting for her to say something.

We stood on the sidewalk in front of the police building. Then she handed me the hard drive and said, "I'll just walk home and check on everything. Let me know if you find anything interesting there."

She headed down the sidewalk. And it was all still unspoken, whatever it was between us.

But then, just as I turned to go in, she came back. In front of all the interested citizens there in the courthouse square, she threw her arms around me and whispered fiercely, "He ran. It was his own fault. Not yours. You just tried to stop him."

"Yeah," I said, and kissed her. No need, I supposed, to discuss that high-speed chase, the adrenaline rush of danger, the triumph—we both understood. That was our secret.

That was why she wanted me, after all. And why, probably, I wanted her.

I looked up the steps to find the interested regard of two young officers. "Don't you have streets to patrol?" I said, and pushed past them into the building.

When I arrived at the Wakefield house that afternoon, the front drive was full of cars. I recognized Tom O'Connor's black jeep next to his wife's Audi. I'd been married long enough to read the cards there— he'd gotten tired of waiting for Ellen to give in, so he figured he'd better come back and give in himself. Women, even the most congenial ones, could be a lot more stubborn than any man, and the sooner a guy learned that, the better.

Next to the jeep was the kid's beat up sedan, and beyond that a nondescript Ford with rental plates. I pulled in beside Laura's Porsche, and got out, carrying the manila folder.

In the front parlor, Mrs. Wakefield was sitting straight up on the couch. She looked fragile and pale, but that was apparently no excuse for slouching or for putting her feet up on the coffee table. Her youngest daughter—or her granddaughter, I supposed—was in the armchair next to her. They didn't seem comfortable together. Too much to adjust to too quickly.

"Mrs. Wakefield," I said. "Maybe we could get everyone together."

Theresa left to gather the others, and Mrs. Wakefield gave me with a sharp glance. 'You handled this very efficiently."

I assumed she meant that as a compliment. "Thanks. It would have been simpler if—" No use finishing that sentence. Mrs. Wakefield wasn't going to learn any lesson from me. She thought things had turned out well. "How's Theresa taking it?"

A shadow passed over her face. "I wish . . . I wish there had been a way that she—"

"Was kept in the dark? I don't think that was going to work out. She was already suspicious."

Laura came in then, trailing the kid. He was finding himself in clover, I guessed—a rich grandmother, a couple nice aunts, and even a helpful half-sister. The new father maybe wasn't so easy, but at least he hadn't prosecuted.

I didn't think young Brian ought to get off so easy. So I fixed him with a cop scowl, and he glanced away, and sat himself on the window seat, out of range.

Pretty soon Theresa arrived back with Ellen and Tom O'Connor, who was probably wondering how his long-ago indiscretion led to all this coming to light. At least his action seemed pretty minor comparatively. Even Ellen looked halfway to forgiveness, sitting in the love seat next to him. Not touching, but close enough.

I opened up the folder. "There wasn't much retrievable on the hard drive. No logs of chats. "

"So—" Ellen's hands were gripped in her lap. "But it must have been important, if Urich went out in the dark to get rid of it. I mean, that's a sign of guilt, isn't it?"

I knew what she wanted—what I wanted too, to tell the truth. Something concrete that said he deserved to die. Laura didn't need that, I guess. She had a certain ruthlessness I kind of admired. As far as she was concerned, Urich had done plenty to deserve death, starting with seducing a fourteen-year-old girl.

I withdrew the single page. "There wasn't much on there. But the tech found this." I rose and took the sheet to Mrs. Wakefield, and Theresa shifted to sit beside her.

For the benefit of the others, I said, "It's an email from a couple months ago. He'd dumped all his Outlook files, but there was a—the tech called it a shadow. A saved draft, deleted differently. An anonymous hotmail account. Anyway, it's to a girl he'd been in correspondence with. It sounds like she was talking about telling her parents. I don't think she'd figured out who he was exactly, but she had some idea he was important. And I guess he'd threatened her back. This seems like it's his second email on the subject, backtracking from a threat he'd made in the earlier email."

Mrs. Wakefield was staring at the page, and finally Theresa took it from her hand. She scanned it and then, slowly, read it out loud. "No, I'm not threatening you. I said with that other girl, it was just an accident. But accidents happen when you start talking out of turn."

I looked at Mrs. Wakefield. "After she had to give away a second baby, Cathy knew something was wrong. That something was broken in her, that she'd go so far. She came to you and said she wanted to go to the authorities, report this former teacher of hers. You didn't think it would work, and you were probably right. It's hard enough to make a case like that, but there would be statute of limitations problems since it had been more than a decade since the original crime. But Cathy couldn't let it rest. So she must have arranged to meet him. He'd want it away from the college, away from where someone might see them together. So they went back to where they used to climb together—the river gorge. He probably thought he could persuade her to keep quiet, that she had as much to lose as he did."

"But she wasn't going to give in," Mrs. Wakefield said. "And she would have told him that. Told him that she didn't care how much damage it did, she was going to make sure he didn't do that to another girl."

"And maybe he shoved her. Just in anger. But she went over the guardrail—"

Ellen drew in a breath, and her husband reached out and took her hand. But Mrs. Wakefield was tough. She'd already been through worse than this in her imagination. She said evenly, "And then when he realized what he'd done, he tried to fix it. He got her rope and harness out of her car, and set it up so it appeared that she'd buckled the harness wrong. An accident."

"Or suicide made to look like an accident," Laura said. "So no one wanted to look at it too closely."

"And he kept on doing it—going after young girls," Theresa said. She set the page down on the table and looked away. "At least this girl."

"There were probably others along the way." I looked at Mrs. Wakefield. "You said his ex-wife wanted nothing to do with him. Maybe she found something suspicious. Maybe he wasn't stupid enough to be going after the youngest girls anymore, but the high school students he found in recruitment chats—he probably approached them later using a different identity. Maybe it was all just in email—or maybe he arranged to meet one or two. But it was enough that he thought we might find something incriminating on his computer."

"What are you going to do now?" Ellen said.

I shrugged. "Not much I can do. He's dead. We don't know his victims, and not likely to find them now. And even if we did, we can't prosecute a corpse."

"He got what he deserved," Laura said coldly. "Not enough. But he won't hurt anyone else."

Very quietly, Theresa said, "Is there some way you can get word to that girl? That he's dead and won't bother her anymore?"

I agreed to give it a try, and Theresa rose. "It is over, isn't it?"

Ellen said, "I hope so. Some things have changed, but not everything. We're still—still a family, aren't we?"

"Of course." Mrs. Wakefield's voice was strong. But I saw her glance at Theresa, and after a moment she said, "Are you going back to the cloister now?"

Theresa shook her head slowly. "I don't think so. The prioress told me she thought I was hiding there, hiding from something. And that's not a vocation. I think—I think maybe I'll stay here for a while. With you. Help with the house. Maybe get a job at a clinic in the county. For now."

Mrs. Wakefield let her breath out—the only sign she'd ever give of anxiety. "That would be nice, dear. You'll always have a home here, you know."

Theresa rose, smoothing her skirt front with her hands. "Mother, you need to rest. Let me take you to your room."

Mrs. Wakefield accepted her hand and slowly got to her feet. But instead of walking towards the hall, she came to me. "Thank you," she said.

And then she and Theresa left the room.

Tom O'Connor stood up then too. He looked over at the boy. "Well, come on. Let's go introduce you to your sister."

The boy's face lit up, and he didn't look so much like a punk. Just as well, if he planned to come back to my town. He bounded out the door, and more slowly, Ellen and her husband followed. I have to say, the former felon in me admired this. I mean, the guy got away with it—well, there was that kidnapping incident, but otherwise, looked like he got off scot-free. Hell, Ellen got away with siding with the kidnapper and leaving Tom to rot in an old jail cell. Looked like they'd just, I don't know, agreed to move on. Found a way to stay together.

That was what Michelle and I couldn't manage. The "I" mattered more than the "we", once we got to that point. And by then, we just didn't bother to find that way to stay together.

Love had to matter more than that. I had to make it matter more than that.

Now it was only Laura and me, standing on the faded rug in the formal parlor. The afternoon sun was streaming in through the wide windows, and Laura's hair and face were touched with a golden light. She looked beautiful and unattainable—but she was mine, goddamnit. I'd made her mine. Again.

"So how long are you staying?" I said. My voice sounded rough.

She moved a little closer to me, her hand rising as if to brush my chest. But she didn't touch me. "I have to go back to the beach house."

"To the renovations."

"Yes." Now her hand splayed across my uniform front. "I need to make sure it's all done in time to sell the house."

Hope opened up in me. A dangerous feeling. But what else was there, really? "You decided you don't want the house?"

"I don't actually love the beach," she said. "Too sandy. I'm more of a mountain girl, when it comes right down to it."

"So—"

"So maybe I'll make this my retreat. Come back when I'm not working, and for long weekends. Keep Mother and Theresa on their toes."

"Maybe you'll start a trend."

"Yes—like Demi did with that Montana town. Maybe all the Hollywood types will decide Wakefield's just the sort of quaint place they can go to relax."

"Oh, great. That's all I need. Sunset Boulevard east. Cocaine and paparazzi."

Finally she came into my arms, her head against my chest. "Let's do it right this time, okay?" she whispered.

"Okay." And then, as she lifted her face for a kiss, I said, "This time looks like we've got your mom's blessing."

For just a second, she looked stricken with horror. But then I kissed her, and it was all okay. Again. This time.

For Readers' Groups

Discussion Questions

1. *The Year She Fell* is set in the mountains of West Virginia, a beautiful but impoverished state. Discuss the situation of the Wakefield sisters, growing up rich but surrounded by poverty.

2. Both Ellen and her sister Theresa have religious vocations, but while Ellen's faith is low-key, Theresa's requires constant sacrifice. What about their personalities and experiences might account for the difference in religious intensity?

3. Mitch Price is an artisan, a man who works creatively with his hands in a traditional craft (wood-carving). In his own way, he is as much a throwback as Mrs. Wakefield. How might the remote setting (mountainous West Virginia) lead to an embrace of more traditional forms and roles?

4. Jackson McCain was a delinquent who grew up to be a cop. What sort of experiences might account for such a transformation?

5. Mrs. Wakefield is a society matriarch of a sort not seen much in these days of grannies in hiking boots. Tom calls his father "a professional Irishman," deepening his accent and Irishness to impress the Americans who come to his pub. Trevor O'Connor. and Mrs. Wakefield are both most comfortable in the personas imparted by their social class and situation. Is that sort of role-inhabiting a thing of the past in our fast-changing society? Contrast this with the discarding of early roles (delinquent and debutante) shown by the younger Jackson and Laura.

6. Laura and Jackson never got over their early love, and they reunite as adults. Is this sort of "reunion love" an example of self-deception, or can what attracted us at 16 still be alluring in midlife?

7. In his reckless youth, Tom betrayed Ellen. Do you think it's possible to forgive and forget in a case like theirs? Is she a fool if she believes him when he says he loved only her?

8. Cathy is the great enigma, and her death the mystery that her sisters must solve. Consider the damage she has done to each sister. Does her reason absolve her of guilt? How much should childhood trauma excuse adult misbehavior?

9. Were Mrs. Wakefield's attempts to protect her family admirable or lamentable? Chief McCain thinks she's crazy, as are most rich women. Do you agree that wealth distorts reality for the wealthy?

10. All families have secrets, though the Wakefields have more than most. Have you discovered secrets in your own family? What did your parents and grandparents hide from you, and why?

About Alicia Rasley

Alicia Rasley grew up in the placid old mountains of SW Virginia. She was the second of eight children of a math professor and a scientist, and could rebel best by majoring in English. She teaches writing at a community college, and is a guest lecturer and writing advisor at a state university. Between sadistic bouts of grading papers, she hangs out and talks sentences with co-blogger Theresa at the Edittorrent blog. She lives for semi-annual trips to England, and her children (Andy, JJ, and surrogate daughter Kate) are gracious enough to travel there with her once in a while. She lives now in the flatlands of Indiana with her husband Jeff, who is also a writer and runs a foundation to benefit villages in Nepal. For a two-writer family, there is remarkably little artistic temperament. But the house is filled with crammed bookcases and overflowing magazine racks.

LaVergne, TN USA
03 December 2010

207282LV00003B/52/P